Running away from myself

RUNNING AWAY FROM MYSELF

A dream portrait of America
drawn from the films of the forties

by BARBARA DEMING

GROSSMAN PUBLISHERS · NEW YORK · 1969

Copyright © 1969 by Barbara Deming
Published by Grossman Publishers, Inc.
125A East 19th Street, New York, N.Y. 10003
Published simultaneously in Canada by Fitzhenry and Whiteside, Ltd.
All rights reserved.
Library of Congress Catalogue Card Number: 77–76094
Manufactured in the U.S.A.
First Printing

To Quentin and Vida

Acknowledgments

I wish to acknowledge the stimulation of many friendly discussions with the late critic, Dr. Siegfried Kracauer. And I thank Quentin and Vida Ginsberg Deming and Anniewill Siler for helpful comments during the writing of the book.

For help in collecting the movie stills which are used as illustrations, I thank Leo and Florence Ardavany, then of the Broadway Theater in Haverstraw, New York, and John Houseman, then with RKO Pictures.

The first two chapters appeared in installments in the magazine *City Lights* in 1953, 1954 and 1955. The book was at that time entitled *A Long Way from Home: Some Film Nightmares of the Forties.*

 Contents

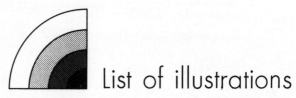 List of illustrations

Foreword

Wellfleet, Mass, 1969

The original version of this book was finished in 1950—entitled then *A Long Way from Home: Some Film Nightmares of the Forties.* No one was ready to publish it—except for the magazine *City Lights,* which began to serialize it, but shortly went out of existence for lack of funds—and I put it aside and turned to other writing. Then in the 1960's I became active in the nonviolent movement, and as the struggle in which this engaged me brought me a new kind of knowledge of this country, I began more and more to recall certain images with which the book had dealt. When I wrote it, I knew that it could be read as a psychological study of America, but my own experience of America was so limited still that writing it was a curiously abstract though fascinating labor. When I finally took out the manuscript and reread it—a little over a year ago—I found that it was very much more alive for me than it had been when I put it away.

This was especially so, perhaps, of Chapter 4, in which I deal with the distracted heroes and heroines of various "success stories." Some of these heroes exhibit a strange split in consciousness. They boast openly of being out for what they can get and of not caring what means they use. At the same time they utter piteous cries, claiming to be misunderstood—to be innocent of the cruel charge that they are out for what they can get. I began to recall these figures sharply as I studied this country's involvement in Vietnam—reading, on the one hand, bald statements like Eisenhower's explanation of our support of the French war to keep Vietnam a colony ("When the U.S. votes 400 million dollars to help that war, we are not voting a give-away program. We are voting for . . . our power and ability to get certain things we need from the riches of . . . South East Asia"); reading also pronouncements made by Eisenhower and others about our selfless fight to help the South Vietnamese preserve their freedom—the same men making the one kind of statement and the other, and in some strange fashion able to believe both.

All the characters whom I trace in *Running Away from Myself* can be seen to be products of a deep crisis of faith. It is striking to me that the period in which this country is most aggressively trying to impose its will upon the rest of the world follows a period of suffering from this deep uncertainty. And again a particular character in Chapter 4 holds a new interest for me: the one who in effect declares, "Believe in me or I will have to destroy you!"

As I write this introduction, we are nearing the end of the 1960's. The reader of today will find, I think, that the imagined world I examine in this book is still projected upon our movie screens—a world I sum up in Chapter 6: "a nightmare realm . . . where visions tantalize but deceive, what seems substantial may prove insubstantial, what promises life may bring death. Nothing is sure."

Even more film dreams today offer us the relief simply of giving it all up. We thrill as everything goes to pieces, everything flies apart —or threatens to. Or perhaps we laugh. In our comedies, still, "the line between the laughter they evoke and an outcry of pain or hysteria is a thin line."

There are still dream figures offered us whose triumph is that they are able to survive in this world that falls apart. The tough boy hero I describe in Chapter 7 can still be recognized. Note the theme song of the hero in *Duffy*: "If there's no skin off my hide, I'm satisfied . . . Long as I'm neat inside, I'm satisfied." The changes that have taken place in this hero would be interesting to study carefully, however. He is hardly the tense ascetic figure portrayed by Humphrey Bogart in the forties. As Duffy says of himself, comparing his style now to that of his youth, "I'm cooler, more mentholated."

Another survival figure, the laughing old man in *The Treasure of the Sierra Madre* (whom I describe in Chapter 9), can be very directly related to the figure of Zorba in the current *Zorba the Greek*—who teaches the younger hero of that film to laugh and to dance as the project into which he has put so much energy and hope collapses.

Still another survival figure is recognizable, though in very much altered form: the figure of the Innocent (described in Chapter 4). The heroines of *Candy* and of *Barbarella* are two examples—able somehow through their special variety of "innocence" to survive Chaos itself essentially unharmed.

Barbarella is one of the new genre of space odyssey. In the film dreams of the forties it was almost always the setting of the modern city that conveyed the psychic wilderness in which hero or heroine must try to survive. Now a new landscape is often provided—one even lonelier, more bewildering and treacherous, though sometimes also full of wonders, the landscape of outer space.

Those heroes who are not shown traveling through outer space are shown, very often, leading an existence as eerie, as encapsulated. Compare, for example, the experience of Anthony Quinn as the first Russian to be pope, in *The Shoes of the Fisherman*, with the experience of the hero of the space odyssey *2001*. In *2001*, the hero, in the middle of a long space flight, sees his companions killed off by a treacherous computer machine and he has to dismantle the machine and try to handle the entire spaceship all by himself. In *The Shoes of the Fisherman*, Quinn, who has been suddenly freed from exile in Siberia to become a bishop in Rome, then as suddenly the pope (in spite of his protests: here again is the figure of the Innocent), must face the problem—quite by *himself*—of how to avert World War III and the end of the world. The film moves him about the globe and through the awesome rooms of the Vatican, a figure quite as lonely, quite as far-out, as the other hero—his yearnings to make a visit incognito to the streets of Rome, "where people are living, just simply living," comparable to the yearnings of the space traveler to feel his feet touch ground again.

In Chapter 5, I describe certain restless heroes and heroines who seek to break away from a life they feel is not real life. Counterparts of these figures too are still to be found on our screens today. The most obvious example is *The Graduate,* whose hero complains, "I feel like I'm playing games in which the rules don't make sense. They're made by all the wrong people." One should make them for oneself, he adds. There are a number of current films, each superficially very different from the others, but in each of which the characters are seeking just this—to make the rules for themselves. Think of the heroine of *Rachel, Rachel* or, in different modes, the hero and heroine of *Bonnie and Clyde* and the two brothers in *Duffy.*

In each of these films, as in the films discussed in Chapter 5, the venture proves difficult indeed. There are moments of excitement in which the protagonists seem actually to be their own masters. There are longer nightmare moments in which they move as under a crippling spell. In the films of the forties, however, the attempt at independence always came to naught. In current films it shows a little more promise. *Bonnie and Clyde* does end with the death of those two rebels of a sort—their only triumph the perverse triumph I describe in Chapter 8: when they realize that they are doomed creatures, they are able at last to love each other. And *Duffy* does end with the frustration of the two brothers who had hoped—with Duffy's help—to prove their independence of their wealthy father by pulling off an elaborately cunning theft of some of his millions ("a sort of morality crime," as they see it). Everything seems to go off perfectly, but at the last the old man turns up, master of the situation still—the money still in his possession and, what is more, the young woman they had thought was one of them revealed as his ally in the game. In both these films, however, the sequences in which the young *think* they are finding their freedom contain a joyful excitement not present at all in the comparable films of the forties. And both *The Graduate* and, in more sober fashion, *Rachel, Rachel* end on this note.

In *Rachel, Rachel* the heroine's rebellion is seen again in terms of an effort to break free of the constraining world of one's parents. At the film's end, Rachel has not only made "the first decision of her life that shows any respect for herself," a decision to bear the "illegitimate" child she had thought she was carrying—before she learned with anguish that she was not really pregnant; she has also left her parental home (though she is taking her widowed mother with her) and set out on a bus to seek a new life. She muses, "Where I'm going, anything may happen." She adds quickly, "Nothing may." But at least the future is now an open one. And *The Graduate* ends with an act of the hero's that more audaciously still declares his independence of his parents' world. Throughout most of the film he is shown in even more painful bondage to that world (the dazed captive most especially of his parents' friend Mrs. Robinson, who has seduced him). But at the very end he too supposedly learns to take his life into his own hands. He abducts Mrs. Robinson's daughter Elaine, whom he really loves, from the church in which she is allowing herself to be married off to another man—abducts her not before but after the wedding ceremony, in a wild and exuberant scene in which he swings a huge crucifix to hold the enraged parents at bay. He and Elaine race off down the street and, like Rachel, climb onto a bus to start seeking their future.

However, if rebellion finds a life on our screens today that it did not have in the forties, a cynical despair finds very much more frequent expression. The majority of films today offer us, at the end, the release of giving everything up. In the forties those films that ended as all that had been strained for came to nothing, added usually one softening note: love was born among the ruins. Most films today omit this note. Their nihilism is stark.

But I have omitted mention of the Beatles, who introduce a note all their own—and one that represents the most decisive break with an older generation. They are rebel figures whose rebellion has in fact been accomplished. They are who they are and stand in no awe of those who would like to frustrate them—the Blue Meanies, as they characterize such opposition in *The Yellow Submarine.* Of the chief of those one of the Beatles can remark lightly, "He reminds me of me old English teacher."

The Beatles are British, of course, but so much a part of American culture at this point that it does seem appropriate to speak of them. And they very clearly represent liberation from the cynicism that is so general. The landscape in which they move is a threatening one still, inhabited by "monsters" and by "lonely people." But their lives are felt to be charmed lives. They cannot be lonely; they have one another. It is not exactly that they know yet *where* they are. When

(in *The Yellow Submarine*) they meet "a real nowhere man . . .
who knows not where he's going to . . . poor little fellow," they
add without hesitation, "Isn't he a bit like you and me?" But "All
you need is love," they sing. (Here is the Innocent again, in new
guise.) They confront and oppose in their persons—in fairy tale
fashion, simplistically, but with a great deal of wit—precisely the
spirit of nihilism, the spirit of the Meanies ("I only take 'No' for an
answer"). The Beatles remark of these Meanies, "They look almost
human." "Join us," they are innocent enough to suggest. This rebellion against despair has been contagious already. May the con-
tagion spread!

Running away from myself

 1

A portrait of ourselves

New York City, 1950

"Abandon all hope, you who enter here!" Dante found these words written above the entrance to Hell. I should give the same warning to anyone about to enter the world through which this book will lead him—a world that has been shaped upon our movie screens. That world is the image of ourselves, and the image is discouraging. The reader can comfort himself with the thought that the portrait is incomplete. I am not speaking of any direct likeness that Hollywood films offer. It is not as mirrors reflect us but, rather, as our dreams do, that movies most truly reveal the times.[1] If the dreams we have been dreaming provide a sad picture of us, it should be remembered that— like that first book of Dante's *Comedy*—they show forth only one region of the psyche. Through them we can read with a peculiar accuracy the fears and confusions that assail us—we can read, in caricature, the Hell in which we are bound. But we cannot read the best hopes of the time.

[1] I am of course not the first to note it. See most especially Siegfried Kracauer's brilliant book on the German film, *From Caligari to Hitler*. Princeton University Press, 1947.

If our films reveal only this hapless side of us, it is because of the role most film makers choose—that of giving the public "what it wants." Most films made in Hollywood offer—as certain dreams do—wish fulfillment. In wishful dreams one can discern quite clearly the condition from which a man wants to escape, but never the more difficult, the *real* hope he might have of escaping from it—never, that is, his real strength.

As in wishful dreams, Hollywood films offer an escape that is disguised. The fact is less obvious than with dreams, which often, if taken literally, make no sense at all (some films, to be sure, make almost as little sense), but the drama here, too, is secret. The thrill that movies hold for us is usually thought to be that of identifying with persons unlike ourselves—of imagining ourselves Ingrid Bergman (or one loved by her), Humphrey Bogart (or one loved by him), or of imagining ourselves a millionaire or a musical genius or some equally remote figure. The truth is that the spectator always knows very well—in essence—the dramatic situations in which these screen figures are placed. The heroes and heroines who are most popular at any particular period are precisely those who, with a certain added style, with a certain distinction, act out the predicament in which we all find ourselves—a predicament from which the movie-dream then cunningly extricates us. But the moviegoer need never admit to himself the real nature of the identification—never admit what that condition really is from which he is being vicariously relieved. Virgil describes Hell to Dante as that blind world in which the good of the intellect has been surrendered. His words could also be used to describe the darkened world of the movie theater.

If the dreamers are unaware of what it is they dream, the men who contrive these dreams know little more than they do. They consciously enough indulge the public—because it pays.[2] But their cunning at providing blind comfort is, itself, largely blind. I have remarked that the plight from which these dreams extricate hero or heroine is disguised for us. The film makers might very well deny

[2] One can speak also of a political instinct here. Films that open no eyes stir up no trouble. The film industry, like many another, is not without its stakes in maintaining the status quo. Within Hollywood ranks one can find a variety of political opinion; yet all, more than they would like to admit, involve themselves in this conspiracy. The Committee on Un-American Activities need not really have excited itself about our movies.

having intended this. But no art is involved here. Rather, it takes art to be always aware of what the actual subject is with which one is dealing. One may be shrewd at spotting a subject of general appeal and at the same time quite ignorant of the true nature of that appeal. Often in these films, the hero's extrication from his difficulties is effected by sleight of hand. The film makers could again protest that they were unaware of executing any such feats. Cunning of that sort need not be plotted; it is instinct. The least knowing among us cunningly enough delude ourselves. It takes again precisely art to avoid these motions which, even when one attempts an honest representation of life, have a way of intruding themselves spontaneously.

The film medium lends itself especially to sleight of hand. The spectator, in the first place, plays a more passive role than he does in relation to any other art and so is in a more suggestible state. He is seated in darkness. The screen, the only source of light in this darkness, easily usurps his attention. This is so of the lit stage at a play, of course, but at a play, at least, the eye of the spectator must move to take in the scene. At a movie, the camera performs the work *for* the eye. We need not even turn our heads to follow the action; the camera does that for us. It squints for us, to note details. It is alert; we need not be.

As a movie communicates both at the visual level and at the level of the word, it is easy for it to distract us with words spoken, with a name given an event, while the underlying sensuous appeal it makes remains unacknowledged—and may have very little to do with those words. This is possible in the theater also; and something comparable is possible on the printed page; but in the movies it is so to a new degree, because of the freedom the camera has to range through the physical world—quite casually, it would seem. (To those who make the film, it can seem casual too; here is always much that is involuntary.) It is very possible for a person in the audience to ridicule the film he has seen, to point out glaring absurdities of plot—and still, in spite of himself, to have responded to it very actively, at a less obvious level. A man can wake from a dream too and say, "I have just had the most absurd dream"; yet he has dreamed it.

Even if he laughs at his dream, the dreamer often carries the taste of it with him through the day—troubled by his memory of it, unless he can decipher it. This book attempts to decipher the dreams that all

Eddie Bracken in
Hail the Conquering Hero (1944).

Humphrey Bogart in
Casablanca (1942).

Robert Walker in
The Clock (1945).

Dick Powell in
Cornered (1946).

ary Grant in
one but the Lonely Heart (1944).

John Garfield in *Pride of the Marines* (1946).

obert Alda in *Rhapsody in Blue* (1945).

Mark Stevens in *Dark Corner* (1946).

Gregory Peck in *Spellbound* (1946).

of us have been buying at the box office, to cut through to the real nature of the identification we have experienced there—to that image of our condition that haunts us, unrecognized by most of us, unacknowledged, yet troubling our days.

Because it is a blind comfort they offer, our movies are hard to read in this way individually. But in unison they yield up their secrets. If one stares long enough at film after film, the distracting individual aspects of each film begin to fade and certain obsessive patterns that underlie them all take on definition. Film after film can be seen to place its hero in what is, by analogy, the identical plight—the dream then moving forward carefully to extricate him. From such a series of instances one can deduce a plight more general, sensed by the public (and by the public-minded film makers)—a condition that transcends the literal situation dramatized in any single film.

The heart of this study has been the juxtaposition of many texts, and the number of films that I have studied in this way is a substantial one.[3] But the number of films to which I will actually refer is small. This is so because I felt that I should tell each film story in some detail. One who writes about the movies can never assume that the text he is discussing is common both to him and to the reader. With the exception of certain favorites which do tend to be revived fitfully from year to year, films make their sudden appearances upon the nation's screens and as suddenly disappear. No comprehensive film library exists. The reader cannot turn to a certain text at will. Even if he were able to do so, to check a particular film is a much more complex process than to pull a book from a shelf; but the films are not even available. The Museum of Modern Art in New York has pioneered in this field, but its selection remains, appropriately enough, a limited one; and this collection stands as yet virtually alone. In 1942 the Library of Congress undertook to establish a national film library, but three years later, when Congress balked at voting the

---

[3] For 1942, 1943, and 1944, in the capacity of film analyst for the Library of Congress, I saw a quarter of all Hollywood feature films released. For 1945, 1946, 1947, and 1948, I saw fewer than this, but I carefully selected the films I did see—on the basis of published synopses—with a view to missing no new trends. With the exception of several films simply mentioned in footnotes, I talk of no films I have not actually seen. And I do not rely upon memory. At each film I took lengthy notes in shorthand—a very literal moment by moment transcription. Quotations I make may not be verbatim but are very nearly so.

necessary funds, it abandoned the project. Not even film scenarios are readily available. Even the Gassner-Nichols publication of *Best Film Plays for the Year* was discontinued after only three editions. There has been insufficient impulse among either the makers of the films or the public to review the substance of all these spellbound hours. In writing this book, I felt that I should provide the reader with some sort of substitute for the text to which he cannot turn—should try my best to evoke it for him, so that he could judge for himself whether or not the pattern I trace is there in fact. I could not do this with very many films, without entangling the reader in plot after plot. Nor could I examine certain films in detail but refer to many more in passing. The real substance of a film never lies on the surface, and so cannot be "noted briefly." If by the end of this book those analyses I do make seem legitimate to the reader, if the images I trace in films representative of a variety of genres seem together to compose a world that is consistent with itself, perhaps the reader will be willing to assume that any other films chosen from these years would contribute to the same portrait of ourselves.

I offer no interpretation of that dream portrait. My feeling is that it stands by itself; that if it is presented—as I try to present it—not in fragments but all of a piece, it will wake in the consciousness of the reader echoes more resonant than any special reading I might give it.

2

"I'm not fighting for anything any more—except myself!" (war hero)

"What is this pumpkin pie Americans are fighting for?" cries a youth just arrived in this country (in *They Live in Fear*, 1944). "Gosh," he is very soon writing to his mother, "people are quite willing to die for it, and I too!"

At a casual glance, our films about the Second World War would seem well summarized in this child's cry of delight. Listen to the voices which join themselves to his: "In other wars, men haven't always known why they were fighting; in this war we are all fighting for the same thing—our lives!" (*Cry Havoc*); "We all see eye to eye!" (*The Yanks Are Coming*); "This has been a happy home" (*Cross of Lorraine*); "When it's all over . . . just think . . . being able to settle down . . . raise your children . . . and never be in doubt about anything!" (*Thirty Seconds over Tokyo*). I could go on quoting from film after film.

My warning in the past chapter would seem a curious one. Where is the unhappy portrait of ourselves of which I spoke? Men die in these films, for this is war, but they fall on a battlefield bright with visions of the life they "almost happily" die to secure; each with his family photograph, his letter from sweetheart, wife or Mom, with news of the home town he is proud of, tucked in his pocket; or the page he has torn from a magazine—"Your Ideal Home." "We shall utterly defeat the enemy," the government film *A Prelude to War* quotes General Marshall. And at his words, a bright bright globe eclipses a dark.

A few songs in the musicals of those years announce that the soldiers look forward to "a world that is new." But the words only mean that, through this war, the rest of the world will come to know some of the happiness that we already know. After the war, "the people of the whole world will meet together at one big table" (*Three Russian Girls*), and there the whole world will come to know the taste of— "What did you call it?" the Russian girl asks the American aviator. "Pumpkin pie!" he tells her again. When an American in one of these films wants to explain American life to a stranger, pumpkin pie comes most readily to mind: we set it out for all who want to gather round, and everybody gets an equal share. "One big family—that is America," someone sums up (*They Live in Fear*).

On the field of battle, clear evidence of this happy family meets the eye wherever it turns. *Guadalcanal Diary* (1943): Here is Catholic side by side with Jew; here is Brooklyn cabbie next to philosophy teacher; here is—briefly—black man next to white. *The Purple Heart* (1944): Here are artist, laborer, lawyer, football player, arm in arm; one of Italian extraction, one Irish, one—again—Catholic, one a Jew. *Eve of St. Mark* (1944): Here on the one team are a boy from a small New England farm; a poor city boy, Irish Catholic, who is a Dodgers fan; a rich southerner from an aristocratic family, who likes to quote poetry. Again I could continue for pages. Slight tensions are sometimes dramatized, but they are always quickly resolved. In *A Wing and a Prayer* (1944), there is a little bit of tension between officers and men; but before long the men come to understand why the officer had to behave as he did. In *Cry Havoc* (1943), there is a little bit of tension between rich girl and poor; but their differences vanish. In *Destination Tokyo* (1943), there is a little tension between the doctor, who claims to be a materialist, and one of the men who is deeply religious; but events soon prove just how serious this difference is. After the usual operation at sea such films feature, the doctor, to the boy's muttered prayer, mutters a fervent "Amen!" Fundamentally "we all see eye to eye." "This is America!" confident voices chorus.

The voices are always just a little too confident; the tableaux are too carefully composed, one-of-each-of-us placed too punctually in the happy group. There is another invariable that one can note, also. In film after film there erupts some really harrowing moment of violence. One could put it down to realism and pass on. But this is not the mere documentation of reality. The jugular vein, pierced, spurts its blood directly at us, spurts, it almost seems, straight from the screen (*Cross of Lorraine*). As the "Jap" screams, the armored tank charges right over us, as if we were its victims (*Guadalcanal Diary*). The hand-to-hand fight between the "Yank" and the "Jap" is protracted endlessly. We suffer in close-up each killing blow (*Behind the Rising Sun*). The emergency operation will never end. The camera cannot take its fill of that face, where teeth bite lips, eyes suddenly roll in a swoon (for this, name at random almost any film). Here is no controlled rendering of the facts of war. The camera voluptuously involves us in the destructive moment, moves in too close and dwells overlong, inviting us to suffer the ecstasy of dissolution, the thrill of giving it all up.

This compulsion, betraying itself in film after film, belies the bright tableaux arranged, the bright words carefully mouthed, and hints at some very different sense of the actuality of things, repressed but secretly insistent. And a long look confirms just this. The figure of the clear-browed soldier with the dream in his eyes turns insubstantial, and another figure claims attention, member of no happy clan, a figure of bitter aspect, withdrawn upon himself, who cries, *"Don't you ever wonder if it's worth all this—I mean what you're fighting for?"*— who cries, *"I stick my neck out for nobody . . . I'm not fighting for anything any more, except myself! . . . All hail the happy days when faith was something all in one piece!"*

These particular words are taken verbatim from one of the most popular films of 1942—*Casablanca*. They might seem blunt enough to catch one's attention at once. One might ask why some official ear did not note them and have the film withdrawn. But the truth is that the film is one of the last a censor would notice. It is one of the last that would shake up self-questioning and doubt in an audience. The reverse is its very design: to relieve any such agitations. At the film's beginning, the hint is dropped that the hero may be speaking words he does not mean. He is presented as a cipher, a man behind a mask, and the film poses the question: if it should come to a trial, might he not be shown to possess a fighting faith more real than all the rest? Just such a trial is gradually framed, and the film delivers its answer in the affirmative. The very nature of the drama here—the very nature of the question which makes the wheels of the film turn—might still seem to give much away. And here on paper, I believe it does; but not on the screen itself. This is the film's real magic: not only does it bring to the question the right answer; it brings the right answer without letting the audience become fully aware of what the question is; it drowns out the bitter cries without letting the audience become fully aware of what the cries have been all about. (I repeat that all this is likely to have been unconscious on the part of the producers.) But here is the film itself, in synopsis:

It is set abroad, and just before Pearl Harbor, the fight in question not yet our fight. (This, to begin with, makes the tale seem more innocent.) The hero, Rick (Humphrey Bogart), runs a café in Casablanca. Next to his café lies the airfield from which planes take off to Lisbon—and from there to America; so Casablanca is crowded with people trying to flee occupied Europe. Visas are pitifully hard to obtain, legally or illegally, and while they seek, and wait, "everybody goes to Rick's." Among all these displaced people, Rick himself is marked out for us, a homeless one among the homeless, exile in some special degree; and in this case alone the nature of the exile is not an apparent one. Our curiosity about Rick is provoked long before we are allowed to see him. The manner in which we are finally introduced to him carefully prolongs the suspense: a waiter has just informed an eager newcomer that Rick never drinks with customers; we see a check handed across a table; a hand puts an okay to it; the camera draws very slowly off to take Rick in—and we are left more curious than when we started; our introduction is to the very figuration of that question on which the film turns: Rick's glooming deadpan. He sits alone, staring at a drink, "no expression in his eyes."

As the drama unfolds, various facts about Rick's background are provided for us by the characters who press upon him, each, for his

Dooley Wilson and Humphrey Bogart in *Casablanca* (1942).

Jean Gabin in *The Impostor* (1944).

own purposes, seeking to guess him right. But always the sense is conveyed that the key to the puzzle, that which would make all the other pieces fall into place, remains to be found. Almost everyone wants something from Rick, starting with poor little Yvonne, "fool to fall in love with a man like" him; but there are two characters who most particularly strain themselves to decipher him. They are Renault (Claude Rains), French prefect of police, and the Nazi Major Strasser, who is in Casablanca to prevent the escape to America of underground leader Victor Lazslo. Two German couriers have been murdered, and letters of transit have been taken from them. Strasser is concerned to see that these letters do not get into Lazslo's hands. He and Renault both come to suspect that Rick knows where they are hidden. We know that he knows. We have seen the little "rat," Ugarte, leave them in his keeping ("Just because you despise me, you're the only one I trust"). And Rick may do what he wants with the letters, for Ugarte, who had his own plans—he helps those who are desperate, at a price—is promptly arrested for murder. We first see Renault trying to figure out how Rick will behave in relation to this arrest, for he plans to take Ugarte at Rick's place. "I stick my neck out for nobody," says Rick. And when the time comes and Ugarte goes scrambling to him, he *doesn't* move to help. This tells us nothing, for why should Rick risk anything for one like Ugarte? The episode— with several others in the film—is a teaser, keeps the guessing going. But Renault has also tried to sound out Rick about Victor Lazslo. In the process, he has provided us with our first tangible facts about Rick's background. A flicker of interest has crossed his face at Lazslo's name, and he has bet Renault ten thousand francs that Lazslo will manage a get-away; but what makes Renault think that he, Rick, might do anything to help? "I know your record," Renault brings out, watching him. "In 1935 you ran guns for Ethiopia, in 1936 you fought in Spain on the Loyalist side." "And got well paid for it on both occasions," Rick returns, deadpan.

Another note out of his past is sounded for us, but this more vague. Rick has run into the interview with Renault by wandering onto the terrace of the café. From here the airfield is visible. The sound of a plane warming up pulls Rick's eyes in that direction and he watches mesmerized as, caught in the glare of the floodlights, the plane speeds down the runway and turns to a speck. "You would like to be on it?"

Renault probes. "I have often speculated on why you do not return to America. Did you abscond with the church funds? Did you run off with the President's wife? I should like to think you killed a man." "It was a combination of all three," Rick grunts, eyes still captive of the speck of plane.

Renault introduces Rick to Strasser, and Strasser in his turn tries to get some rise out of Rick with Lazslo's name. Rick lightly comments that his interest in Lazslo is a sporting one (he refers to his bet)—"Your business is politics, mine is running a saloon." But "You weren't always so carefully neutral," says Strasser. He has a dossier on him. "Cannot return to his country," he reads, watching him; "the reason is a little vague." His words fail to disturb the expressionless mask.

And then, suddenly, the film takes a turn. Suddenly we sit up, expectant. Enter Ingrid Bergman—(Mrs. Victor Lazslo). She walks into the café with her husband, and from their table she spots Sam, the Negro pianist, Rick's only intimate. Sam spots Ingrid too, and his glance is nervous. When Lazslo leaves the room for a moment, he crosses to her quickly. "Leave him alone!" he begs. "Leave him alone, Miss Ilse!" And we hold our breath.

We are at the point at last, we feel, of finding Rick out. When they come face to face, this feeling is confirmed. She has insisted on the music that brought him: "Play it once, for old time's sake. Play it, Sam. Play 'As Time Goes By.'" Sam, mumbling words of resistance, has played it, and Rick has come storming in: "I thought I told you never—" his face at last registering an emotion. In the few tense sentences they now exchange, it is obvious that Rick's past confronts us right here, in Ilse's person. We cut to a later hour and Rick alone over his drink, the lights out, the customers all gone, everyone gone but Sam, who pleads, "Don't just sit and stare a hole in that drink, boss." But "Tonight I've got a date with the heebie jeebies," Rick announces. "You know what I want to hear. If she can stand it, I can. Play it!" So Sam, at the piano, fingers out the song. The veil is about to be torn. The music, we know, will softly rend it. "The fundamental things apply, as time goes by . . ." Sam murmurs out the words. "Woman needs man, and man must have his mate, that nobody can deny . . ." We move up on Rick, on the drink before him, and dissolve—into a day in 1940.

An idyl: Rick and Ilse in Paris, in love. They have met only recently, we gather; know nothing about each other's pasts. "Who are
you really?" he asks, gazing, love-struck. But she: "We said no questions." Love-struck, he acquiesces. In the background, Sam plays
their theme song; they drink the last champagne. For the Germans
are advancing on Paris; they will have to flee; but they will flee together. They name the train at which they will meet; Ilse has one
thing first to which she must attend. But then we cut to Rick waiting
at the station, in the rain; and Ilse does not come. He waits; she does
not come; the train is about to pull out—the last train out of Paris.
Suddenly Sam arrives with a note: she cannot see him ever again,
she writes—but believe believe that she loves him. The raindrops
pour down upon the letter, smudging the writing; the train utters its
baleful departing whistle, and we dissolve back to Rick over his drink.
He looks up and there is Ilse standing in the door, come after all these
months to explain. Rick doesn't give her a chance. He mimics her
words back there in Paris: " 'Rick dear, I'll go with you any place.
We'll get on a train together and we'll never stop. All my life, for-
evermore!' . . . How long was it we had, honey? . . . All hail the
happy days," he lashes out, "when there were no questions asked, and
faith was something all in one piece!" She gives up and leaves. Rick,
giving it all up too, sags over the table; his drink tips, spilling over the
cloth; the scene fades out.

So we know him now. The veil has been torn aside for us. He has
had his "insides kicked out by a pair of French heels." This is his
secret. And this, note, is the context in which he utters that cry: "All
hail the happy days when faith was something all in one piece!" As
uttered here, this is not the cry at all I seemed originally to report. It
is a wounded lover's cry—nothing more.

Actually, a veil has been subtly drawn before our eyes—not parted
for us. Look again and see the sleight of hand. Review the puzzle
pieces which supposedly assemble for us into the portrait of a man
betrayed in love. He never drinks with the customers and is cold to
poor little Yvonne—this will fit. The man who fought in Spain and
ran guns for Ethiopia will now stick his neck out for nobody—claims
to have done what he's done only because he got well paid for it. One
who is embittered in love, of course, will often extend that bitterness
to life in general. But note too: for reasons unknown he cannot return

to his own country. Here is a piece that refuses to be fitted into the place assigned.

It refuses, that is, on paper; but not upon the screen. Rick's "date with the heebie jeebies" is worth going over again, this time in full detail. In this scene, all the variant notes I have just mentioned are introduced again—but in the instant are gathered up, and blur into the one note. As one *watches*, it is persuasive.

When we see Rick sitting there at his bitter drink, he is lit through the café window by a circling finger of light from the airfield—which dramatically enough recalls that trip to America he can never make, an exile quite distinct from the exile he suffers because of Ilse. And listen, now, to a more complete text of what passes between him and Sam. "Don't just stare a hole in that drink," Sam pleads, but Rick answers that this night he has a date with the heebie jeebies. Then he breaks out—"strangely," comments the script[1]—"They grab Ugarte, then she walks in. That's the way it goes. One in and one out. Sam, if it's December 1941 in Casablanca, what time is it in New York? . . . I bet they're asleep in New York. I bet they're asleep all over America. Of all the gin joints in all the towns in all the world, she walks into mine!" Then "Play it!" Look at all the notes that are casually woven in together here. "One in and one out" of Ugarte and Ilse. Ugarte is an opportunist who serves a good cause for a price —as Rick claims to have done, himself. Rick's cold familiarity with this sort of betrayal of a faith here blurs in one split second with his cynicism about love's promises. Note, next, the date, "December 1941"—making this just pre-Pearl Harbor. "I bet they're asleep," in the light of this date, takes on, automatically, political overtones—and Rick's cynicism about the state of his country too is blurred with the very special cynicism of the jilted lover. Finally, when at the fading of the flashback, Ilse appears at the door, it is the circling finger of light from the airfield that picks her out for us, materializes her; so even *that* variant note, with which we began, is gathered in—visually confounded, in a moment, with the other, the lover's bitter loss.

As Ilse stands there now, all bitterness can be said to have been focused on her person. From here on, Rick can come out with whatever cry he wants; it will be harmless. And note: if the film can

[1] *Casablanca* is included among the Gassner-Nichols *Best Film Plays of 1943– 1944* (Crown, 1945).

somehow dispel that very particular disillusion of his, in this girl—by
subtle act of substitution, all other harsh notes that have been introduced and blurred into this note will be dispelled.

As the film proceeds, Rick does come forth with ever more cynical
outcries. The way to listen to them, as I quote them, is to forget his
characterization as the jilted lover, to abstract the cries from this context, and listen to them in themselves. The film proceeds:

After Ugarte's arrest, Lazslo is advised that Rick may have the letters of transit. But when he goes to Rick, Rick turns him aside coldly
—"The problems of the world are not in my department. I'm a saloon
keeper." When Lazslo retorts that once, he's been told, he was a man
who fought for the underdog, Rick comments, "Yes, I found that a
very expensive hobby." The characterization of sulking lover is
quickly reanimated for us; we are quickly reminded that it is love
Rick found to be expensive. He goes on to say that he may not ever
use the visas himself, but he won't give them to Lazslo; and when
Lazslo mutters, "There must be some reason . . ." replies, "There is.
I suggest that you ask your wife."

Then Ilse herself goes to see Rick for her husband. "Richard!" she
begs. "So I'm Richard again?" he mocks her. "We're back in Paris.
I've recovered my lost identity." But in this interview too, one can, if
one wants, listen to his words in terms of a lost identity not simply
that of the happy lover. "Do I have to hear again what a great man
your husband is and what an important Cause he's fighting for?" "It
was your Cause too . . ." "Well, I'm not fighting for anything any
more, except myself. I'm the only Cause I'm interested in now." In
desperation Ilse pulls a gun. "You'll have to kill me to get them," he
tells her. "If Lazslo, if the Cause means so much to you, go ahead!"—
with this equation again safely reducing all to a wounded lover's
terms.

She cannot shoot, of course; she breaks, she drops the pistol—and
flings herself into his arms. "I tried to stay away . . . If you knew
. . . how much I loved you . . . still love you!" And the film fades
in on them a little later as she explains at last what happened on that
fateful day. She had been married to Lazslo already when she met
Rick, but she had heard that he had been murdered in a concentra-
tion camp. Then that day she had learned that he was alive, had

escaped, was waiting for her. She had had to go. But now, she cries, she'll never have the strength to leave Rick again. "I can't fight it any more. I don't know what's right any longer. You'll have to think for both of us, for all of us."

"I've already made up our minds," Rick answers her. But he does not reveal his decision. The question of how he will act is stretched out to the very end. Rick continues inscrutable. The script notes with regularity, "His expression reveals nothing of his feelings." And he continues to utter the most cynical statements. Of course we more and more tend to suspect that such utterances mask his real intentions. We suspect this, even, with some anguish.

Lazslo ducks into Rick's to elude the police, who have broken up an underground meeting, and Rick, sending Ilse off by a back way, gives Lazslo a drink to settle his nerves. Here it is that Rick demands, "Don't you ever wonder if it's worth all this? I mean what you're fighting for?" Lazslo retorts that he sounds like a man "trying to convince himself of something that in his heart he doesn't believe." And we in the audience at this point would gladly be convinced, ourselves, if we could. There is only one level of meaning at which we would think of taking his words, and the price asked does seem a dreadful one.

As Lazslo and Rick stand there, Renault's men burst in and declare Lazslo under arrest on suspicion of having been at that meeting. Rick grimaces at Lazslo, a dark smile: "It seems destiny has taken a hand." And now he takes his most seemingly cynical step. He calls on Renault and suggests a deal. If he'll release Lazslo, Rick will give Renault a real charge against him. He, Rick, does have those visas. He'll pretend to give them to Lazslo, and this will give Renault the chance to walk in and arrest Lazslo for complicity in the murder of the couriers. Under cover of the excitement—if Renault will help—he, Rick, will make use of the visas himself, to leave for America with Ilse. Which should put Renault's mind to rest about his desire to help Lazslo escape. He's the last man he'd want to meet in America. "I'll miss you," Renault tells him. "Apparently you're the only one in Casablanca who has even fewer scruples than I." So Rick goes to Lazslo and offers him the visas for a hundred thousand francs. He tells him to come down to the café with Ilse, a few minutes before the

Lisbon plane is to leave. When Lazslo tries to thank him, he cuts him short: "Skip it. This is strictly a matter of business." One cynical gesture is here wrapped within another.

This particular gesture is soon enough annulled, in a little sequence all to itself. When Lazslo does try to hand Rick the money, he refuses it gruffly: "Keep it; you'll need it." In this small instance, at any rate, his cynicism has been proved insubstantial. But we wait to see how he will act in the main matter. Ilse thinks that what he intends to do is send Lazslo off on the plane alone. But nobody at this point really knows how anybody else is going to act. Rick is not at all sure about Renault. The film has been building him up as a minor puzzle. "Rick, have you got those letters of transit?" Renault has asked. "Louis, are you pro Vichy or Free French?" Rick has retorted. "I have no convictions . . . I take what comes," Renault has declared; but on his face too the camera has dwelt teasingly, the smile there ambiguous.

Suddenly everything begins to happen fast—though in a manner, still, that keeps us guessing. Renault walks in and—Lazslo and Ilse stare—declares Lazslo under arrest again. "You are surprised about my friend Rick?" At which Rick pulls a gun and informs Renault that there will be no arrests—"yet." And he orders him to check with the airport that there will be no trouble. Renault pulls a fast one and, pretending to call the airport, really calls Strasser, who races for the field.

At the field, at last, all our questions are answered. While Lazslo is off somewhere checking arrangements, Rick tells Renault to fill out the names on the visas. They are: Mr. and Mrs. Victor Lazslo. Ilse, dazed, protests, but Rick tells her: she knows and he knows that the Cause needs Lazslo, and Lazslo needs her—she is part of his work, "the thing that keeps him going." "What about us?" she cries, but he answers her, "We'll always have Paris. We didn't have it. We'd lost it . . . We got it back last night." And "I've got a job to do," he tells her. "Where I'm going, you can't follow." Lazslo returns—"Everything is in order." "All except one thing," Rick adds, and he tells him of Ilse's visit. She did it to try to get the visas, he tells him. To get them, she tried to convince him that she was still in love with him. And he let her pretend. "But that was long ago." "Welcome back to the fight," Lazslo salutes Rick. "Now I know our side will win!" And he and Ilse walk off toward the plane.

Strasser bursts in. Further decisions are called for. Renault cries out that Lazslo is on the plane. Rick has Strasser at gun point, but Strasser calls his bluff: he jumps to the phone and asks for the radio tower. Rick shoots Strasser. The French police burst in; and the next move is Renault's. There is an extensive pause as he and Rick exchange stares—faces, to the last, expressionless. Then: "Round up the usual suspects!" Renault barks, and the police dash off. The roar of the ascending plane is heard. The two men turn their eyes. The beacon light sweeps them. The plane roars up over their heads. It might be a good idea to leave Casablanca for a while, says Renault. There is a Free French garrison at Brazzaville. The ten thousand francs he owes Rick—"that should pay our expenses." "*Our* expenses, Louis?" says Rick. "I think this is the beginning of a beautiful friendship." Arms linked, they walk off into the dark.

Look where the film has brought us out: the embittered one, who would stick his neck out for nobody, steps briskly into battle. Look what has been accomplished: the final note here is the very one documented at this chapter's beginning. Arm in arm with comrade, he steps forth, to music, the dream in his heart intact. "Everything is" indeed "in order," magically. The film has permitted a most disturbing figure to take shape, and there before our eyes has comfortably recruited him. Lazslo may well cry out, "Now I know our side will win!"

What is more, the dream has recruited this unlikely warrior without even leaving us with the sense that we have witnessed a remarkable translation. The love story has borne the brunt of the work: it is the guise of the jilted lover that has allowed the figure to take shape at all and utter his bitter cries; and it is the scene in which he regains his lost faith in the beloved that enables us to cancel out those cries and believe in his entry into the fight. But note a further magic: the impression we are left with at the end of the film is that even if Ilse had never returned to explain her leaving him, if it had come right down to it, Rick, for all his gloominess, would of course have rallied to the Cause. This the dream accomplishes by having him continue his bitter gesturing to the end. When we are given proof of how insubstantial is the cynicism about "the problems of the world" that he professes after Ilse has returned to him, automatically we extend even to his original bitter aspect the same judgment; retroactively we dismiss it too. Thus, as the film ends, that glum mask, shaped there before our eyes, has been interpreted as no disturbing sign but sign, rather, of a faith deeper than other faiths. "Just because you despise me, you're the only one I trust," Ugarte has blurted to Rick. The film, in effect, manages the tour de force of defining Rick's relation to the Cause analogously. It leaves us with this half-conscious feeling: just because he wears the aspect of utter cynicism, one can be sure that he is the real man of faith. Precisely by this contradictory sign, one can spot the man who really cares, the man to be relied upon. And so, in the dark, the shadow of our dim disquiet is dispelled.

Some readers will perhaps protest at this point: why cannot the film be taken at face value? Here is a love story, and it is complicated by the fact that the bitterness the hero feels toward his beloved he transfers to life as a whole; but that, they may protest, covers the matter; to read any more into it is artificial. Even at a strictly literal level, however, the label of jilted lover cannot be made to adequately cover Rick's case. At the end of the film one thing remains altogether unexplained: why it was that he could never return to his country. For the purposes of the dream, this stray end is gathered up neatly enough with Ilse's final departure. As Rick's eyes turn this last time to follow the plane's flight, the one exile is fused forever with the other; an audience is unlikely to remember that they are actually separate matters. For our purposes, though, the distinction stands and—even to be altogether literal—does raise the whole question of a wider reference for the drama enacted than any love alone provides. In that last cry of Lazslo's—"Now I know our side will win!"—the producers of the film themselves unconsciously acknowledge the more crucial identity of the hero, the more general nature of the crisis of faith he suffers.

But it is in unison that films most clearly yield up their secrets. It is the joint evidence of other war films that above all exposes the drama of Rick as something more than a drama of love in a war setting. I can name film after film about the war which raises dramatically the question of the hero's faith, then moves forward to confirm that faith and steps him briskly into battle. Among these films, the hero is by no means always a disillusioned lover—though this note too is repeated.

He may be any one of a variety of figures. Of any of these figures, viewed individually, one could say, as of Rick: this is a very special case, or a case, at any rate, without any general application for the American public. The hero very often is not even a citizen of this country. But line them all up and the question one has to ask is: why do the American film makers so persistently seek out remote cases of just this sort with which to satisfy their public—unless the identification made is actually one that is not remote at all? Here now are a succession of these "special" figures. Look at them all together, as I line them up, and watch the special markings fall away, the figures curiously blur.

Here, for instance, is another Humphrey Bogart film: *Passage to Marseille* (1944). This is one of a number of such films that comfortably tag the hero a Frenchman. His precise identity is again withheld from us for a while—hidden, this time, to be thorough, within not one flashback but an elaborate succession of them. A glum mask is again our starting point, and the question: what lies behind this mask? is again the question that sets the drama in motion. A war correspondent, visiting a Free French unit at a British airfield, singles out the hero and asks about this strange grim man ("I have never seen a stronger face, nor a stranger!"). The commanding officer (Claude Rains again) nods darkly. Off the record, he could a tale unfold. So he unfolds the tale of his own attempt to puzzle out the man. He, Rains, had been first mate on a French ship ordered back to Marseilles during the defense of France, when a little raft was sighted, a bunch of ragged half-starved men taken aboard, Bogart—Matraux—one of them. The men identified themselves as gold miners from an out-of-the-way place, set forth to join the fight for their country; but this story did not seem convincing. Finding Rains sympathetic, the men opened up to him, one after another (in one flashback after another) giving him their true backgrounds—all, that is, but Matraux, who sat in brooding silence throughout. But in a further flashback, which unfolds within one of these flashbacks within a flashback, the identity of Matraux is finally revealed to us. And Matraux is no disappointed lover this time. The betrayal *he* has suffered is Munich. Matraux is a newspaperman, and in his paper he savagely assails the pact. We see his place stoned in retaliation. We see him making his escape in his car, Michele Morgan by his side. And watch this

figure blur now with the figure of Rick in *Casablanca*: on his face as
he drives away is the very same grimace that Rick wore that terrible
day Ilse left him waiting at the station in the rain. But France is the
beloved, this time, who has betrayed him. He and Michele themselves
talk of the betrayal in these terms; the parallel is none that I am
forcing. When he proposes to her, she tells him that she had thought
France, her rival, would always stand between them. But "that is all
ancient history now," he tells her grimly. And so they do get married.
But "a sigh is still a sigh, as time goes by." This broken love even has
its musical leitmotif, a little song that runs through this film much as
"Time Goes By" runs through *Casablanca*. "Some day I'll meet you
again," it moans, as Matraux glooms—even on his honeymoon.

Soon those whom Matraux has outraged by his criticism of the pact
have sent him off to Devil's Island on trumped-up charges. There we
see him grimly pacing a solitary cell; and the scene again could almost
be a scene from *Casablanca*, that scene where Ilse walks in on Rick
and he rails at her. But here Matraux rails at France: "Beautiful deca-
dent France! Rotten France! I hate France!" Matraux has *his* "date
with the heebie jeebies."

Just as in *Casablanca*, the question of whether or not he really does
mean these words he speaks is raised many times before the answer is
given. He manages an escape from the island, with a small group of
convicts of various backgrounds—eager, in spite of all they feel they
have suffered there from their country, to return and fight for it.
They look to Matraux as to their natural leader in such a venture.
And he does lead them in the escape. But all the while the question
hovers for us: are his intentions in escaping really, as *they* think, to
fight for his country? Back on shipboard, as the film begins to reel in
some of its flashbacks, this question is very much the concern of
Rains. In mid-ocean the Vichy armistice is announced. The camera
moves among weeping faces, then hesitates before Matraux's face as
before a code. A ghost of a smile distorts it. Rains and an officer who
are watching him argue the meaning of this smile. The officer gives it
a dark reading, but Rains is willing to stake his life that Matraux is
"more of a Frenchman than any of us." He goes to him now and asks
his help in seizing the ship for de Gaulle. As in *Casablanca*, here just
before that moment which will prove the hero indeed such a Frenchman, the disquieting image at the heart of the dream stands out in

sharp relief. "I don't care anything about my country any more!" cries Matraux. "Her death is complete! I'm trying to get back to my wife. I have never intended to join the fight!" His words are promptly annulled—more promptly than in *Casablanca*. (The very beginning of the film has told us in advance the outcome, but we tend rather to forget this.) When certain villains on board try to hold the ship for Vichy, the first man to the guns to keep them at bay—is Matraux. When a Nazi plane, in answer to a wireless message from these villains, dive bombs the ship, the one to bring it down—is Matraux. The film now returns us to the British airfield—and to that image so many films have made familiar, of the fighting group that is one happy family. Rains, concluding his story to the correspondent, leads him among the men from Devil's Island, identifying them at their tasks. At the opening of the film, the correspondent had remarked not merely upon the strangeness of Matraux but upon the strangeness of that French unit as a whole. The men had seemed to him, all of them, so silent, so grim. Where was that gay banter he remembered from the last war? But here this impression is quite forgotten. The dream has again brought us clear.

It is not only when Humphrey Bogart plays the part that other figures tend to blur with the figure of Rick in *Casablanca*. *The Impostor* (1944) features Jean Gabin. As the film opens, this hero (a Frenchman again) is again cursing his country. But Munich has nothing to do with it here. He is a criminal, about to be executed. (In *Passage to Marseille*, Matraux was introduced to us in the company of criminals and it was the length of several flashbacks before he was clearly distinguished from them. In *Casablanca* too, recall, Renault wondered aloud—only half-joking—whether it was not some crime that was the cause of Rick's exile.) The hero of *The Impostor* is saved from execution by an air raid, which crumbles the jail and allows him to make his escape—and allows the film to unwind its dream reversal of the image we have been given.

This reversal is a more difficult one, and the dream work is managed with the special assistance of one character who, throughout, stubbornly anticipates the final magic effect—through the power of suggestion fools us into seeing what is not really there to be seen. He refuses, that is, to recognize the hero's behavior for what it clearly is. He is Gabin's commanding officer—for Gabin makes good his escape by donning the uniform, papers, ostensible identity of a French soldier he finds dead on the road. Pétain has just broadcast his surrender, so once in uniform, he is immediately involved in all the decisions facing soldiers as to whether or not they will try somehow to continue the fight. As I describe them, the hero's actions will seem all too clear. The men with whom he finds himself are all for shipping out for Africa, to sign up with de Gaulle. He embarks on a ship with them— just as Matraux took part in the escape from Devil's Island; but as a fugitive, this is the practical move for him to make. At Point Noire, where the others rush to join the Free French, he promptly declares his intentions of becoming a civilian. Then he joins up with them after all; but he does so after learning that whoever signs up can ask for advance pay. Collecting the advance pay, he enters a shop to price civilian clothes and to inquire about job opportunities across the river. He decides not to buy the clothes, but only after the shopkeeper tells him that six months' army pay would buy a rubber plantation. He never follows up this tip, either, but he doesn't get a chance: the group is suddenly moved up the Congo. At the new post, he sulks about, holding himself aloof from the others. They are always talking about their beloved country and bringing out photos, reviving memories. He snarls at them, "The past is dead and buried! Let it stay there!" All of which would seem to read plainly enough—if it were not for the eye of the lieutenant upon the scene. All through this the lieutenant is watching him, as Rains watched Bogart in *Passage to Marseille*, laying bets with himself that this man is "more of a Frenchman than any of" them. He is promoting him steadily, to force on him the test which will *prove* him the reverse of what he seems.

The test arrives. The lieutenant falls sick and runs around delirious, shooting off his gun—setting the lives of the men in danger. The hero, at the risk of his own life, disarms him. Soon after, the group goes off to battle in Libya and the hero with a handful of men takes an entire enemy garrison. On the return to camp, his comrades gather around him, singing his praises. "We all fought together," he cries, and arm in arm they drink to one another, and to Britain, and to Russia, and to America too, "who's sending lots of things"—here again the image with which this chapter started: one big happy family.

This film does almost admit that an about-face has been effected. Gabin speaks of the strange effect it has had upon him to assume the identity of another man. We also witness many touching efforts on the part of the men to make him feel less "out of things." At one point he says right out that a great change has come over him—like the change that comes over a man when he falls in love. ("A beautiful woman, our France," the lieutenant nods.) Yet though these words are spoken, the final impression we are left with is that this love has really always lived in his breast. The attitude of the lieutenant helps to build this impression, and also the fact that Gabin (like Rick), with the exception of this one lapse, continues to the end to make cynical statements. On the very eve of battle he comments, "I have just my own skin, and it's not worth fighting for." In our minds two images are intimately linked, as if the one were to be deduced from the other: the gloomy seeming-faithless gesture—and the decisive blow for the Cause. Near the end of the film, one of the soldiers is talking about Gabin to a stranger. His words refer not to Gabin's eventual behavior but to his behavior from the very start. "We were driven from our homes," he says, "into a cruel killing world. We would have died if it had not been for him. He was more of a man, stronger than any of us." The sullen mask is again recognized as the sign of strength, the mark of one to be relied upon before all others.

At one point in this film the hero tries to decline a promotion the lieutenant is offering, and the lieutenant suddenly challenges him: "I know plenty about you. Back in France they had to practically shoot you to make you fall back." It appears that the lieutenant, knowing the record of the man whose name Gabin has adopted, has taken Gabin to be one like Matraux, suffering from political disillusionment. And the one figure, at his words, does easily dissolve into the other. Later in the film he dissolves for us as easily into quite another figure. The story continues a while longer, after the return from battle. In the course of events, the hero's real origins are discovered. The lieutenant promptly defends him against official protests—in this fashion: Many unsung heroes rallied to France in her hour of need. They weren't forced to take up arms and there was "no hope of profit" in it for them. "Simple everyday people" they were, and the hero was "one of that number." He took the other soldier's name and honored it. As the lieutenant speaks, the hero does merge in our minds with these "everyday people," his criminal background dissolves into simply a humble one, and he stands there before us just a guy who had to come up the hard way ("Nobody ever gave me anything" has been his motto).

This translation of the criminal figure into the figure of the everyday guy is not an isolated instance. It is to be found, for example, in an earlier film than *The Impostor*—*Mr. Lucky* (1943).

Mr. Lucky also provides an example even more pronounced of the film's ability to outface the very facts it arrays before us. This film has more to outface, for it dares to make its hero an American, and the setting is the States. The time set is, of course, to ease things, pre-Pearl Harbor, and the hero is no everyday citizen at first glance but a boss gambler. A light touch is also added. This hero enters whistling. Mr. Lucky (Cary Grant) confronts us not with glooming sour stare but, eyes propped wide, with the comic doubletake (Grant adept at this face as Bogart at the other); crying not, in dark accent, "I'm the only Cause I'm interested in!" but, when the draft call comes, "They can't do this to me; I'm a civilian!" In front of the recruiting poster— finger-leveled Uncle Sam: "I WANT YOU!"—he performs a wonderful pantomime: uneasiness he can't place, start of recognition, nimble sidestep. The key is a different one, but the tune is the same: "This isn't my war!" "My war," says Mr. Lucky, "was crawling up out of the gutter. The hard way. I won that war. I don't recognize any other." So he ducks the draft, by assuming the identity of a 4F member of his gang, one Boskopolis, who's just died. Then—he needs money to launch his gambling ship—he sets out to try to milch some thousands of dollars from a certain war relief organization. His plan is to run the gambling concession at their charity ball—all the machines to be conveniently equipped with false bottoms.

In this film too, one can isolate the clear lines of an about-face. Again the new identity the hero has assumed plays its part. A letter arrives from Boskopolis's mother, back in Greece, describing the futile valiant defense of that homeland, and Mr. Lucky is impressed. He also falls in love with Larraine Day, active in War Relief, Inc. Like the hero of *The Impostor,* he speaks right out about the change that has come over him. "I woke up," he says one day. And he doesn't run off with the take from the gambling machines. In fact, he decides to

convert his gambling ship into a transport to deliver medical supplies
for War Relief, Inc. And at the end of that trip he himself joins the
Merchant Marine.

But though the film lines up these facts for us in clear array, a
synopsis in terms of them is altogether inadequate. Here is the more
pertinent synopsis: This is the drama of a man misunderstood, a man
whose girl, to her shame, mistrusts his motives. In the end, this girl
wakes up, recognizes the hero for the hero he is. "You're right always," she comes at last to say.

The dream accomplishes its ends by simple distraction. It carefully
lines up alongside the one set of facts, another set: one episode after
another in which the hero is attacked not on the score of his very real
guilt but for something for which he is blameless. The fact of that
real guilt, in all this, goes barely noticed—and the fact later of his
change of heart.

When "Joe Boskopolis" goes to Larraine Day with his plan, she
tells him bluntly, "I don't trust your motives," and sends him away.
This is our starting point: she knows better than to trust him; so do
we. Next day he turns up again to volunteer as a simple recruit—
saucily, big-eyed, "I'd do anything to help the Cause, anything!" Larraine calls his bluff: she sets him to knitting. But Joe sticks. And he
soon has this "iceberg" thawing. He thinks up a fast one, confides in
her that he has relatives over in Greece. If he's 4F and can't enlist, the
least he can do is help raise medical supplies for "those poor people."
Larraine falls for it and, ashamed of herself, she relieves him of the
knitting. So far so clear to *us*, if not to Larraine. But from here on the
subtle confusion begins.

Joe has a rip in his coat and Larraine takes him home with her to
mend it. Joe interprets her action as well he might and tries to kiss
her. She protests. (Already we sympathize with Joe.) Meanwhile she
has spotted a trick coin in his possession. She has seen Joe put this
coin to use for War Relief, Inc. A certain Scotsman has tried to over-
charge them for some blankets; Joe has flipped the Scotsman for
double or nothing and, of course, won. Larraine, who has just put
that two and two together, challenges Joe: "Suppose we settle it with
the game you played with MacDougall." The game is a matter of
guessing which hand, and the coin has a little gadget to hook it to the
back of Joe's coat. Larraine cries, "Neither hand!" but—this time he

hasn't cheated. He rebukes her, "Never give a sucker an even break, but don't cheat a friend—I live by it." "I lost, but I didn't know the rules of the game," she protests. Poor girl, we feel—no, she doesn't at all know the rules; it is *he* who plays by the rules. He quietly asks for his hat. Blushing again, she suddenly cries out, "Joe, will you run the gambling concession at the ball?" Now she knows that she can trust him.

We know perfectly well that she cannot. In fact, he tells us so himself, promptly reports to the boys, "She laid it right in my lap!" And yet: we are blushing still, with the heroine, for having doubted his morality in this other instance. Our distraction has begun. It deepens. Larraine's grandfather rages upon the scene, wanting to know what's all this about gambling. And now Larraine must blush for *him,* for he in turn attacks Joe on grounds entirely unjust. He first attacks him on the outrageous grounds of the name he bears: "Get that greasy black head out of here!" Then he looks up Boskopolis's record and begins to attack him on the basis of this. Larraine won't believe what he says about him. And she is right, of course, for Joe is not Boskopolis. Nor does he know of the record, which is not a nice one.

But Larraine now, in a quick counterattack against her grandfather, proceeds to misuse Joe again herself. She drives him off to the home of the other side of her family, in Maryland; and there, by phone, she blackmails her grandfather: unless he permits the gambling concession to stand, she will marry this man. It works. "Yeah, why wouldn't it work?" Joe comments, and this time rebukes her at some length. In the drama of *Larraine's* conversion, this is the major scene. "Anything for the Cause!" he taunts. He tells her, "I know where I stand with you once you've cashed in on me." And, he implies, she fails to recognize whom she is scorning.

The moment is worth dwelling over, for it is here that the figure of the criminal undergoes complete translation into the figure of the everyday American guy. "You think the worst thing that could happen to you is to marry me," he says. He turns to the family portraits on the walls. She has led him among these, telling him of each, and one after another has been a man of inherited wealth—except for the last in the line, the earliest ancestor. Joe triumphantly indicates this portrait. Go back far enough and somebody "made all that dough" for the others. The moral looms: in scorning Joe she is in effect scorning that first of her ancestors. Larraine, herself, has prepared the ground for the equation quietly effected here. To her grandfather, another self-made man, she has remarked that he and Joe have a lot in common. "You're both tough," she sums it up. "I know *you* are in a highly moral civilized way," she has thrown in, "but it's fundamentally the same thing: character." "How long since anybody ever had control over you?" she has asked Joe. "Nobody ever had or will." Character. Under the power of this heading, a long series of items now coalesce into one. Her grandfather's hot temper, Joe's liking for flashy ties and his scorn for traffic signals, a long-ago out-of-the-ordinary act of that remoter ancestor—what but the same sort of thing, we dimly feel. Her ancestors "never seemed to behave the way people expected," Larraine had boasted. His descendants "had quite a time living down" the first of the line: he, a slave owner, was killed at Harper's Ferry, fighting side by side with John Brown! Now, as Joe chides her, here they stand, side by side—her grandfather, this remoter ancestor, Joe— marked for us by the dream with the identical sign: all of them rugged individuals. Out of some perverse snobbery, at odds with all most brave in her own background, she has been scorning this man. She doesn't know what to say. So she does the appropriate: she embraces him.

The further drama we now look forward to is the drama of Larraine's definitive awakening. Yet look where literally we are: the hero is still frankly intending to run off with the take from the gambling concession. It is soon after this very scene that we see him give the boys their instructions, cautioning, "No slip-ups!" Perfectly clearly we hear him give these orders. Perfectly clearly we next witness his about-face; we see him receive the letter from Boskopolis's mother; we hear him, arrived late at the ball, blurt out to Larraine, "I woke up!" But we are blissfully confused. The further thrill we stubbornly anticipate is some final act to that drama of her conversion—which is of course what we are given: the final misunderstanding, most cruel of all, and the final total "recognition."

Joe tells the boys that the plan is off: "Our take is nothing." The boys will not have it. They force him at pistol point to make the grab. In on this Larraine walks. She doesn't see the pistols, just Joe there with his hands full of the money that was never turned over to her. "Oh, Joe!" she groans. He even has to knock her out, so that she won't get hurt. "Now I recognize you, Joe boy," says one of the gang. And there he stands, indeed, for recognition—the disturbing figure dominant in all these dreams. But for one in the audience he has been subtly altered beyond all recognition: he is the one, simply, always cruelly misunderstood. Such he now proves himself. At the risk of his life, he tackles these villains single-handed; is shot, sorely wounded, but drags himself off, the money clutched to his breast; then sends the money back by messenger to Larraine—who sees how wrong again she was to doubt him. Further confirmation: her grandfather's agents hand her the proof of that nasty record of which he has spoken—and the photograph attached is not of Joe at all! The film ends as Larraine works out her contrition. Joe, sufficiently recovered, has set sail to deliver those medical supplies. Unable to learn his whereabouts, she has managed to get to the dock only in time to see the ship pull out and to cry across the widening gap, "Oh, take me with you, please!" We see her now, waiting at the pier. Day after day, we gather, she waits there patiently. One would not know the once haughty girl. At the very last her humility is rewarded: out of the fog walks Joe (in the uniform of the Merchant Marine).

All of which, set down on paper, sounds perhaps like ineffective magic. Set down on paper, certain stubborn facts tend to obtrude—like the fact that if Joe is not this Boskopolis of unsavory record, he has, after all, assumed Boskopolis's name for questionable purposes of his own. For the reader these facts may stand out. For one sitting out front the distractions are, to say the least, more lively.

I have not even done full justice to the bravado of this film. Here is an incident I have omitted: Joe has pulled off a bit of fraud on the side. He has bullied a creditor, Mr. Hargrave, into letting him tear up a check from War Relief, Inc.—deftly substituting a blank check at the crucial moment and cashing the real check himself. At the charity ball, Larraine announces to Joe that her grandfather is out of town looking for Hargrave. We see Joe take this in, add two and two; see him proceed upstairs, collect the necessary cash, stick it in an envelope addressed to Hargrave, and stroll downstairs again. When Hargrave and the grandfather storm in and confront him, he calmly takes this envelope from his pocket and hands it across, remarking that he hasn't been able to reach Hargrave, because he has been out of town. Hargrave is disarmed, and the grandfather is disarmed—and we have been disarmed long ago. Here is measure of the film's powers of distraction: in spite of ourselves we comfortably nod: You see!

There are some films, more simple-minded than any I have detailed so far, in which the magic of the dream is abbreviated crudely. A particular moment from such a film will exhibit the essential nature of all these dreams in what amounts to caricature. This is true of *China* (1943). The hero of this film is another American on his way up—a certain Jones, played by Alan Ladd. While Mr. Lucky was surreptitiously identified for us as an everyday figure, Jones can be established as one openly, for this setting is a remote one, and the time is again pre-Pearl Harbor. He is a salesman for a big American oil company operating in the Far East. When a Chinese Intelligence chief chides him for selling to the Japanese, and delivers an impassioned speech about the issues at stake, he interrupts him: "Going to give me more of that tripe? . . . War's your business, oil is mine." On the road to Shanghai, where Jones has a business appointment, he encounters Loretta Young (also American) in charge of a pretty little group of Chinese coeds. They too have an appointment—"with the destiny of China." They are bound for a university in a distant city, and they ask Mr. Jones to take them there. Jones consents to give them a lift, but for a long while he insists that he will not go out of his way. One of the coeds decides to stay behind at the farm of her parents, when the truck makes a stop there; and her parents also take into their keeping the orphaned baby, little "Donald Duck," whom Jones's pal (William Bendix) has picked up along the way. Just as the truck is nearing the crossroad at which Jones has said that he must put them all down, word comes that the Japanese are approaching that farm. Loretta says that Jones must turn back. But if he turned back, he would be late for his appointment. He refuses. At which Bendix challenges him to a fight: he'll have to knock him down first if he wants to drive on. The two have a violent scuffle. Mr. Jones does knock Bendix down. But instead of proceeding on about his business, he here declares in gruff hurt tones: "I was going back anyway!" Off he goes to the rescue—for which he is too late; and from here on he is definitely in the fight. He was going to all along!—here, in this moment, is the substance of all these films in crude shorthand: the faithless gesture given expression, and then denied.

A similar gambit can be recalled in *Casablanca*—there but one sleight of hand among many. In this instance too, it was the cynicism of "business is business" that the dream was concerned to wish away. For among the various guises flickeringly assumed by Rick is also this one—of the man out for what he can make. "I got well paid for it," he has said of his past engagements. When he promises Lazslo the letters of transit, he demands a high price. Skip the thanks, he tells him, "This is strictly a matter of business." Then when Lazslo tries to pay him, "Keep it, you'll need it," he grunts, just a touch reproachfully.

There is a comparable moment in *To Have and Have Not* (1944), another film to feature Humphrey Bogart. Morgan, an American settled in Martinique, makes his living as a guide, and with the boat he runs he could be very useful to the Free French. (Again this is pre-Pearl Harbor). But "You save France, I'll save my boat," he declares. His sympathies? "Minding my own business." He agrees, finally, to run one errand for the underground, but he'll do it, he says, just because he needs the money. When they beg him later to look after one of their wounded, he answers, "Not a chance." His landlady proposes a bargain: if he'll help them, she'll cancel his bill. "Will you throw in *her* bill too?" he inquires, indicating Lauren Bacall (another American who has wandered far from home). She will. At which he declares in bitter tones, "You almost had me figured out right—except for one thing: I still owe you that bill."

The cynicism of Mr. Jones in *China* is specifically established as that of one obsessed with making money. But this is not strictly so of Morgan in *To Have and Have Not*. In the Hemingway novel on which the film is "based," the hero was, of course, a man politically disillusioned. But in the film his background is left quite blank. As in *Casablanca*, we are diverted from doing too much guessing about him by the suggestion that he is the victim of an unhappy love affair. Lauren Bacall offers this diagnosis. "Who was the girl, Steve?" And though this leaves things a bit less definite than they were made in *Casablanca*, it serves to distract us. As in that film, the dream then leans heavily on the heroine's success in breaking down his resistance to *her*. He succumbs to the Free French and succumbs to her vigorous wooing at a significantly parallel rate, and says his definitive "yes" to each simultanously. Off they go together into battle, in fact. Their honeymoon is to be the risky attempt to free an underground leader from Devil's Island.

But there are other films besides *China* in which it is specifically the obsession with making one's way that seems for a while to characterize the hero. Another is *Reunion in France* (1942). In this film, an about-face does not have to be obscured. The drama framed is one of literal misunderstanding. The hero is a French industrialist, and when France falls, he continues to run his factory, at the service of Vichy. So he is abandoned by all those whom he loves. But in the end they learn that all the time he has been working within the enemy camp, turning out defective mechanisms. "How terribly lonely he must be!" wails his fiancée (Joan Crawford), who deserted him with all the rest; and she hurries back to face with him the death he must inevitably suffer when his work is discovered.

I could go on duplicating, triplicating these figures, duplicating, triplicating the sleights of hand, subtle or simple, with which the dream persuades us how wrong we have been—to be disturbed by a cynicism we only *thought* we recognized. I have omitted not merely further examples of figures already defined, but examples of further types of figures altogether. There are a number of films, for example, that question dramatically, then dramatically affirm, the faith of one who is foreign born. One film features an expatriate in the role. To detail more would be redundant. Line up together merely those films I have described and see how pervasive the image is. Figures at the fringes of society, figures at its center, those at the bottom of the ladder, those at the top, some mourning a faith they never had, some a faith they once had but have lost—that bitter light, telling of exile, which swept the room in which Rick sat, catches them all in its circuit. From film to film, the figure takes to itself new aspects. And even, in many an instance, within a single film, through any of a dozen casual ways—through a half-joking exchange (*Casablanca*) or a friend's oratory (*The Impostor*), a misunderstanding (*The Impostor*) or a bitter pretense (*Casablanca, To Have and Have Not*)—it dissolves one figure into some other.

If the image is curiously pervasive, it is also more intractable than I have suggested. It is well to take a more complete look at the endings of all these films.

Look again at the ending of *Casablanca*. Stout words Rick utters to Ingrid—about the Cause, about the job he has to do. And off he goes, arm in arm with comrade—"the beginning of a beautiful friendship," he observes. Off he goes into the fight. But—off goes the plane too, to America, his country, to which he can never return, bearing Ingrid, whom he loves, and whom he will never see again. Nor has the music let us forget that "man must have his mate." A stoic exit, Rick's. One may breathe: he *needs* to be "stronger than any of us." [2]

One may breathe this at the end of all these films. For though in each case comfortably tagged now the warrior who will win for us, there, if one looks twice, is one whose condition closely resembles that of the lonely figure who worried us at the start. The dream has been able to effect no translation too total—lest, it seems, we wake.

Certain of the heroes, recall, must step into battle grievously misunderstood. Here by the very sleight of hand with which the film chooses to deny the hero's acquaintance with one kind of bitterness, it imposes on him a new bitterness. The actor need hardly change his expression—seldom does. This is true of Mr. Lucky and of the heroes of *China, To Have and Have Not,* and even, briefly, *Casablanca*. And some of the films labor the point exquisitely. At the end of *The Impostor,* when the hero's real identity is discovered, the lieutenant defends him vigorously, but military form must be observed: he is stripped of his rank, before all his men, and he is told that he can no longer bear that borrowed name. The lieutenant tells him to choose in its place whatever name he wants, but he chooses to step off into battle bearing no name at all.

Mr. Lucky is the only film of all those I have detailed that ventures at the end to bring its hero home. Even in that film an alternate note has been sounded. A man down at the docks where Larraine waits for

[2] One popular and lively group of war films that I have not mentioned so far is here worth noting briefly. The genre borrows from the documentary manner and dramatizes a group battle situation. *Guadalcanal Diary* (1943), *A Wing and a Prayer* (1944), *Objective Burma* (1945) are examples. Almost invariably in these films the drama is of some stoic stint, some mission the raison d'être of which the fighters cannot be told until the mission is completed. They must fight on grimly, not knowing whether they lay down their lives for some real purpose or not. To be sure, this is often literally enough the nature of battle. And yet there are other battle situations the makers of those films might have chosen. The one image does compulsively take shape, wherever one turns, in the films of these years.

Joe day after day informs an observer that Joe's ship has been sunk. We thrill appropriately to this news, and only at the very last moment of the film is it disproved. In other films, such news is final. In the last moments of *Passage to Marseille*, Matraux's plane returns from a bombing mission and he is lifted out dead. At the end of *The Impostor*, Gabin volunteers for a particularly dangerous battlefront and fails to return. At the end of *China*, Alan Ladd, too, walks into certain death. If I described them in detail, none of these deaths would be called exactly realistic. Here, for example, is the finale of *China*: The Chinese have planned to dynamite a mountain pass through which a Japanese division must file, but the Japanese get there ahead of schedule; and so Ladd takes it upon himself to delay them. He jumps down onto the road and asks the commanding officer for some gasoline for a stalled car. The officer, amused by his audacity, takes time out to bum an American cigarette from him and then to inform him that Pearl Harbor has just been attacked. Ladd tells him that millions of "little guys" like himself will see to it that Japan is beaten. He then sees to it that he, Ladd, will get a bullet in the stomach: he tosses his own cigarette into the officer's face. And the pass explodes over them all, as Loretta on the mountain above proudly weeps.

There is a touch of the suicidal to be discerned in the final gestures of these heroes, a shadow of that impulse in which we have seen them indulge in their hours of bitterness. Dying for their country is the name given this gesture now, but the echo of an earlier despair remains.

At the end of *To Have and Have Not*, Bogart sets out to storm Devil's Island, arm in arm with Lauren Bacall. Jaunty smiles sit on both their faces. Those smiles may be read as the smiles of the valorous—and of two who are very pleased with each other; but they easily waver into the smiles of those who walk into death with a certain reckless pleasure. When this hero said "yes" to the heroine, he had warned her that if she came with him it might be a long long time before she would get home. "Maybe never," she had countered gayly. She might have meant that she intended to stick with him; but she might equally have meant that he and she were very likely to be killed off.

The gesture with which the hero in one of these films steps off at last into battle is not definitively suicidal. The note is sometimes a wavering one, as here. One could say, for example, of Rick in *Casablanca* that he enters the fight without hope of any homecoming, yet determined to fight on for the love, as it were, of what he has not. Here is the range of this final gesture, however: it wavers between the suicidal and the rather bleakly stoical.

 3

"I've got to bring him back home where he belongs!" (a Hollywood Ariadne)

Turn to some films made after the war's end or when the end was in sight and in sight the hero's return, to take up his life again. Turn to some of those boy-gets-girl stories for which Hollywood is famous. Can one find there some happier heroes?

Here are seven representative films of 1945 and 1946: *Love Letters, State Fair, Those Endearing Young Charms, Adventure, Lost Weekend, Spellbound, Pride of the Marines*. The setting for each of these dramas is home ground again, and each features a love story.

The first thing one has to note about all these films is that the old descriptive term—"boy gets girl"—no longer fits. In *Lost Weekend*, it is the heroine, not the hero, who gives the kisses. "Bend down," she says peremptorily. It is *she* who bombards *him* with notes—"Call me, call me, call me!"; and when he doesn't call, she calls—until he begs, "Stop it, Helen, stop it, stop it!" (Even then she persists.) In *Spellbound*, it is *she* who walks into *his* room in the middle of the night. This particular heroine, being a psychiatrist, pauses to remark upon her own behavior: "I thought I wanted to discuss your book with you. I don't! . . . I am amazed at my subterfuge!" But "I am going to do what I want to do!" she announces, and when he takes to his heels, she pursues him around the country. In *Pride of the Ma-rines,* when letters and telephone calls get her nowhere, the heroine resorts to abducting the hero bodily "home," there in the face even of his desperate "Get me out of here!" to insist that they shall be mar-ried. In *Adventure* too, the heroine does the proposing. And the hero-ine of *Those Endearing Young Charms* takes things into *her* own hands: "I'm shameless . . . I want you with me always, even if you don't. I love you I love you I love you!" She tells the hero, "You will come back to me, you'll see," and when he begs, "Don't, Helen . . . You think I love you—" she tells him bluntly, "You've got to." Even the little country heroine of *State Fair,* right after the hero has an-nounced that he intends to remain a bachelor, is bold enough to re-mark, "I could never marry anyone but you, ever." And the heroine of *Love Letters* pursues the hero with an abandon that reduces him at one point to giggling helplessness.

From the account I've given, these heroines might appear to be direct descendants of those villainous ladies of the twenties, the Vamps. But I have omitted the terms of our introduction to them. Here, in each case, is the heroine as the hero first finds her:

Ingrid Bergman in *Spellbound* (psychiatrist at a mental hospital) has been nicknamed "Miss Frozen Puss" by a patient, "Human Gla-cier" by one of the male doctors. "Very much like embracing a text-book," the latter remarks, after trying his best to melt her. The script describes her as "slightly austere." She even wears glasses at times— by which Hollywood tends to make itself very clear. A hotel detec-tive, at one point, takes her to be a schoolteacher or librarian. In *Ad-venture,* Greer Garson *is* a librarian, again bespectacled. We learn from her roommate, Joan Blondell, that men get nowhere with her. A "mild tomato" the hero calls her, their first time out together. In *Those Endearing Young Charms,* the heroine has come to the city from a small town, Ellsworth Falls, holds down a little job behind a perfume counter, lives, very properly, with her mother, and is courted very properly—until she meets Robert Young—by a nice young man also from Ellsworth Falls. He has named her "Snow White," and Robert Young, upon first meeting her, declares that he sees what he means. In *State Fair,* the heroine is a girl on a small farm, for whom even the state fair seems a huge adventure. In *Pride of the Marines,* she is a well-behaved Philadelphia girl. In *Lost Weekend,* she moves in somewhat more sophisticated circles, for she works on "Time" magazine and she goes to cocktail parties, but she's from a "nice respectable" family in Ohio and she gives the impression of being from out of town. In *Love Letters,* she is a foundling who has been brought up by an old maid, "guarded ferociously from the world." Victoria is her prim name until, the victim of amnesia, she takes the name of Singleton. Her amnesia brings her into a state of even greater innocence— though Jennifer Jones does make it look like something else.

In several of these films, in fact, the first round between hero and heroine is one in which she, maidenlike, rebuffs *his* advances. For he is capable of making advances. This hero is not, as one might have assumed from his piteous cries of protest, shy of women. Near the beginning of *Pride of the Marines,* the heroine has to tell John Garfield that if he stops the car, she'll scream; the heroine of *Adventure* has to tell Clark Gable that he cannot come up to her room; the heroine of *Those Endearing Young Charms* has to escort Robert Young very firmly to the door. If she is known as "Snow White" or "Miss Frozen Puss," he has gained for himself the title of "Brown-eyed Devil" or "The Black Prince," "Flying Wolf," "Casanova himself." This hero is not shy of women but of marriage. "It just ain't up my alley," he claims (*Pride of the Marines*). When this question comes up, "Do yourself a favor," he advises—"clear out" (*Lost Weekend*). As someone quips, "He wouldn't even marry his own mother" (*Adventure*).

From this it might appear that the hero is that familiar old-time villain, the Gay Deceiver. But he is no more that figure than the heroine is the Vamp. If he misuses the heroine, he takes no joy in it. "Are you having a good time?" one heroine challenges. "Rotten!" is his reply. "This is no fun!"

The heroine herself is apt to muse for some time upon his true nature (she herself sometimes naming him at first the Cad—but knowing better in her heart of hearts). Let her give the diagnosis. Studying Joseph Cotten, Jennifer Jones speaks at last: "You're broken up inside!" Gazing at Robert Young, Jane Wyman speaks: "You're afraid of yourself!" Garson, the morning after her first date with Gable, muses aloud: "He's like an animal caught in a trap or a maze! You try to help him and he turns on you, afraid that you'll tear his heart out!" "Leave him alone, Miss Ilse," Sam had begged in

Casablanca. The cry of this hero too is: Leave me alone, I am
wounded already. Here is no hero to contrast to Rick. Here on home
ground is the same figure met again.

When Rick lashed out at Ilse it was because she reminded him
cruelly of a faith he had lost—a faith that stood in the dream for
more than faith in a girl. In these films too, the hero sees the heroine
as cruelly unattainable. This is why he cries, "Clear out!" cries "Stop
it, Helen, stop it, stop it!" And in these films too, she is in the dream
only a symbol: in the nightmare of a girl he does not feel that he can
have is shadowed forth the nightmare of a life itself that seems out of
reach.

The dream, of course, stepped Rick into battle, and the dream
brings this weary wanderer home. But it does so with comparable diffi-
culty, does so only through the rather extraordinary exertions which I
have described on the part of the heroine. Here those unorthodox
motions are explained: she is assigned in the dream an Ariadne role
(Hollywood version)—to wind the hero forth from the dark laby-
rinth of his distraction to that final embrace that is (presumably) the
day.

It is her conscription to this task that so translates the heroine,
impels her to throw off her accustomed shyness. One can usually isolate the moment of her change. A special glint enters her eye as she
perceives the labor that must be hers. "Turn around and walk out,"
he begs her. "Walk fast and don't look back." But "You don't know
me," she suddenly cries. And he soon does not. Her assaults must be
full scale, to bring this hero home; for wrapped in his dark plight, he
resists her stubbornly. "The Slugger," Greer Garson comes to be
named in *Adventure.* And the nickname is earned by each one of
them. The films echo, in crescendo, to their battle cries: "I'm going to
fight!" (*Those Endearing Young Charms*); "I'm going to fight and
fight and get you free!" (*Spellbound*); "I'm going to fight and fight
and fight!" (*Lost Weekend*). *To Have and Have Not,* recall, assigned
Bacall an analogous role—to woo Bogart for the Cause. When near
the film's start, at Bogart's request, she walked all the way around
him, then announced, "No strings tied to you—not yet," she too spoke
with the determination of the dream itself. Hers was a more flagrant
wooing, actually, than any of these, and it gained more comment (Bacall playing the role with a pleased self-consciousness of herself going

through the paces that gave it the boldness of caricature—as, giving him a kiss, she offered the suggestion, "It's even better when you help," or waving a bottle of chloroform over a rival she inquired, "All right if I give her a whiff of this?" her famous head-down stare, "the look," leveled at him mercilessly reel after reel). *That* dream had to make her brazen in order to draw him into battle. (*Casablanca* had to strip Ingrid of her modesty and walk her into Rick's room in the middle of the night.) *This* dream has to make the heroine brazen in order to draw the hero into a life that he refuses to believe in for himself—in Hollywood terms, draw him into the heroine's arms (where life begins).

Just as, in any of the war films I have described, the hero's reluctance about entering the fight could seem at first glance a very special instance, so here: the doubts and fears in which this hero is entangled seem hardly applicable to the general public. But again, when one film is lined up next to another, the question confronts one: Why does Hollywood seek out with such regularity the special instance of just this sort with which to satisfy that public? And once this question has been posed, one can see, even within an individual film, the special instance dissolve into the generality.

Here, for example, is the story of *Pride of the Marines* (1946). This hero is given a very special reason for feeling that he cannot hope to build any sort of life for himself. He has been blinded in the war.

The night that Al (John Garfield), lying in a West Coast hospital, is told that he will never see again, he has a nightmare—eerily visualized for us in the photographic negative: He is coming home. He runs down the railroad platform toward his girl. But when he comes up to her, she doesn't know him. Slowly she does see that it is he, and they embrace; but their embrace is interrupted as a blind man draws near. They turn and stare at him, in his black glasses and odd cap— and suddenly, behind those glasses, it is the hero's face that clears; the camera moves up on it in a relentless rush. As he screams, "Ruth! Ruth!" she is hurrying off backwards down the platform, out of his reach. It is when he wakes from this nightmare that Al writes to Ruth, not telling her that he is blind, but writing merely that he is not coming back to her. A kind nurse explains matters when she calls long distance, but it will be a big job, she warns, bringing him "back home where he belongs." It's not too big a job for Ruth. The Navy wants to send him back to Philadelphia to receive the Navy Cross. "It ain't my home any more!" he protests. In spite of his protests, they put him on a train; and Ruth meets him at the station, without his knowing it is she, and drives him to the home of friends, where he used to board. His friends assure him that he can get his old job back if he will take a little special training. He doesn't respond. They leave him alone with Ruth. "You're home, Al," she tells him. But "It's no good!" he cries. It's no good, and he will not be a drag on her! And he begs her, piteously, to let him leave. "I won't," she tells him. So he tries to leave by himself and stumbles over the decked Christmas tree (it is Christmas Eve) and falls to the floor, all tangled in its ornaments. She crouches beside him where he lies conveniently snared, and batters away at him still with her love. And as the film ends, she has had her way, she has wound him forth from exile. We see him next receiving proudly the Navy Cross he had felt only bitter about. At the last, things are a little softened: walking from the field with Ruth, he is able to discern faintly that a cab's top is red. Perhaps there is hope that his vision will return. But they agree, "Whichever it is, we'll do it together." They climb into the cab. "Where to?" asks the driver. And he replies, bringing the dream around to its striven-for end: "Home." The music swells: "A-merrr-i-caaa!"

The dream has been dreamed in terms of a very special case—that of a man who has been blinded. No need for one in the audience to feel that he is identifying with someone in a plight beyond that particular one. Yet there is a scene in the film in which these very specialized doubts and fears flare into those of a more general nature. The film includes a brief scene at the hospital in which a group of G.I.'s has gathered—many of them men who can expect complete cures—and they are talking of what it will be like to return home. Most are wondering how they will be received by their wives, but some go on to wonder what kind of a reception the country as a whole will give them. Will there be a place for them any more? For a moment they recall the years after the First World War, how the fathers of some of them had to sell apples on street corners. "You know something funny?" one of them breathes. "I'm scared." He is quickly reassured: a nurse steps in and informs them all with vehemence that the country has learned something since that first war, that it is now a country of opportunity for all. Her eloquence quiets them; but for a moment the wild cries of the hero, that home is not home any more, his vision of the beloved vanishing eerily from his embrace, these cries, these visions, have found an echo, and that very special figure of the disabled one has wavered into a figure less special.

There is another sequence in the film more important still, because it has been inserted for less conscious reasons and because too (as in some of the war films I described) it is the hero himself who stands before us, caught up in the same gesture, yet in other guise. Even before his blinding, Al may be seen to go through the very motions later explained to us in terms of that blinding—the same motions of wild resistance to the heroine, of wild resistance to all talk of "home." The film strains twice to relieve him of the one plight. It opens with the hero's first meeting with Ruth, at the home of the couple with whom he boards, and in their first moments together he gets the idea that she is out to "hook" him. When she remarks what a nice home it is, "I suppose *you'd* like one!" he cries, and throughout the evening, quite hysterical, he behaves like "an animal caught in a trap." When he finally realizes that she has no intentions upon him, he makes a turnabout and begins to pursue her—but he makes it clear to her that he is a rolling stone, hit the road at the age of fifteen, has a decent job now at a factory, but is not the kind to stay put anywhere. And he still teases her about wanting to hook him for good. We are soon shown that his hesitations have not been grave. Just before leaving for the wars, just before the train pulls out, he thrusts a ring into her hands. But the film intends to put the two of them through the same paces more strenuously.

This figure of the rolling stone is worth tracing further, beyond the limits of this particular film. For in various other films it is precisely this figure against whom the heroine must launch her full-scale assaults.

One film in which the figure reappears, featured, is *State Fair* (1945), the Rodgers and Hammerstein musical version of the earlier Will Rogers film. The motions of this figure are shadowy motions; production numbers constitute the film's main fare, the hesitations of this hero just one of several story threads—very slight, a shorthand jotting of the pattern I have described. (But the fact that the pattern can be left this vague—even in shorthand can be counted on to reach an audience—does in its own way mark the pattern a live one.)

The hero, Dana Andrews, is a roving reporter, covering the state fair. He meets the little country heroine on the roller coaster. They share a seat and as the roller coaster begins its dives, the heroine, in spite of herself (an ancient Hollywood tradition compelling her), dives into his bosom for comfort. When the ride is over, he suggests that they see the rest of the fair together too and, smooth of tongue, he quiets her maidenly misgivings by pointing out that she can "break it up" whenever she likes by simply losing herself in the crowd. So she is persuaded and they see it all together—in technicolor. To Rodgers and Hammerstein's song, everybody is "fa-lling fa-lling in love" and they too are soon very obviously enchanted with each other. On a little hilltop he tells her all about himself, and his story is much like Al's early story. He's "been everywhere." The Des Moines "Register" has him "hogtied" for the moment, but he intends to break that up. And does he perhaps want to "break this up" too, the heroine inquires, anxious. But he assures her that if he should want to do that, at the next appointment they set she just wouldn't find him.

He is always there, though, at those appointments, and one night, as they lie under the stars, the question of marriage comes up. He asks her about the boy back on the farm whom she has mentioned, and she counters by asking if he ever plans to get married. And here he comes out with the duplicate of Al's cry after he has been blinded—that he wouldn't be a drag on Ruth: "If I really cared for a girl, I'd care too much to wish a guy like me off on her!" Boldly, for one of her upbringing, Margy blurts out, "I could never marry anyone but you, ever!" and runs off down the hill.

Then at the next appointment he isn't there! The fair is packing up and she waits and waits, the camera eyeing her from way above, as all about her the Ferris wheel, the roller coaster, the gay booths are dismantled—with them, it seems, all her good hopes. Sadly she returns to the farm.

It turns out that he has unavoidably missed the date: he has suddenly had to catch a plane to Chicago or miss the chance at an important job. He calls her on the phone from somewhere very near. Will she be the wife of a columnist? She jumps into a startled neighbor's jalopy to meet him on the road halfway. The music lovingly whirls the two cars to a face-to-face stop—and all our anguish is resolved.

A very sketchy story; and the figure of the hesitant hero a very sketchy one: vague restlessness, vague doubts about himself resolved in the flurried happy ending without ever having been particularized. For one in the audience this story easily enough reduces itself to the story of a young charmer who has tended to think himself incurably the wolf—until the strength of this new love ends such thoughts. That hinted restlessness on the job is easily forgotten—easily enough (since never defined for us) dispelled by the acquisition of the columnist's post.

In *Those Endearing Young Charms* (1945), the story is less sketchy and improvises at somewhat greater length upon the theme of the restlessness, the self-doubts the hero suffers. He emerges more visibly as one who, in his drifting, seeks a kind of life that he despairs of finding. But he is also very much more carefully defined as the gay one who does not expect ever to find the proverbial girl of all his dreams.

This hero is a pilot, soon to go overseas. We meet him as he is giving the air to one young lady, with whom he's become bored. Then he runs into Bill, an army pal, who boasts to him about *his* girl, Snow White, and in spite of Bill's protests he tags along on this date. He manages adroitly to stick along for the entire evening, throws a lot of money around, quite takes over the party; and at the end of the date, after they have both left, he returns to Snow White's apartment. "Smooth as a silkworm," Bill has described him bitterly, watching him get his way all through the evening. The heroine, deftly eluding his passes, gets him to talk about himself, and his story is composed of the familiar elements. He worked for his father for a while but found that unbearable. He was never happier than when he got out of his home town. He became a flyer, he blurts out, because it makes one feel "tough and alone." Again he turns on the silkworm charm and tries to make love to her and, true to her name, she shows him the door.

But when he continues to woo her, she goes out with him eagerly. Her mother is full of warnings, and the warnings seem sound. He is used to having his way, it is obvious—with money or with charm (he dispenses one like the other) buying whatever he wants. The heroine has continued Snow White in her behavior, and to break her down he pulls an old trick: pretends to leave for overseas, then calls her that weather has forced them to turn back and he has another day to be around. She does go running to him—but not in the spirit he had planned. The special glint of which I spoke has appeared in her eye. She had been wavering, "stupid and frightened"; but she has made up her mind. "He just pretends to be cynical and tough!" she cries to her mother. Deep within him, she has decided, lies dissatisfaction with the way of life in which he has been caught up, a nostalgia for something different. "Yeah, this is real!" he had cried out one day at the airport. "You can't kid anybody in the air!" She is sure now that the fact that he can't kid *her* is what makes up the attraction she holds for him. They ride out to a lonesome beach. Here she at last allows him to make love to her and he asks her what has happened. She isn't frightened of him any more, she tells him—"You will come back to me." It is his turn to be frightened: "You're trying to make something out of this that isn't there! . . . I'm not what you want!" he cries—as Al had in *Pride of the Marines,* as Dana Andrews had in *State Fair.* "It would be slow murder!" In his helplessness he lashes out at her: "You made up your mind to spoil my last evening, didn't you?" And he discloses to her the cynical maneuvering he had employed to get her to come to him. But she does not flinch. When he still resists, she leaves, chin up, but before she goes she delivers her challenge: "You're afraid of yourself, not of me!"

Back in his room, her words work on him with a strange power— "What did this girl do to you?" a startled pal demands—and just before he is really due to leave for overseas, he hurries to her. He had been in such a rut, he tells her, that he hadn't even known when things had changed for him; he'd been kidding women so long that he hadn't even known when he'd stopped kidding. To drag out the suspense, the film has her doubt him for the moment, but after he has left realize that he has spoken from the heart and chase him to the airport, arriving just in time for a final embrace through the wire fence of the airfield before his plane takes off.

This film, like *State Fair* before it, manages to keep things pretty tightly within boy-meets-girl terms—everything triumphantly resolved, supposedly, when the hero allows himself to be captured by this girl he "can't kid." ("How to catch a flying wolf," the advertisements read, and the wolf is in the net.) And yet there are hints here of a larger quest that agitates the hero and drives him, in his bitterness, to play it "tough and lonely"—a quest for that role in relation to society at large in which one would not be kidding anyone, either. This quest the audience does not see resolved; the token satisfies it.

But *Adventure* (1946) is a film that contains more than hints of a deeper restlessness stirring its hero than can be covered quite by the explanation: he is a wolf. This hero (Clark Gable) is defined as the wolf clearly enough too. He is the traditional sailor with a girl in every port. But as Greer Garson says of him to Joan Blondell, he "has a rather complicated mind for a sailor." The film is maudlin, an unwitting caricature of its kind, but it is worth recounting in detail, for it serves to bring into greater visibility the heroes I have just sketched.

Our first sight of Gable matches our first sight of Young: we see him taking leave of one of his ladies at a foreign port, and she is gamely asking him to tell her that he loves her; she'll make believe that she believes him. Then he is off to his merchant ship. There we get our first glimpse of the complications of his nature. An old man commits his grandson to his keeping: "I know he'll be safe with you," he says, "and the sea's a good school." But Gable snaps back bitterly, bitterly, "Yeah, for smart seagulls and sharks!" Later he comes upon the boy on deck, yearning up at the evening star and mumbling about the hopes of the world, and again he becomes very gruff, snaps at him not to get to thinking he can walk on the water. It is obvious enough that, like Young, Gable "only pretends to be tough." He cares too much. "I'd care too much to wish a guy like me off on anyone I loved!" "I'd be no good for you!" "It would be slow murder!" those other heroes I have sketched cried to those who wanted to put themselves in their hands. Their behavior might have seemed, as I noted it, that simply of men who couldn't imagine remaining faithful to a marriage vow; but in this film, echoed and exaggerated, it takes on more clearly a further meaning. The conspicuous sense in which Gable feels he shouldn't be wished off on anyone is that he feels bound to destroy in those he cares for all bright hopes. Yes, if he growls at the boy out there under the stars, it is because he too is full of yearnings, but he has come to feel that all yearnings come to nothing. (Aptly, the boy dies in his keeping; the ship is torpedoed and out on the raft on which he and Gable and a few others escape, he wastes away.)

Always poor Gable must suffer this helplessness toward those in his care. Back on shore, his pal Mudgin gets into terrible trouble. During a binge held by the crew to "drink the ship down," Mudgin breaks a solemn oath he has sworn, and as the party is breaking up in some disorder he has a hallucination—seems to see his soul flit from his breast like a firefly and drift away in the fog. The rest of the crew mocks him when he tells them about it, but Gable hushes them. He knows what it is like to feel that one's soul is gone from one's breast, and he follows Mudgin out onto the streets. But again there is no help he knows of and again this makes him very gruff. They pass the public library and the words inscribed above the door suggest to Mudgin that there may be help inside: "The tree of knowledge is rooted in the ages." "Wisdom is peace." Mudgin turns his eyes here as the young boy had turned his eyes to his star. "So they're wise! So they got peace!" Gable growls. But he enters with his friend. And it is here, behind the desk, that he finds Greer Garson, bespectacled. "I can't find it, the tree," he says, marching up to her. "Come in, it says, and get under the tree." Miss Garson coolly suggests that he look for it at the nearest bar. But he rebukes her: he has a sick sailor with him, "looking for hope." Mudgin explains his plight and asks her whether she has a book on the soul. Solemnly she drags out a "Symposium on Modern Thought." But all it has to offer is that a large body of contemporary thought denies the soul's existence. "Some tree!" cries Gable; and suddenly wild, he backs her down the library aisles. "There's nothing in here!" he yells. Poor Miss Garson tries to stand her ground: "What do you want?" "That's it—just it!" he cries in his great vague anguish.

It is worth stopping the film for a moment, for here, as these two face each other, one can in effect study too all those other pairs I have introduced. There is something about Greer that "gets" Gable. When the young sailor turned his eyes to the evening star, when Mudgin turned his eyes to the inscriptions over the library door, that moved him to utter bitter comment; but there is something about Greer that stirs up in him more than mutterings. "There's nothing in here!" he yells. "The only difference between us is that I know it!" It is this that gets Gable—that Greer serenely, stubbornly refuses to see that there is "nothing here." And—look back—this is what "gets" all these heroes. "It's no good!" one cries; and "I suppose *you'd* like (a home)!"; and another: "You're trying to make something out of this that doesn't exist!" In *Pride of the Marines,* the nightmare the blinded hero suffered was that of a homecoming that proved to be no such thing, a welcome that had seemed secure receding eerily. Each of these heroes, faced by the heroine, suffers in effect this same nightmare. In her eyes he sees a vision of a life; but the vision, he is sure, is false, a cruel promise.

He cannot turn away. Even when Mudgin leaves, Gable cannot turn and go. He loiters, tantalized. He has to rid her of that look that tears the heart out of his breast. The public library is soon agog. Blondell, Greer's roommate, arrives—"How you don't fit in here!" he greets her (none of that look in *her* eye)—and the scene moves on to a night spot, for he's taking them both out, he announces, and though Greer says no, Joan accepts for them both. At the night spot, he continues his frenzied abuse, flirting and dancing with Joan, but Greer the real object of his attention ("Fight with *me!*" Joan begs). First thing in the morning he turns up again at their apartment, and all that day the abuse continues. Joan invites him to drive them both out to Greer's little farm. And there his wild gibes reach their pitch. Flirting with Blondell, but one eye on Greer, and all his words aimed really at her, he asks Joan whether she was ever married and proceeds to enlarge on the subject: *"It all ends nowhere,"* he cries. He isn't just picking on marriage, he adds. *"There's nothing on land that doesn't leak itself to death!"*

It is here that Greer gets to her feet and begins at last to hit back. That very first evening she had abandoned mildness in one flare-up: Gable's shipmates had rolled in, and in the inevitable free-for-all winding things up, she had joined in to hit Gable over the head with a plate. "Taking on the Black Prince single-handed!" Mudgin had cried, in boundless admiration. The morning after, amazed at herself, she had announced, "That exhibition was my first and last." But we had not believed her. The familiar glint had entered her eye. She had continued, though, like Snow White, a bit frightened, a bit sulky, until now. Now at last she gets to her feet and the real slugging begins. Gable is raving on: the ocean provides at least an imitation of the real thing (for Young, recall, the air was the one place you couldn't kid anybody), but the ocean is the only place that even *seems* to lead to it. It is Greer's turn to back Gable across the floor. What is this "it" he is always crying after like a baby—"it it it!" "You you you!" he yells. He is seeking that excitement that doesn't die! The ocean comes nearest to it, and if he picked on her it's because the ocean is in her eyes. "I never found it in any eyes before!" he cries. "I'm sick to death of you!" And he rushes out into the night. She walks right out into the night after him and soon has him in her arms. In the next scene they are on the road and she is reciting Elizabeth Barrett Browning to him with determination: "Unless you can dream that his faith is fast . . . Oh never call it loving." A roadside sign, "Marriage Licenses," draws near, and Greer points. Gable murmurs meekly, "All right," and they are pulling into the next town, Reno, to be married.

Nevertheless, when they get back home and Blondell and Greer begin to discuss where Blondell will live now, Gable interjects, "Hold it! This needn't make any difference to you two!" He's off to sea again in a couple of days and he may well be gone for a year. Greer comments that she had sort of thought he might want to stay. "Shore job—me?" he exclaims. Blondell begins to gabble that a man should want a home of his own—a garden, or a baby. "You want a baby, pal?" Gable demands of Greer, the look of a trapped animal upon him again. And he is off in haste for a drink with the boys.

"A tricky one," this hero, with "tricky twisty ways to him," as Mudgin puts it. Mudgin pays a call on Greer. She ain't bruised too bad? he wants to know. But she's a "pretty tough mug" herself, she assures him. And "he's not nearly the champion he thinks he is," Mudgin adds. A pretty tough mug she proves herself, and she has the right blow ready for Gable when he returns: she wants a divorce. And now we see him sailing his "black ocean," not at all the man he was before. "He's hurt harder than I'd thought!" Mudgin muses. He can tell this when Gable becomes rough on the men, for the first time in his life hits a man who has his hands down! He even breaks with Mudgin and for weeks will not speak to him. But at a foreign port Mudgin is in an accident and lies dying. Then of course Gable does hurry to him, and Mudgin dies in his arms. Just before he dies,

Mudgin regains his soul: a shooting star flicks across the heaven and he reaches out his hand, crying, "God gave it back to me!" This little sequence provides us with a hint that Gable too will find peace at last. And to be sure, when at the end of the voyage he gets back to home port and discovers from a very angry Blondell that Greer is out at the farm bearing his child, "If I'm a father, I'm a father!" he says—simply enough—and is in a cab, yelling at the cabbie, "Get going!" "Will you marry me, Harry?" she asks when he comes walking in. "Sure, any day," he says. Like Snow White, she is not quite ready to believe him. But when the baby arrives, and the old country doctor can't get it to breathe, and Gable grabs it up and shouts the life into it— "Breathe for us, boy!" (the dream here, note, reversing at last the death of the little sailor)—then she believes. "Did you hear him?" he asks as the baby hollers. "He's here to stay." "I heard *you*," she says. And they name their little son Mudgin.

So "Gable's back and Garson's got'm," as the advertisements promised us. But if at the end of *State Fair*, at the end of *Those Endearing Young Charms*, the element of hurry hurry, meet him halfway, catch him before he leaves! seems a necessary distraction—lest one look too closely at all that has been reversed—the distraction here of the excitement of the birth is more essential. For this film in its gauche way has very much more visibly marked its wandering hero as one who questions not simply the possibilities of a particular marriage but the possibilities of any sort of life "on land," any sort of life within existing society. His cries have been a bit inchoate: "it it it" is lacking. But, however inchoate, they have not been very decisively hushed.

In most of the films in which this heroine must wind the hero safely home, outcries against society itself are very much more fleeting. Not doubts about society but—the other quantity in the equation—fears concerning one's own identity find sharpest utterance. Most frequently too in these films, the cries are from the lips of a hero who, like Al in *Pride of the Marines*, suffers some obvious disability— something more than the vague disorder of temperament to which one could if one liked reduce the doubts suffered by the heroes of the last three films.

In *Lost Weekend* (1948), for example, the hero is an alcoholic.

And "the reason is me," he explains—"what I'm not." He has tried to be a writer, but cannot make the grade. "I've never done anything . . . Zero zero zero."

When this hero (Ray Milland) meets the heroine (Jane Wyman) —over a mixup of coat checks at the opera—and he learns that she works for "Time" magazine, "perhaps you could do something for me," he quips, "help me to become Man of the Year." And for a while it looks as if, under her influence, he *will* find himself and become, if not man of the year, at any rate a man again. The very day he meets her, he goes on the wagon. As he recounts to Nat, the bartender— giving him the substance of the book he wants to write about himself: under her spell, "he thinks he's cured. If he can get a job now, they can be married and that's that." And then "one day, one terrible day" —the heroine's parents have come from Ohio to meet him; he is wait- ing for her in the lobby where the introduction is to take place and by chance he overhears the parents talking him over in advance: "He ought to have a job"—"He's a writer"—"What does he write? I never heard of him"—"It'll all come out, his background, prospects." In the nightmare Al suffered in *Pride of the Marines,* recall, as the heroine was welcoming him home, a stranger drew near who was suddenly revealed as the hero himself, disabled. The nightmare here is the same. Don has to have one drink first now before he can go through with the meeting. Then he has a second, and then a third, cannot help himself—the "other Don Birnam" is back. This is where the heroine first learns of his weakness. This is where he tells her fiercely, "Clear out . . . walk fast . . . don't turn back." But she, of course, is going to "straighten it out."

As he hits out at her now in the familiar fashion, the vision of a life we have glimpsed ("If he can get a job . . .") dissolves before our eyes and here too dissolves the bright deception of the dream—the special nature of his disability. As she presses him, he suddenly blurts out that he couldn't hold down any of the conventional jobs anyway. "Most men lead lives of quiet desperation! I can't take quiet despera- tion!" Here, for a moment, is echoed Gable's wild cry. Here for a fleeting moment the plight he suffers is made general. (The hero can see for himself only one role that would not lead to desperation, and that is a role in which he would attempt precisely to set down as a familiar one this situation of his: "Out there in that great big concrete jungle," he muses later, as he drafts in his mind an opening for his book, "I wonder how many others there are like me.")

But this is for a moment only—a drunken cry. The bulk of the film elaborates the "special case" of his inability to write that book—and so of the nightmare intrusion of that stranger to himself, "the other Don Birnam." The story of his first meeting with Helen, and early hopes for a life—the opening chapters of his book (all there in his mind, he claims, except for the ending)—is told in flashback to Nat, the bartender, in the middle of a weekend bender. It is three years after that "terrible day." The heroine is still at her labors—still fighting, still believing, the hero comments wryly to Nat. The film has opened as she has appeared to send him off to his brother's for a few days of country air. She hasn't managed to get him on the train; he has contrived to stray off on "another binge, another bender, another spree"; and the greater part of the film details this terrible spree as, cunningly evading Helen, who hunts for him, who calls, who waits outside his door, he seeks from "that bottle of his"—as Gable had sought from sailing his "black ocean," Robert Young high in a plane—the nearest imitation he knows of a sense of identity. "It pickles my kidneys, yes," he cries, "but . . . suddenly I'm above the ordinary . . . I'm walking a tightrope over Niagara Falls. I'm one of the great ones!" The film describes the spree from his first elated sense that he is no longer "zero zero zero," through all the ensuing helpless deepening of that very plight. "You can't cut it short," he says. "You're on the merry-go-round and you've got to ride it . . . till the blasted music wears itself out and the thing . . . clunks to a stop." The film draws those who watch into the helpless round. As the music grows eerie, whirly, and involves us in its whirls, as the camera moves us up on the interminable jigger glass and plunges us deep, we enter the vortex with the hero, to lose all bearings.

In a night club where he goes the first night, he finds that he has not enough money to pay the check and in a panic he sneaks a girl's purse from the bench beside him. He is discovered, is loudly accused, is surrounded by outraged faces (we are surrounded). Crying, "I'm not a thief! I'm not a thief!" (as Al at the hospital had cried, "I'm not blind, not blind!"), he is ejected onto the street. At the end of the next day, after an endless trek down Third Avenue in search of a pawnshop that will give him a few dollars for his typewriter (shop

Eleanor Parker and John Garfield in *Pride of the Marines* (1946).

Jane Wyman and Ray Milland in *Lost Weekend* (1945).

after shop is closed, because it's Yom Kippur), he falls down a flight
of stairs and comes to in an alcoholic ward. Here the camera gives us
first only the close-up of his face as he wakes confusedly and we,
disoriented as he, hear all about us strange moans, terrible half-animal
mumblings. "Where am I?" he cries. A listless man in a faded bath-
robe gives no answer, drifts away. A mocking male nurse finally appears to inform him. He will not let him leave and, horribly, as night
falls, patients in neighboring beds begin "seeing little animals," begin
trying to climb the walls. Don is able to escape and makes his way
back to his room through the empty early-morning streets. But at the
end of the bottle that he manages to bring back with him, he endures
the final horror: he himself for the first time experiences the D.T.'s.
Again we are allowed to see what he sees, cowering in delirium: out
of a hole in the plaster of the wall a small mouse peers, a bat makes
low swoops through the room, with a final swoop applies itself to the
mouse; blood seeps from behind the struggling wings as Don bursts
his throat screaming. And it is here that Helen finds him at last,
comes rapping at the door. When he will not let her in, she hurries
off down the stairs for the passkey. Too weak to stand, he drops to the
floor and drags himself to the door to chain it against her, more frantic
than Al trying to escape from Ruth, but she pushes her way in before
he can get the chain in place, merciless as Ruth was.

However, even the heroine acknowledges this hero to be beyond
help. The next morning she admits, "It's finished." What has brought
her to this has been his sneaking off, as she slept, to pawn her leopard
coat—the very coat which, in the mix-up of the coat checks, had
brought them together. If he is *this* far gone, surely all labors are in
vain. Actually, Don has pawned the coat for a gun; and after Helen
leaves him out on the street, he returns to his room to end it all. It will
be "just a formality. Don Birnam is dead already." Here the story
logically "clunks to a stop."

But not in the dream. For in the dream the heroine, though she has
wavered, puts up her chin again and finally works her way. When
she goes to the pawnshop for the coat and learns that he has pawned
it for a gun, the glint returns to her eye and she goes rushing back to
him. "Do you want me to give you another of the promises I never
keep?" he asks when she comes bursting in. "What do you expect—a
miracle?" But "Yes yes yes!" she cries. Suddenly the doorbell rings

and in walks Nat. He is carrying Don's typewriter, which he had left at the bar. He has oiled it up for him. "She writes real good," he says. And here, of course, is an omen, like Mudgin's recovery of his soul. "He gave it back to me!" Mudgin had cried, and Helen now cries in *her* delirium, "Someone, somewhere, sent this typewriter back. Why? Because you're to stay alive! Because he wants you to write!" On and on she talks, and all at once he has been wound in one great motion home, all at once he stands before us Man of the Year; she has brought him here quite as he had requested, fliply but gravely, so many months before. Now he can write his book, she has persuaded him, because now at last he knows the ending—his own death. (A nice bit of irony; but in the flurry, it slips by.) The film ends as Don stands there by her side, imagining a bookstore window and "a great pyramid of books! 'A Novel by Don Birnam'!" "That's by my fellow!" Helen boasts.

The reversal here has been more drastic and more abrupt than in any of those other films. The heroine's has been a true feat. And from one film to another her labors do become increasingly prodigious, the depths—the doubts—out of which she must draw the hero, increasingly great. The film makers take the most far-fetched situations to dramatize.

In *Spellbound* (1946), for example, the hero is an amnesia victim who fears that in real life he is a murderer—and one who might be driven to kill again. *Lost Weekend* contained the hint that even if its hero were to be cured, and so enabled to take up a normal role in society, quiet desperation would result. Here the threat is posed that if the heroine should succeed in restoring the hero to himself, he might discover that self to be a deadly one.

"A woman like you could never become involved emotionally with any man," a fellow psychiatrist has announced to this heroine, but the dream is to involve Ingrid as few women have ever been involved. The head of the mental hospital where she works is being retired and the new man, Dr. Edwardes, is awaited. When he arrives, it is the hero (Gregory Peck). He and Ingrid meet at dinner. As usual, it is the gesture of the wounded one, of the trapped beast, that lights in her eye the look we have not seen there before. She is discussing the pool the hospital hopes to build and begins to sketch it with a fork on the tablecloth, and suddenly Gregory Peck exclaims about her marking up the linen, and with his knife he hurriedly erases the lines she has made. Everyone else laughs, but she covers up for him, strangely affected as she watches him erase those lines. That afternoon he calls her in for a consultation. A patient has been confessing to him that he has killed his father. Gregory appears disconcerted by the case— though, as she reminds him, he has written a famous book on the subject of guilt complexes. Abruptly he breaks off the interview, asks her to go for a walk with him. That night she cannot sleep, a great restlessness is upon her. Rising, she wanders to the library and takes down Edwardes' book. Then, passing his room, she sees a light under the door and suddenly, quite helplessly, she raps and walks in. Like Greer in *Adventure,* she now stands bewildered at her own actions: "I thought I wanted to discuss your book . . . I don't . . . at all!" Gregory gently nods, "Something has happened to us"—and they are in an embrace. It is a very special embrace, designed by Alfred Hitchcock: the camera moves us up on their faces, first one and then the other; her eyes fill the screen, his eyes, and begin to blur; and then beyond the blur a door opens, and beyond it another and another and another, a succession of doors opening in ecstasy down an endless corridor.

The moment fades abruptly, and with it the glimpsed life, glimpsed promise of successive ecstasies. Gregory looks down at her shoulder. We are shown in close-up the dark lines woven in the white of her robe. And he pushes her away. "It's not you! It's something about your robe—the lines!" Before she can question him, an emergency call sends them both hurrying to the operating room: the patient with the guilt complex has run amok and stabbed a doctor. Gregory breaks again: "You fools! Babbling about guilt complexes! . . . He *did* kill his father!" And he collapses in shock. And now, sitting by his bedside, Ingrid slowly opens the autographed copy of Edwardes' book and compares the signature with Gregory's signature on a note he had sent her earlier. The two do not match. As he opens his eyes, she whispers, "Who are you?" And he cries, "I remember! Edwardes is dead! I killed him and took his place! I'm—someone else —I don't know who!"

A more frightening stranger here intrudes himself than in any of those other nightmares I have reported. But a more unabashed heroine takes her stand, eyes afire. There is no longer any look of shyness about Ingrid. As he paces the floor in anguish, she faces him bold and assured. Absurd, his conviction that he is Edwardes' murderer. "That is a delusion you have acquired, out of illness." In the morning she will "straighten everything out." In the morning they will begin to try to remember his childhood.

In the morning he has fled from her. She pursues. He has left a note: "I cannot involve you . . . When the police step in, tell them I'm at the Empire Hotel in New York. I prefer to wait alone for the end." So she pursues him there. What happened in his childhood? "Try remembering!" The police are by now on his trail. A bellboy has recognized Ingrid and they must flee from the hotel. But even as they flee, even in the railroad station, even on the train, she probes at him. (They must flee the harder as her probings tend rather to draw attention to them in public places.) "Stop it!" he begs; he doesn't like her any more, he warns her. But this heroine has a ready answer: that is what happens in analysis—"You're going to hate me a great deal before we're through." She decides to take refuge at the home of her former teacher, Brulov, in Rochester. She pretends to the old doctor that she and Gregory (Brown, she names him cunningly) are on their honeymoon and cannot find a room. He invites them to stay, and up in the little room he gives them she takes up her labors again. She has got out of him so far that he is a real doctor; that he has been in the army and suffered a slight injury bailing out of a medical transport plane. ("I probably deserted!" Gregory has cried out. "I hated it, hated killing!" But she always has an answer: "Your guilt fantasies were obviously inflamed by your duties as a soldier.") "On our side" also she tells him is the knowledge that the color white frightens him —white, and dark vertical lines. There is a white coverlet on the bed in their room, with lines running its length. This has again had a horrible effect upon him. "Look at it! Remember!" she has commanded him, and he has pitched forward onto the bed—has fainted away to escape her. Tenderly she has revived him and helped him to the couch—always provided such lovers by Hollywood, that they may be virtuous in comfort. Shiny-eyed she has assured him, "We are making progress!"

But if Ingrid is more and more confident about the progress she is making, we begin more and more to thrill to the possibility that the

guilts Gregory suffers are as real as he insists they are; more and more
we begin to share the hero's terror of himself. In the dawn he wakes.
He goes to stand beside Ingrid's bed, gazing down at her. There she
sleeps under the white spread with its dark vertical lines. He frowns.
To distract himself, he goes into the bathroom to shave. He makes a
white lather in the white shaving mug. He stares at it and sets it
down. The basin on which he sets it down is white white. He turns
away. And the table is white, the chair is white, the tub is white
white. He runs out of the bathroom, razor in hand. The white coverlet again meets his eye, aglare in white moonlight. He approaches—
and we are not so sure that "we have the word 'white' on our side."
But suddenly he turns and runs from the room. Downstairs is Brulov,
at his desk—doing a bit of work, he says. He asks the hero to have
some milk with him. Babbling away, he disappears into the kitchen,
his white jacket, in close-up, filling the screen. He returns with the
milk. The hero raises the glass and drinks—and again the camera
gives us what the hero sees: the milk whitely rising as the glass is
tipped, to fill the screen. When Ingrid wakes and finds the hero gone,
and hurries downstairs, there is Brulov slumped in a chair, head lolling.

We have merely been given—with Ingrid—a violent start. Brulov
yawns and wakes, and then Ingrid sees Gregory asleep on the couch
across the room. However, Brulov promptly informs her that he is calling the police. He had noted the hero's condition the moment they
arrived and had sat up to be ready for anything; he had seen from his
face, when he came downstairs, razor in hand, that he was dangerous,
and slipped him a bromide in his milk. He knows too of the Edwardes
case, and he thinks it "good and certain" that Gregory is the murderer.

Brulov is an older and wiser psychiatrist than she. And yet—she
couldn't feel that way toward a man who was bad, she insists. Brulov
must give her just a few days! Brulov suggests that they can penetrate
his secret most quickly through dream analysis, so they wake him up
and ask him to describe his most recent dream. It is visualized for us
in a sequence specially designed by Dali. They are puzzling together
over the decorative clues it offers, when bobsled tracks on a snowy hill
outside the window give Ingrid an idea. Dr. Edwardes, she has heard,
was fond of skiing. Ski tracks in the snow are what those dark lines

on white recall! A death on skis must be the horror the hero is trying
to forget! And the dream gives them the name of the sports resort
where it must have happened. When it featured a valley and hover-
ing wings, it "was trying to tell him the name"—obviously Gabriel
Valley! "We have to go to Gabriel Valley!" she cries. But Gregory in
his turn now begs that the police be called in. "I know about last
night," he cries. "I've had enough of it!" "Nothing happened," she
argues. "But it will!" he cries. She will not listen. Edwardes obviously
met with some accident. The two of them will go skiing together, and
when he sees the hill, he will remember what really happened. He
will automatically do the same thing he did on that day. "And what if
I killed him?" Gregory demands. Does she believe in him enough to
take that chance? Of course she does, she cries, and turns to Brulov.
Brulov turns grimly away. And for a moment, in close-up, the heroine's own expression of confidence falters.

But this is no ordinary heroine. For then we see her on the train
with Gregory, and then we see her with him on the snowy slope. She
skis a bit ahead of him, looking back to urge him on. As the white
slope speeds beneath them, his face begins to assume a look that is
more and more menacing. But then all at once our accumulated anguish is relieved. A deep chasm rushes into sight. Gregory flings himself in front of Ingrid, falling with her at the very edge—safe. And
just before he flings himself, the "something" in his childhood is revealed to him, in quick flashback: a bannister, and a little kid sliding
down it, he, not much bigger, sliding after; alarm distorting his face,
for he slides too swiftly upon the other, who is flung onto a spiked
railing and impaled! And Gregory lies there beside Ingrid, sobbing
with relief. "I didn't kill my brother! It was an accident, an accident!"
She adds her joyous cries to his: *that,* then, is what has haunted him
through all the years, caused him to take upon himself all those other
guilts; "inflamed" him with the guilt of killing when he served as a
soldier; convinced him, under the shock of seeing Edwardes fall into
this chasm, that he murdered him. And next we see them sitting in
front of a cheery fire at the lodge and his memory is all coming back
to him. He recalls how he was invalided out of the army after that
plane crash, how Edwardes invited him here to recover from shock.
He is still a little foggy about the accident but—she would look wonderful in white, he gayly proposes.

Once again there opens out before them glimpsed joys, a glimpsed life. But once again the moment is shattered. In walk the police, who have trailed them here, and they announce that they have discovered Edwardes' body at the bottom of the chasm—with a bullet in his back. Gregory relapses into his former conviction of guilt. A court swiftly finds him guilty too. The prison gates clang to.

"It is over," Brulov tells Ingrid. "The evidence was definite." But "Don't ask me to stop!" she cries. "I can't!" (as of course she cannot, until the dream is done). And at the film's very end she does work her way—a small miracle again assisting. For she returns to the hospital, where the former head of the place, Dr. Murchison, still retains his job because of Edwardes' death; and from a remark that slips from him in an unguarded moment, the admission that he has known Edwardes slightly, and from the still unfigured pieces of that dream of the hero's, which now fall into place, she realizes that he, Murchison, murdered Edwardes—of course, out of jealousy, unwilling to resign. So obvious now that he is that sinister bearded figure that puzzled them in the hero's dream. When she faces him with her accusation, he kills himself off. And as the film ends, the two lovers are setting off by train on their real honeymoon, at long last.

It is against all seeming logic that Ingrid has wound Gregory home, quieting all the terrible doubts that we have shared, naming them fantasy—all explained by that long ago childhood accident. For a startling moment we have seemed to see this explanation exploded, the doubts all flaring up again; but for a final time she has laid them all to rest—a heroic labor.

In *Love Letters* (1945), Jennifer Jones lays to rest doubts just as dreadful. In this film, for variety, the heroine is amnesiac. Her amnesia, though, is pictured as a happy state—not like poor Gregory's. "What shall it profit a man to gain the whole world and lose his own soul?" she quotes. "That was written for me!" And the bishop himself agrees with her: in losing the world, she has gained a "contagious serenity." Yet she is willing to sacrifice this enviable state to bring Joseph Cotten into a fuller life. In this film it is the door to her own past that the heroine has to force, but again it is for the hero's sake. And again the hero's dread is that, if she succeeds in her labors, he may stand revealed as a murderer. This is a good film to examine next to *Spellbound,* which it parallels in many ways; for though the case it sets up is as extraordinary, the hero can be clearly identified, as Gregory could not, with the heroes of *State Fair, Those Endearing Young Charms* and *Adventure,* with Al in the early part of *Pride of the Marines*—with that restless figure whom I have shown to be one suffering a more than personal plight.

As the film opens, Jennifer (or Victoria) is not yet amnesiac; she is in a state of lovely innocence foreshadowing that later state. "You are to me a distant promise of beauty untouched by the world," Joseph Cotten writes to her. But as we meet him, he is fretting over the possibility that he has endangered this perfection. He has never seen her; he has been writing to her on commission for a fellow soldier, Roger, who's wanted to spare himself the trouble (Roger having met her only briefly, back home in England, and having other ladies on his mind as well). Though they have never met, Joseph and Victoria have fallen deeply in love through those letters. He had always wanted to say to someone the things he had written, but never before found anyone who would understand. But of course, as the hero cries out now in his anguish, Victoria thinks it is Roger she has come to love; actually "She's in love with my letters—a man who doesn't exist!" What is more, what is worse, Roger has just informed him that he's been given a furlough and will be calling on her soon. Joseph Cotten begs him, frantically, not to see her. "I'm afraid for both of you! Give me your word of honor!" But "honor's old-fashioned," Roger gayly replies. Cotten's fears are soon realized. Wounded in the next action, he receives news in the hospital that Victoria and Roger have been married. Then further word arrives: Roger has met with some kind of accident, is dead. "I knew something would happen!" he moans.

Here is but a prelude to still more dreadful fears. After his release from the army, he decides to look up Victoria, but learns that she is now a victim of amnesia. He hears her story from the friend, Dollie, who cares for her. Dollie had seen very little of her after her marriage, knows only that she was not happy. Then one day Miss Remington, the old lady who had raised Victoria from an orphan, had telephoned, hysterical. By the time Dollie got there, Miss Remington had suffered a stroke and stood unable to move or speak; Roger lay on the floor, stabbed to death; and Victoria crouched at the fire, her

white dress spotted with blood, trying to rake out of the coals the remains of her love letters—in a state of complete shock; she could
remember nothing of the stabbing. She has been tried and sentenced
to a year for manslaughter. (But "I am the guilty one!" the hero dis-
mally interjects.) Now, happily, she remembers nothing of any of it,
remembers only her earliest years in the orphanage. And she answers
to the name she was given there—Singleton. Does she remember the
letters at all? Joseph wonders. For if she does, she is still in love with
him. But of course he could never tell her. "Hopeless, isn't it?" For if
she should ever find out that it was he who wrote them, she would
be sure to despise him. More than that, the doctor has warned that
if she should ever be brought to recall the happenings of that day,
she might lose her mind. Yes, he might prove to be her destruction
a second time. This obsession of his now becomes the insistent leitmotif of the film.

Here is the extraordinary trap in which this hero finds himself,
very special background for his distraction. But just as in *Pride of the
Marines,* though one could nod that of course this hero had doubts
about building a life for himself, as he was blind—if one looked twice
one could note that he showed the same hesitations even before he
was blinded; so here. One can see this hero too going through the
identical motions even before he has been trapped by those very special circumstances. In the first scene of the film, in which he begs
Roger not to visit Victoria, he declares impulsively that he would
never want actually to meet her himself. "A pinup girl of the spirit"
she is to him. Thus when he cries out that she loves "a man who
doesn't exist," one can read his words two ways: read them to mean
that Roger, whom she will welcome home as the man she loves, is not
that man; but read them too to mean that all the words he, Joseph,
has written to her, all those expressions of a yearning he could never
speak of to anyone else, give a misleading picture of him too, for there
is a part of him that is unable to believe in such dreams.

One may, if one pleases, still describe his distraction in terms of a
girl he does not dare to meet. But there is one sequence in the film
where these terms are clearly overstepped. After he is released from
the army and before he goes looking for Victoria, we see the hero for a
while back home with his family. They keep asking brightly whether
he hasn't been back long enough to know what he wants to do. So

does Helen, who was his girl before the war. She urges him to forget the war, find useful work. ("Take a nice job," as the hero of *Lost Weekend* has mimicked bitterly.) "Try to understand," he tells Helen. "I'm not the man you knew and loved before I went away." She soon does come to understand this and breaks things off. He might well have added, with the hero of *Spellbound*, "I don't know who I am." He decides very soon (as Al in *Pride of the Marines* had decided early in life, and Young in *Those Endearing Young Charms*) that the first step for him, at any rate, is to move away. So he goes to live in an old house in the country left him by an aunt he never knew very well. Off there he feels immediately more at ease (just as Young had "never felt better" than on leaving his home town). And his aunt had carefully left untouched the little room where he used to stay as a child; all his childhood treasures are there to greet him—a pleasant and touching surprise. ("All hail those happy days when faith was something all in one piece!") Just before he leaves for the old house, on the eve of his going, his brother drags him to a party—at Dollie's. The hero drinks too much. We cut to a later hour, when everyone has left except for Dollie and the hero, who stands at an open window fervently addressing the outside air. The focus is now, in the usual fashion, shifted easily, even as one watches, from any larger quest that one may have thought to be agitating the hero, to his more special yearning—for the mysterious Victoria. "We perform unspeakable crimes," we hear him raving, "and yet always there stands before our eyes that vision of beauty." And note the "we." He speaks like one who is obsessed by the predicament of an entire society. But when he comes to and Dollie tells him that he has been talking to himself and he inquires, "What was my theme?" she replies, "The usual—a girl. Who's Victoria?" she adds, studying him.

From here on, all narrows down indeed to his obsession with Victoria. We see him up at his aunt's isolated old house, more at ease but still full of a great restlessness. Every time he is out walking and passes the sign that points to Long Reach, the place to which he used to address those letters, that is when he feels restless (and a haunting musical theme stirs things up, the notes beckoning but faintly mocking). One day he decides to set off down the road. When he finds the house where she once lived falling into ruin, some cryptic words Dollie had spoken return to him; he grabs a train for London;

he looks up Roger's death in the newspaper morgue; and then it is
that he hurriedly calls on Dollie again, to ask her to tell him Victoria's
further history.

At Dollie's he finds Victoria herself. He spends, in fact, a rather
overwhelming half hour with her alone, before Dollie returns. But he
is not aware that it is she, since she introduces herself as Singleton.
When Dollie does return and, startled, sends Singleton off on an
errand and then explains things to Joseph, he leaves, determined
never to see her again. But "Don't let him get away!" Singleton has
cried to Dollie. (Having no past and no future to constrain her, she
can just be completely herself.) "I don't want him to be unhappy!"
she has cried. For she has sensed at once his deep distraction—"You're
broken up inside!" He has admitted to her that he's heard disturbing
news. Does she know Victoria? He's in love with her, isn't he? she has
guessed. No, she doesn't know her. And he has lost her? She hopes
he'll find her! And when he has sighed, "I never will," she has chal-
lenged, "You will if you want it strongly enough!" For he must be like
her, she has urged him—unafraid of life. Now when he gets back to
his old house, he finds her waiting for him, giggling. She sets out to
infect him with her "contagious serenity." He must talk to her about
Victoria, she tells him. "Some day you'll be very happy with her!"
And she doesn't mind, she adds, because right now he's happy with
her.

Before that evening with the amazing girl is over, Cotten has had
his mind quite changed for him: he will marry Singleton. What
about Victoria? she wants to know. "That is gone and finished," he
assures her. He cannot really know until he finds her again, she urges;
but he tells her that he is sure. And so they are married and he takes
her with him to live in his aunt's sweet old ugly house. But something
has happened in the middle of the marriage ceremony. "I, Singleton,
take thee, Roger . . ." she has stumbled. Later, standing with Joseph
Cotten up in the little room that was his when he was a child, and
emerging from a happy embrace, she recalls that moment. Was it
something in her past? "Don't you worry about that!" he begs her. He
sets the little old music box to tinkling, twirls her desperately in a
loving dance. But she is not to be distracted. "I'm only half a person,"
she cries. "I care now!" She is haunted by the thought that she is not
all that Victoria would have been to him. There is nothing the hero

can do. She must unravel the past, or never feel that she has stilled his restless heart once and for all.

Doggedly she sets out to remember, and from here on that haunting musical theme sounds interminably its mocking notes—as he tries to obstruct her labors, but helplessly, for she always senses it (as Ingrid had): "There's something there you don't want me to see!" And gradually memory does begin to return, in broken sequences. It begins to be a disturbing thing for her too, but she keeps right on. "I don't understand myself any more," she cries. And yet she persists. His happiness is at stake. And then, picking berries one day, she looks down at her hands and the berry stains streaking them bring back nightmare imagery, her white dress horribly stained—bloodstains! "What did I do?" she screams. Yet even as she cries out, she presses forward in her mission: "I must know!" The hero at this point, frantic, tucks her into bed and rushes off to London to consult Miss Remington in the nursing home where she has been recovering her speech. Miss Remington has left the place. And when he returns home, he finds Singleton gone! For while he is away a letter arrives for him, and Singleton, battling that strange dread she always feels at the postman's approach, forces herself to accept the letter for him. It is from Miss Remington at Long Reach. "I have come back," it reads, "because I want to be near Victoria." The letter drops from her hand, she turns pale as death, and that musical theme thunders in our ears—but the indomitable girl leaps onto her bicycle and pedals off down the road. She steps, trembling, into the cottage at Long Reach and stands before Miss Remington. "You don't know me," she cries, "but I need your help." She must find Victoria, she cries. Her husband needs her. She had thought that he could forget her, but she is convinced now that he never can; convinced too, suddenly, that she herself is not fit to live with him.

Now Joseph Cotten, trailing her here at last, pulls up quietly in his car; and standing outside the door, in dreadful expectation, he listens to Miss Remington disclose to Singleton the identity of Victoria and the happenings of that terrible day. The scene is replayed for us in flashback: Roger sulks in a corner. Victoria rereads her love letters for the millionth time. Roger begins to curse her, drunkenly: why must she always be reading and rereading these things? Because she loves him, she cries, and doesn't want to stop! He seems to her so often a stranger, but "these letters are you!" At that, he bursts out with the truth, and he tries to grab the letters from her, to hurl them into the fire. She resists. He strikes her. And now we hold our breath—but of course: not Victoria but Miss Remington, who happens to have a bread knife in her hand and who goes momentarily crazy at the sight of this violence done to her child, stabs Roger to death. The old woman concludes bitterly: she hopes that Victoria never learns the identity of the man who did write those letters, for surely he is the real murderer and the one to hate. And we hold our breath again, for Joseph Cotten calls to her from beyond the door and she goes out to him. And in anguish now he quotes to her from these old letters: "You are to me a distant promise of beauty . . ." Does she hate him, he cries, or can she possibly forgive him? She takes him in her arms: "It was terrible waiting for you! But finding you is such a great miracle that anything seems but a slight thing to suffer in return!"

Miracle indeed. All had seemed headed for ruin. We had thrilled, rather, to that prospect—as we thrilled to it in *Spellbound*, the white slope speeding beneath us, as we thrilled to it in *Lost Weekend* when the little animals began to stir. In each of these films the heroine has accomplished miracles. And she rather shows the strain. Hers is a role that is hard for an actress to play without coming up with something a bit unnerving—a little grim around the mouth in Greer's case, a little suggestive of the nymphomaniac in Jennifer Jones's. The other woman who sometimes briefly enters these films tends really to be more sympathetic. Blondell is much more appealing than Greer in *Adventure*. In *Lost Weekend*, Gloria, a nice little tramp who hangs out at one of the hero's bars, is more appealing than Helen. And Dollie is really more attractive than Jennifer in *Love Letters*. Cotten has a moment's flirtation with Dollie after the party at her house. He tries to stay the night, but she tells him gently that it isn't really she whom he wants. A pity, we rather feel. It is a wistful moment. She makes so few demands, this other woman; she is willing to have the hero as he is. They move toward one another, these two, not tortuously, as hero and heroine do, but by a simple affinity, lost soul inclining to lost soul for a little warmth. Here is a reversal, note, of the ancient pattern. It was once the lost woman, the Vamp, from whom the hero had to endure wear and tear. This Home Wrecker is now extinct—since the hero no longer knows where he lives. It is the heroine who is the disruptive element in his life—wants to set her mark on him. She wants to "plant trees in (his) blood," as Gable complains. It is strenuous work. Gable remarks to some girl who eyes him in *Adventure* that she's a nice redhead but "I'm looking for a girl with green hair and purple eyes." The image is not inappropriate. For trying to keep hold in her mind's eye of a vision of a home and a life does put a strain on the face of this heroine, lends her a slightly freakish look.

 4

"I keep running away from myself!" (success boy)

1. "Part of me is lost"

One figure is supposed to dominate the American myth: the success boy, the self-made man. By definition, he has overcome hesitations, found a place for himself. Here, if anywhere, is a hero to contrast with the figures the past two chapters presented. The success boy *is* still to be found in the films of these years. Here are four spectacular careers:

Rhapsody in Blue—The Jubilant Story of George Gershwin (1945): A struggling musician from the Bronx has "ideas that are different," doesn't want to be "just a concert pianist." "When I get started, nothing will ever stop me," he declares. And nothing does. "Up like an elevator" he goes, "looking for new buttons to push." Up he goes to penthouses and fame, the idol simultaneously of Broadway and Carnegie Hall. "How does it feel to be sitting on top of the world?" they ask him. He stands in his expensive new apartment, across whose spaces the camera seems able to travel forever, stands in front of a self-portrait he is trying to paint—and here is his jubilant cry: *"I keep running away from myself! . . . Part of me is lost somewhere! . . . I don't want to hurt anybody!"*

Incendiary Blonde—"The skyrocket story of Texas Guinan"

(1945): A little tomboy of humble origin (Betty Hutton) wins a contest in a rodeo, which gives her the chance she's "been waiting for all her life": the owner invites her to join. Once in, she rapidly makes herself its star. Silver pistols she's wanted and she gets them. One day she decides to "have a look at" Broadway. "Have a look at it? You could *be* Broadway!" her agent tells her. And soon she is just that. She decides to open a night club and soon she is "Queen of the night clubs." "One of the immortals," they name her. She set the town "on fire." "My little girl!" crows her poppa.

And *her* cry? "Sure, I got everything I ever wanted—except the one thing I wanted more than anything. There's a black curse on me! I'm scared!"

Humoresque (1947): Another struggling musician, like Gershwin a poor boy living over his father's grocery store—but this time the name fictitious as well as the history, Paul Boray (John Garfield), violinist—again has ideas: "Nobody's going to sit on my head . . . Nobody's going to step on me, not me!" And nobody does. He becomes the protégé of wealthy Mrs. Wright; she manages his debut and he's "in." Soon the camera is traveling lengths of concert hall lobby, hung with one life-size poster portrait of him after another; soon his picture is on the cover of "Today"; and his proud poppa, visiting his penthouse, exclaims in wonder, "It's an eagle's nest!"

And he? His eyes turn wistfully to the little photo on his mantel, photo of himself as a kid, holding the first fiddle his mother gave him: "All my life I've tried to do the right thing and it's never worked out! . . . *I keep feeling I'm far from home, and where home is I don't know. I can't get back to that simple carefree kid I used to be!*"

Or here is an earlier film, set this time in England, *Random Harvest* (1942): A victim of the First World War, another amnesiac (Ronald Colman), yearns to "be someone again," and with the aid of a noble-hearted show girl who believes in him, very soon is. The show girl (Greer Garson, cast again as Ariadne) helps him to escape from the rest home where he feels like a prisoner, flees with him to the country; and there soon encourages him to start upon a writer's career; there too encourages him to propose, and sets him up in a humble little cottage (comfortable poverty, MGM style). Nor has he long to struggle along. A bump on the head restores him to his real identity and he discovers that he belongs to an aristocratic family. (The ladder could hardly be ascended more swiftly.) The family fortunes are in a bad way and to recoup them he enters industry. Soon he is a great success in this role; soon he is a Prince of Industry. Then he is elected to Parliament. He is even mentioned as material for the cabinet!

But he? He fingers wistfully, obsessively, the little key that dangles on his watch chain—key to the humble dwelling (on one of its walls hangs the sampler "Home") where he lived as a struggling young writer: *"I keep feeling that there are people I have hurt! . . . I keep feeling that there is something I have lost!"*

Here they stand: success girl, success boy, Queen of Broadway, Prince of Industry, Man of the Year. If the heroes of the past chapter cast looks of doubt and apprehension ahead (there's nothing that won't leak out, nothing that won't hopelessly shatter at their touch!), the heroes of this chapter cast looks of dazed nostalgia backwards— among their riches, cries of loss, of lack, a wrong road helplessly taken.

I have not described these four films in detail, of course. Nor have I told their stories as anyone would who had seen the movies casually. For the movie audience at large, as always, the dream is safely veiled: in each case, it *seems,* what spoils the happiness of the one who climbs the ladder of success is the fact that he is never united with the one he loves.

Gershwin's father sums it all up in *Rhapsody in Blue*: "Success is not enough—it should've been Julie." Gershwin has met Julie early in his career. It is to her that he blurts out his eager dreams. When his first shows are produced, she stars in them. And " 'swonderful 'smarvelous that" they should care for each other. But then he goes off on a trip to Paris, where he meets Christine; and when he returns to America, Julie sees that she has been forgotten. "Don't be a naughty baby, come to momma, come to momma, do!" she sings at his coming home party; but he is not listening. Christine has watched this, and one day she walks out on Gershwin. She leaves a brave little note: "You think of yourself first," she writes. "That is as it should be . . . You don't need anyone or anything . . . Your destiny lies straight ahead." She will travel in Mexico for a while. Gershwin goes back to Julie. "I've been all mixed up," he tells her. But he has shown her

Christine's letter; and if he doesn't need anyone or anything, he doesn't need her either, she tells him. "With you it's different," a friend assures her, but she is not to be dissuaded; she rushes off to Florida. And when Gershwin follows, she bravely pretends that she's engaged to another. But Gershwin does need Julie. He goes driving ahead in his work ("gotta make time, gotta make time!")—more and more successful, more and more lost to himself. "What are you trying to forget?" his friend Max Dreyfus asks him. "Julie?" And Gershwin with an anguished cry confirms this guess: "Way down deep I'm a family man without a family!" He drives himself at last to the verge of a breakdown. And now Julie hears of it and she calls. "Oh, Julie!" he cries. "Oh, Julie! . . . Meet me! . . . Make up for all the lost years . . . Hurry, darling, hurry!" She is coming at last, and he sits at the piano and he can play again, and he plays "Love walked right in and drove the shadows away . . . I found a world completely new!" But it is too late. He is a very sick man.

In *Incendiary Blonde* again, "it just wasn't in the cards for (Tex and Bill, the rodeo owner) to get together." "It had to be you . . . had to be you," the music throughout the film reiterates. But first Bill is married already. His wife has been in an asylum for years, but he doesn't tell Tex this, just that he's married—"Better run along, kid." And she runs along, not knowing that he cares. A couple of years later a friend tells her what "the angle" really is; and she goes running off to Bill, to say now listen to her, she is willing to wait, no matter how long. And suddenly, then, news comes that his wife has died. But to Bill comes news too that Tex and her father are due to land in jail, because of some phony theater stocks for which her father is responsible. To save Tex, Bill buys them both out, keeping his real motive from Tex, bravely bluffing that he's out "to make a killing" at her expense. "I guess I'm lucky at that!" she cries. "You'd be too much for a little country girl like me!"; and once again, not knowing how he cares, she "runs along." A year later her father spills to her what the angle has been this time. "Bill! Oh, you big lug! That's another year of my life wasted!" she cries. But at last they are going to be married. The justice of the peace is waiting, the wedding cake is baked, with a diamond bracelet baked right into it, and then—some gangsters make a raid. Bill must kill one of them in self-defense. The sentence is five years. And—the doctor has just informed Tex that she has only two more years to live. Bravely she does not tell Bill this and he, bravely, will not marry her before setting off to jail, for fear of hurting her career. No, it just hasn't been "in the cards" for them to get together. Of course this poor girl cries of wasted years.

In *Humoresque,* it is the same story. This time it should have been Gina. Gina is a girl rather like Gershwin's Julie—Garfield's childhood sweetheart, and again the girl to whom he blurts out his early dreams. But when he becomes Mrs. Wright's protégé, he forgets Gina. Mrs. Wright (Joan Crawford) is a married woman. And besides, the two of them seem able only to torture each other with their love—"What is this thing, this funny thing called love?" the music asks. "Let me alone," she tells him. "You're a hangman's noose to me!" Then comes the news that Mr. Wright will grant her a divorce. And "I want to marry you," and "Don't try to fight it," Garfield tells her; and "I can't fight it," she tells him. So they are going to be married. But "You don't want me, not really!" she has cried; and one night, out at her place by the shore, as the music from his distant concert swells on the radio, she walks out on him, farther this time than to Mexico or Florida or jail—walks into the ocean. No wonder this hero feels confused.

In *Random Harvest,* when the bump on the head restores his early memories to Ronald Colman, it simultaneously robs him of his most recent ones. He is away at the time from the little cottage and Greer and the son she has borne to him; and he never returns. Greer after years of searching (during which their little son dies) catches up with him—but he doesn't know her. She becomes his secretary and waits patiently, patiently for recognition—but it does not come. (Nevertheless, when he is about to be married to a nice young girl who has wooed him, and at the wedding rehearsal the organ plays "Oh perfect love," the girl can see, from the suddenly vague and gently troubled look that comes over him, that there has been someone else in his life whom she could never replace, and she makes *her* brave exit.) After a while Ronald makes Greer his wife again, but it is on a strictly social secretary basis. Still—though he sometimes stares oddly at her red hair in the sunlight and she holds her breath—recognition does not break. And the years wear on. This hero might well have the sense that there is something he has missed.

At the very end of this, the earliest film of the four, just when

Greer is ready to walk out on it all, Ronald comes by chance to the scene of their early meeting and, memory stirring at last, finds his way back to that cottage. Greer, getting word of it, is there before him; and when he pushes open the creaky gate, walks down the little path, pushes aside the blossomy branch—all just the way it once was, as in a fairy tale—the door opens and there she stands, calling out to him the old name she had for him—"Smittie!"—and he remembers his lost love, and falls into her arms.

Yes, viewing any one of these films by itself, one could say: Here is one who mounts the ladder of success, who also just happens to be unlucky in love. But viewing them in conjunction, the question one has to ask is: why is this note always added, and always fatally—the one film granting us a happy ending granting it, in effect, at the foot of the ladder again: it is as "Smittie" that he embraces her. Why is it added even in two biographies, where it has little to do with the facts—and not just easily added but strained for, far-fetched?

If these frustrations in love are carefully examined, at those points especially where the credibility of the story is most strained, one sees how closely they are interwoven with the stories of success. The pattern that is strained for is apt to be worth study. The fact that, labored as it is, an audience accepts it time after time, is indication that it veils some deeper pattern of experience they feel in their bones to be true.

In both *Humoresque* and *Rhapsody in Blue,* the drama becomes most forced when the hero's second love walks out on him. The various explanations the two films offer here are a little inconsistent. Each of the ladies remarks to the hero at some point that she is leaving him because he is the "ideal bachelor." "You're married already—to your work," says Joan Crawford. "You don't want me." And Christine: "You don't need anyone . . . your destiny lies straight ahead." Here the suggestion is that she walks out on him, nobly, so that she will not distract him. But neither woman really seems the self-sacrificing type, and at other moments we are given reason to suppose that she is jealous of his career and walks out because she feels that she cannot sufficiently possess him. At still other moments, each of the women seems to hunger to possess him precisely through his work. Christine eagerly plays the part of Gershwin's press agent; Joan Crawford even more eagerly takes John Garfield's career under her management. In

Robert Alda in *Rhapsody in Blue* (1945).

Susan Peters and Ronald Colman in *Random Harvest* (1942).

Humoresque, in fact, the most intense love scenes are the concert sequences: as John Garfield plays his violin, the camera moves up on Joan Crawford in her box, lips pouting wetly, then parting in little gasps, eyes swooning shut—while his mother stares up at her from her seat below, deeply shocked. It would hardly seem that a woman *could* possess a man more utterly through his work. Grant this woman her jealousy of his work, however (or, if you prefer, her noble decision not to stand between him and that work), the films offer us a further reason why she walks out on him. In the very speech in which Crawford declares to Garfield that he doesn't want her because he has his career, she declares to him, "You need the home maker type!" Garfield's mother makes a similar statement: "Inside, you want a wife, home, children!" And recall that Gershwin's friends offer this diagnosis too, and he agrees: "Way down deep I'm a family man without a family!"

They cannot be happy together, then, first: because he is married to his work, and second: because he is at heart a family man. The two reasons do not add up—at the literal story level on which I have been presenting them. They add up only in terms abstracted from the context of the doomed love affair—into the clumsily labored picture of one who loses much that he needs from life in the process of making a way for himself. In both films, note, it is when the hero finds himself definitely on the way up that he becomes estranged from the girl he really needs, the girl with whom, as Garfield puts it to Gina, he can "be himself." This point of timing is not obtrusive for one in the audience; it is then simply, it seems, that he meets the other woman. In *Random Harvest,* it is most distinctly when he starts his upward climb in earnest that the hero becomes estranged—not just from a "home maker type" but from an "ideal home." The estrangement is marked literally with the neatness of a bump on the head. I omitted in my synopsis to say that he is away from home at the time precisely to keep an appointment about a job. "A start in life!" he declares, leaving for the city. "A career!" And the stroke descends; he wakes to fortune—and loss.

As usual, it is when several films are examined together that the pattern with which the film makers are really concerned (whether or not they know it) stands out clearly. Ronald's amnesia in *Random Harvest* is the strained-for, the far-fetched element (if one can say any longer that Hollywood fetches this situation from afar). Set this film next to *Rhapsody in Blue* and *Humoresque* and the hero's amnesia drops its literal character, appears as a transparent symbol. Note how closely, really, Ronald's story matches the stories of those other two heroes. Greer Garson plays a role equivalent to the separate roles played by two women in each of the other films. When she finds the hero again and manages to make herself his secretary, she devotes herself to his career in very much the fashion of Christine and Joan Crawford. When she decides at last that his amnesia is permanent and she will never be really married to him, "Your capacity for happiness is buried!" she wails. Gershwin's father had uttered the same cry to his son, who had suffered no bump on the head: "Take time to be happy!"

If the story of *Random Harvest* opens out for us when it is set in conjunction with *Humoresque* and *Rhapsody in Blue,* the hero's amnesia suddenly taking on a less literal character, conversely that image brings into a clearer focus the plight of the other two heroes. *Humoresque* and *Rhapsody in Blue* suggest that the women involved make themselves unattainable. *Random Harvest* clearly names the hero's own "illness" as the root of the trouble. If *Rhapsody in Blue* is unconvincing when Christine walks out on Gershwin, it is even more unconvincing when Julie walks out on him too after he has realized that he needs her. His failure to find in her arms a "world completely new" makes real sense only in terms of his own distraction, his not knowing what it is that he is missing. *Humoresque* is more persuasive here at least. This hero admits that he doesn't know "where home is." Perhaps one reason that the women are made to take the decisive steps in *Humoresque* and *Rhapsody in Blue* is that these two films too strain to present a picture of estrangement *helplessly* suffered. From the three films a common pattern emerges—of one who, when he casts himself into the race, succumbs to a sort of amnesia, in which he loses the original dream that he had, loses the knowledge of where home is. To dull the sense of his loss ("What are you trying to forget?") he engages himself even more frantically ("gotta make time, gotta make time!"). But the faster he runs, the more and more lost to himself he becomes.

2. The innocent

I have been slighting mention of the fourth film of this group, *Incendiary Blonde,* because it does not quite parallel the other three. The crucial estrangement here, recall, results from Bill's apparent decision to make a "killing" at poor Tex's expense. Tex herself (whose career it is we follow) is not responsible. It also turns out that Bill never really did abandon her: his was an act of loyalty, really—misunderstood. In this film, at least, it might seem that one could call the story of success and the story of frustrated love coincidental and nothing more.

But if *Incendiary Blonde* fails to display the exact pattern of forgetfulness that I traced in those other three films, it displays another pattern not at all irrelevant to that one. It offers us on the one hand the pathos of innocence misunderstood: this hero is unjustly suspected of not *caring* if "there is someone (he has) hurt" along the road to success. It offers us at the same time a zestful exhibition of hero and heroine boasting about the the unscrupulous methods they use to make their way. "Hello, sucker!" is Tex's battle cry. "Clip'm and tell'm!" (or sometimes she doesn't bother to tell'm, as when in her rodeo days she hired a midget to dress in baby clothes and crawl out into the ring, and then made a thrilling rescue). What is the special attraction between the two lovers? Here is their first meeting: Tex enters a bucking broncho contest, disguised as a man; is bucked off but charges that the girth was loose; demands another try and this time carries off the prize; then barges in on the owner of the show, the hero. Was he responsible for that loosened girth? No, he says, "but it's an idea." He offers her a job. They bargain in lively fashion. When they have reached a compromise, "Put that in writing!" one cries; and this becomes a sort of byword between them throughout the film. Clearly the very ground from which their love springs is an exciting mutual wariness: they keep each other on their toes, teach each other new tricks.

A funny lapse is evidenced here on the part of the film makers, who flaunt for our pleasure the enjoyment these two take in pulling off tricks, and simultaneously offer us the pathos of innocence wronged—the hero in effect crying, "I never really did it!" the heroine, "You'd be too much for a little country girl like me!" Here, one could say, is another case of amnesia—and it is worth examining at greater length, for it gives further definition to the vague pattern of distraction observed in those first three films.

It can be examined in a whole series of other films, and in a form very much more pronounced, because in these films the one misunderstood *is* the one whose career we follow. Over and over in a series of for the most part "Grade B" productions, featuring most often an attempt to break into the entertainment field (for the films are musicals and here is an easy framework for assorted production numbers), over and over the hero suffers estrangement from one who is dear to him when he is charged with advancing his career at his loved one's expense. Over and over time proves him to have been misunderstood; and here, for a change, the lovers do finally come together. But over and over, too, the happy acquittal of the hero of the charges against him is curiously inconsistent with certain other general impressions the film has given us.

In a number of these films the hero is shown to be clearly innocent at least of the particular offense with which he is charged. For example, in *My Best Gal* (1944), a young playwright is accused by all his friends and by his best gal of having sold them out, by giving his musical to a producer without holding out for an agreement that they will be cast in it. "He got his bank account!" they sneer. The hero *has* sold the script without them, but he has refused first many times and sold it only upon learning that his girl's father is gravely ill and has no money to pay for the doctor he needs; has sold it on any terms he could get so that he can take care of the old man—anonymously, of course, silently suffering their scorn. The incongruity here, as in *Incendiary Blonde,* is simply the manner in which the film quite shows off in *other* instances how this hero, and his friends too, stop at nothing to sell their wares, gayly *disdain* innocence.

But in a great many films it is even a question whether the hero is innocent of the particular act with which—we are made to feel—he is so unjustly charged. Here, for example, is a film called *Hi Beautiful* (again 1944). This hero suffers most pitifully when accused by his sweetheart of cheaply exploiting their love by submitting an intimate photograph to the Brisbee Patent Pills "Happiest G.I. Couple" Contest. A telegram arrives, informing them that they are the winners. "It's horrible to get money that way!" she explodes; and she walks out on him. It's been a "screwy mistake." He never submitted the photograph at all. The maid did it, without his knowledge. But—we *have* seen him wistfully yearning to submit it, murmuring, "It didn't say you had to *kill* anybody . . . A guy has to work so hard and long . . ." Nor when he learns what the maid has done does he tell the Brisbee Pills people that it's been a screwy mistake—and a fraud as well, since he and his girl are not married. Instead, he quickly fakes a happy home, so that he can claim the prize when it is delivered. And he tricks his girl into playing along with him. She has a job with a real estate firm, tending a "Postwar World of Charm" model house, and he pretends for the occasion that this is their home—borrowing some neighbors' children and animals for a finishing touch. When the real estate man walks in on the game, which has begun to get out of hand (but "I can't let anything happen to him until I get that check!" the hero cries in an aside), a little bribery and blackmail save the day. The hero suggests to the irate real estate man that if he wins his prize his first purchase may be this very house; and he scares Brisbee with the suggestion that he may lose face with the public if he announces that his winners are phonies. "There's no end to his lies" and his tricks, the girl exclaims in distress. But the maid steps in now and explains everything; explains that it was she who submitted that photograph—the hero, as she puts it (as we happily accept it), merely tried to "fix up" what she had started. The two lovers fall into each other's arms. "Happiness is good for you," chirrups the maid, turning to face us from the screen and recommend, "You too!"

Other films can be said to show us the hero caught in even more precisely the act of which he is so cruelly accused. In *Swing out the Blues* (1943), the hero is a crooner, does a show with three friends: they are the Four Vagabonds. But one day his partners accuse him of planning to walk out on them for a Hollywood contract his agent has tempted him with; and his wife accuses him of carrying on with the agent behind her back. "Why, I've just been stringing her along," he cries, "just to keep your jobs! . . . I never wanted a Hollywood contract!" "But now," he cries, "I'm going to grab it!"—he is so hurt. And he goes rushing out of the house. And if they've assumed that he has taken that contract even now, they are wrong again; for when he turns up—he has joined the R.A.F. Now they really do feel sorry about what they said.

Run the film through again. When his agent tells him, "You should get rid of those barnacles," the hero declares, "I'm not leaving them." But some days later, when he is resisting her suggestion that he escort her about town and forget about his wife, she has merely to breathe the possibility of Hollywood and we see him sit right up and do what she wishes, putting off his wife with elaborate lies. Nor is it straight to the R.A.F. that he goes on that bitter day; first he goes to his agent, asking what about that contract now. When he learns that she has simply been leading him on, he throws a cream pie into her face—sign of just how disinterested he has been.

In a film like *Swing out the Blues*, there is some room for argument about the hero's real intentions at certain moments. (There is room for such argument at many points in this whole series of films, the film makers are in so little control of their material: for many a film one could easily enough draw up several alternative synopses.) But in certain films the hero openly announces cynical intentions. Here, for example, is *Once upon a Time* (1944). The hero of this film, Flynn (Cary Grant), is a big-time Broadway producer who's just had three flops in a row and is about to lose his theater—until he runs into Pinky, the urchin, and Curly, his dancing caterpillar. When Pinky plays "Yessir, she's my baby" on his mouth organ, Curly stands on end and wiggles, "dances!" "Caterpillars come and go, but that one has talent," as Flynn remarks. "A miracle!" he exclaims next. "I'm going to hold on to my theater!" And he promptly forms a "partnership" with Pinky. The caterpillar has soon been given nationwide publicity. Pinky has joined the partnership, of course, only after making Flynn promise that he'll never sell Curly, for the two mean everything to each other—he's raised the worm "from a pup." And Flynn has given his solemn word. But the first chance he gets to sell (Disney is soon willing to give him the $100,000 he needs), he says bluntly, "I can't worry about that kid; I've saved my theater." "You liar!" cries the heartbroken kid. "We were wrong about you!" For Pinky, who's an orphan, has looked up to Flynn as to a father—has even begun to

dress just like him. "You know something? Once I thought I wanted
to be like you; but now I never want to be like you. You're a mean
man, Mr. Flynn, you're a mean man!"

And it would certainly seem so. We even see Flynn, when Pinky's
elder sister threatens to stand in his way, growl to his sidekick, Moke,
"I'll get her fired!" then "Find out what big Mike's doing!" "Twenty
years," Moke replies, closing that subject. Yet this film too dramatizes
its hero as one who is cruelly misunderstood, and acquits him in the
end of all harsh charges. "Some day you'll understand," it has Flynn
cry to the boy; and it has the boy come one day *to* understand. It
features at one point a hint of shame on Flynn's part. As I have remarked, these films are not consistent with themselves. But this is a
note that is soon drowned.

The way in which the drama offers this hero's justification is particularly flagrant. The film begins by gayly flaunting his ability to sell
anything. The banker who comes to tell Flynn that he is losing his
theater almost succumbs instead to backing another superproduction.
"Just what the public needs," Flynn improvises. "Set in Egypt . . .
the sphinx . . . the pyramids . . . the soul struggling upward!"
"Beautiful, yes!" the banker croaks, but then comes to himself: "No!
That's the way you sold me the last time!" When Flynn begins to
exult to Moke that the dancing caterpillar will save his theater, Moke
has his doubts. "Wait till I tell the public what he means," Flynn tells
him. "What does he mean?" asks Moke. To which Flynn replies, "I
don't know yet, but I'll think of something." When he very soon does,
the film continues to treat as a source of fun his gift for putting it over
on the public. He sells the little worm as a symbol of the spirit of
man—much as he had planned to sell his Egyptian scene: "The
worm was crawling around in the dirt, and suddenly it heard music; it
raised its head and danced. It brings us all a message: if you feel lost
crawling around, look up!" And the public buys. Flynn's office is soon
mobbed with people begging permission to make Curly cookies,
Curly toys. But Flynn's justification to us in the end? Chided with
trying to take the little worm from Pinky, he cries, "You can't understand what the caterpillar has begun to mean to the world!"

(In somewhat similar fashion in *Sing, Neighbor, Sing*, 1944, a
radio entertainer humbugs a small women's college, usurping the

place of a visiting psychologist who's been detained somehow; has a lot of fun faking lectures, hypnotizing people. Suddenly in the end— when he must face up to a lot of charges against him—we are made to feel that he has done the entire community great good.)

But the film adds one more turn, still, in the clearing of Flynn. When Pinky cries out his accusation, Flynn, very hurt, sets Curly right down (in the little shoebox cage in which he lives) and walks out. But when Pinky goes to talk to Curly, he isn't in the box! Pinky thinks Flynn has taken him—here really does misjudge him (a turn, recall, that I analyzed in certain war films). Though Flynn and Pinky miss each other sorely, neither will approach the other. But one day some of Pinky's little friends take things into their own hands and march Flynn to Pinky's house; and as Flynn sits there at the upright, waiting for the kid and idly picking out on the keys Curly's old tune, a little butterfly emerges and begins to flutter about in time to the notes. Pinky comes running in and of course the butterfly is Curly: that's where he had gone, to spin himself a cocoon! "And he's never going to leave us again, is he?" cries the ecstatic boy. "He belongs to us!" But Flynn gently counsels him now, as a father would: they cannot really keep him. How could they? And Pinky begins at last to understand. No one's been trying to rob him of anything. One just can't hold onto these things for oneself. As the butterfly flutters out the open window, "He belongs to the world," says Flynn (just what he's always said, we nod). And the two, arms around each other, wave happily: "Thanks for everything!" (Flynn may well wave his thanks, for though when the deal with Disney fell through he lost his theater, it has been restored to him. The banker has suddenly announced that he's going to back him again—he's been so impressed with what he made of that bug.)

Unlike the heroes of *Rhapsody in Blue, Humoresque,* and *Random Harvest,* the successful one here utters no pitiful cries toward the end—anxious about something he has missed, someone he has hurt. This hero always regains the love from which he has been estranged, and always stands at last acquitted of all trespasses against others. But, as I have noted, in the process of giving us this happy ending—sparing us the portrait of the poor amnesiac—the film makers themselves display strange lapses of memory. And we in the audience, dreaming the dream we are offered, succumb to a kind of amnesia ourselves—disavowing at one moment feelings that have engaged us just a moment before.

There is a more direct sense too in which these films reinforce the image noted in the others—the image of one somehow helplessly lost to himself. Listen, in each of them, to the hero's cry when he is faced by his harsh accusers. Over and over, to clear himself, he cites his helpless commitment to the deeds for which they account him responsible. Here is nothing *he* has intended, he cries. The maid did this; or his agent was to blame. Tyrannical agents abound in this genre, and publicity departments "set loose" on the hapless hero; or meddling friends or meddling parents. Events quite out of his control intervene —poppa's illness, or the fact that caterpillars, after all, have to turn into butterflies and flutter away. Here is always none of *his* doing. This hero may stand there at last securely at the top, and cleared of all charges against him; but what has become of the familiar myth—the youth striking out boldly after his dream, the self-made man proudly surveying the fruits of his own enterprise? That myth has been overturned.

In the films of Preston Sturges—in *Hail the Conquering Hero* (1944), for example—this overturn of the old myth can be seen very clearly. For Sturges, refining in a comic vein upon this dream, managing more nimbly than all the rest to move his hero unsullied to the top of the heap, borrows for his purpose a familiar figure from early films —one brought to life in the twenties by Buster Keaton and Harry Langdon: the clown figure of the Innocent, the unworldly one, pure of heart. The contrast between his version of this conquering hero and the original is a telling one.

Sturges's hero never reaches out his hands to seize what he finally gains, and one does not need to listen to his wild cries about it, one can see that he is not responsible for the path he takes. There is no room for argument at all as to the nature of this hero's intentions. He is a little guy who loves his mother very much, and his girl, and his home town, and yearns to make a place for himself in that town, however humble—he'd proudly be dog catcher. But as the film opens, he sits in gloomy self-imposed exile: he has tried to join the Marines and he has been rejected because of hay fever. Son of a Marine hero, he is ashamed to return home. He has written his mother that he has been sent overseas, has written his girl not to wait for him, and as we meet him he is moping over his beer in a tavern in the big city, far from home, trying hard not to hear the four singing waiters, for "Home to the arms of mother!" they wail. He need not grieve. Home to the arms of mother, to the arms of his girl, to a hero's welcome, to election as mayor of the town, the film brings Woodrow LaFayette Pershing Truesmith (Eddie Bracken). But it brings him home protesting all the way.

Six Marines on leave, treated to beers by Woodrow, impulsively give him his start. Learning his sad story, they decide that his exile is not fair to his mother; they cannot have her thinking that he is over there in danger; so one of them, Bugsy—who feels the most strongly because he's never had a mother himself—gets Mrs. Truesmith on the phone and tells her that her son is headed home, honorably discharged after heroism at Guadalcanal. Woodrow, dragged to the phone, wildly stammers out his denials, but the lie has been told; his protestations sound like a hero's modesty. They march him to the train. Among their firmly stepping feet his two feet balk and drag, but in vain. They hoist him aboard; there, though he struggles and squirms, force onto him a corporal's uniform hung with medals. And they decide to stick right along with him so that he cannot thwart their plan. That mother of his mustn't "worry no more." When Woodrow spots the welcoming committee drawn up at the station, he cries, "Let me outta here!" and tries to hide in the lavatory; but the six deliver him into the arms of the crowd. If he wanted to cry out his denials now, he couldn't, for his words would be lost in the din of the competing brass bands. And besides, he cannot even speak, for a little girl has thrust a great bouquet of goldenrod into his face and he is sneezing helplessly.

From here on, the town itself takes over and events sweep him along. A statue is being erected in his honor. At a special ceremony, his mother's mortgage is torn up. Woodrow writhes, stammers, doesn't know what to do. The six Marines keep careful watch to prevent him from doing anything. ("See that look in your mother's eye?" they gloat.) A crowd of citizens moves on his house. "Here it comes," says Woodrow. "I'm ready." He assumes that the hoax has been discovered. But this turns out to be a committee to draft him as a candidate

Eddie Bracken and the Marines in *Hail the Conquering Hero* (1944).

Buster Keaton in *The General* (1927).

for mayor. He tries to protest. He loves his mother very much, he stammers, and he loves this town, and the very dogs and cats in the streets; but he isn't worthy, and he's no hero, he protests—"I'm not running!" "He could be president!" the crowd murmurs. "He has a natural flair for politics!" "Why, you couldn't stop from being mayor," they tell him. "A miracle couldn't stop you." So he tries to leave town, but the six prevent him. At last from the platform of Town Hall, where he is swept in a tumultuous parade, he flatly names himself a phony, gives them the whole history of the lie (absolving the six of all complicity, though); and now he quickly heads for the railroad station, to leave forever. Again a mob moves down upon him. He thinks this time that they have come to lynch him. But they have come to *insist* that he be their mayor; for, they cry, he has given them proof of his courage and honesty. "No! No!" he stammers, unbelieving. And there he stands, his very heart's desire his—and swept to victory without ever trying for it. In *Once upon a Time,* the theater was handed to Flynn as it were gratuitously, after he had given it up; but this hero has made no gesture *ever* toward the prize that is handed to him. In stammering innocence as to how it all happened, he stands there. "I knew the Marines could do almost anything, but I never knew they could do anything like this!"

In those earlier films of Keaton and Langdon, the hero too is wondrously innocent of half that goes on about him. He too is carried to victory by a sort of preposterous good luck. At a glance, these heroes might seem to be identical. But it is not so. In the original, the old myth—here declined—still precariously stands.

At the beginning of *The General,* a Buster Keaton film (1927), the hero sits in sad exile too. He too has tried to enlist (in the Civil War) and has been rejected—on the grounds that he is more useful at his job: he is an engineer; "the General" is his beloved engine. He is unaware of the reason for his rejection. Furthermore, his girl, believing that he has not tried to enlist, has turned him from her door. We see him sitting dejected on the side of the big engine, so rapt in his grief that when another engineer starts up the train, he doesn't even notice—still sits, listlessly riding the slow-galloping piston rod. But the two exiles with which the films commence are not the same. When this hero steps out onto the street, after the Army has turned him down, he turns solemnly to address them: "If you lose this war, don't blame me!" Disdained by his girl, he walks off in a grief profound but haughty. It is no self-imposed exile that he suffers, meekly convinced of his own ineffectualness.

Nor does this hero wait for others to launch him upon the way. One day some enemy soldiers make off with his "General" while he and the passengers are having lunch at a station—make off with it up the track back toward their own lines, taking with them, too, the hero's girl, who has stepped into the baggage car to look for something. Open-mouthed, everybody watches the train vanish, our hero's mouth open wider than all the rest. But gesturing for others to follow him, he promptly starts running after it. Those others who join him as promptly give up the chase, for it is obviously mad to try to catch the train on foot. But our hero, glancing back and finding that he runs on alone, runs on still, doggedly. This is the stamp of *his* innocence: to persist even when the race seems impossible.

Those more sensible who have stayed behind think to wire ahead to the next station, but the enemy has already stopped to cut all the wires. On the hero, in crazy pursuit, everything now depends. A little hand car that he finds and boards (quite out of hand for him) is soon derailed. Abandoning it—in a huff—he runs on to grab up a bicycle, pedals headlong until this spills him; on foot again reaches another train finally and commandeering it, gives more effective chase. This train is full of soldiers and he thinks he proceeds in force now; but the engine has not been coupled to the rest, and glancing back, again— blinking—he finds himself alone. But again he keeps on.

Superficially this could be the Sturges hero. Amazement drops his jaw as continually as it does Woodrow's. And he too is the beneficiary of crazy chance. The enemy uncouples a rear car to impede him. With it in front of him he must proceed quite blindly. He manages to switch it off onto a side track, but this—unknown to him—rejoins the main track; agape, he finds the car right there ahead of him again. Then while he is busy at something else, a log thrown onto the track by the enemy to further hinder him manages instead merely to derail this one car. When he looks again, it is no longer there. He has spied a small cannon in a shed and coupled it to his engine, and he wrestles with this now—managing only to lob the cannonball weakly into his own cab. He stuffs in a larger powder charge, but this time gets tangled in the couplings, as the jogging of the train aims the cannon muzzle squarely at him. But just as more jogging sets the cannon to barking, a sharp bend in the track brings the enemy into the line of fire. Meanwhile the two trains enter enemy territory. He is unaware of this. He is busy chopping wood for his fire, first with a hatchet, then patiently with the head of the hatchet after it flies off the handle. Beyond him we see, in panorama, streaming by, one army retreating, another, the enemy, advancing—horsemen, wagons, foot soldiers. He chops on, unaware—until suddenly he puts his head up and his jaw drops again. But luck goes with him all the way—enables him, after he hops from his train, to find the cabin where the enemy proceeds; there to rescue his girl; there too to overhear the enemy plans; then steal off, in a borrowed uniform, with the girl in a sack over his shoulder, to board his "General"—under their noses—and drive off back toward his own lines. And every time the enemy soldier who is on the train, unknown to him, starts to creep up on him, some random hunk of wood that he tosses as he stokes the fire knocks the man senseless. The news of the enemy plan he brings back helps his side to win the ensuing battle. And that dazed enemy soldier, noticed at last by the hero and led into camp, turns out to be an important commander.

Of either success, Woodrow's or this hero's, one could declare: magic. Yet it is a very different magic in the two films. Woodrow's success is gratuitous and ironic, one of life's pranks: his protests of unworthiness gain him the heights—turn out to equal a flair for politics. Whereas in the case of this earlier hero the impression is that by special persistence, the intensity of his belief that he will succeed, he magically does—this luck generated, as it were, by his faith itself.

The innocence of these two heroes is of a very different sort. They are oblivious in quite a different way to what goes on about them. Woodrow displays an almost epileptic bewilderment,[1] but Keaton has, still, the air of one distracted by a compelling vision.

The endings of the two films sum up the contrast. "Where did you get that?" the commander of the armies demands of Buster Keaton, who has dressed in a second borrowed uniform. "Take it off!" And

---

[1] One can study the dissolution of the old myth here even in terms of the slapstick staged in the two films. In *The General*, it has all the precision and the delicate poise of ballet. It is virtually danced. Whereas in *Hail the Conquering Hero*, the slapstick resembles a football melee.

Keaton does so, expecting—as Woodrow does at the approach of the mob—to be punished. "Put this on!" comes the next order, and he is climbing into the clothes he is handed before he recognizes them as a lieutenant's uniform. The commander next hands him the sword of the enemy officer he has captured—to be his own. "No! No!" Woodrow sputters, when presented with *his* heart's desire—a figure of helplessness even at that moment. But Buster Keaton assumes his new rank gravely, even haughtily—as one who knows his due. And it is in this same spirit that he then walks off with his girl—the spirit of the deserving knight; whereas Woodrow continues to the very end to cry to *his* girl, "You are well rid of me!"

There is a further sense in which the myth, still live in these earlier films, is overturned in the films of Sturges. Swept home to the arms of sweetheart and mother, the status of hero, election as mayor of his town, Woodrow Truesmith does gain his heart's desire. In all the world he loves best his mother, his girl, the Marine Corps, his home town. Though accidental, his victory might seem at least tangible. But even as Woodrow stands there, his dreams all come true, laughter can be said to explode those dreams. Where the innocence of Keaton proved to be inspired, that of this other dreamer stands revealed as the innocence of the dupe. All that Woodrow Truesmith adores so faithfully is winked away for us in the course of the film. His love for his mother is slyly spoofed by the very inclusion in the cast of Bugsy, the Marine with the mother complex. His worship of the Marines is spoofed in the staging of the solemn visits the boys pay to the portrait of Woodrow's bemedaled father, which hangs in the parlor as in a shrine. And his home town is savagely caricatured, the elaborate welcome home it offers Woodrow revealed as obscene, each citizen shown to be looking simply to his own advantage. "There's something rotten in this town," someone says right out. And even Woodrow declares to them that they are attracted to him because he is a big phony. Supposedly at the very end he accomplishes the spiritual reform of the town, a reform the town itself has been yearning for. But a kind of sly laughter envelops even this event. Sturges in this film cunningly crowns his hero a victor—and then, as it were, winks at us over his shoulder.

3. "Believe in me!"

One hero, then, stands at the top of the ladder of success uttering piteous cries—part of him lost, his belief in himself and in all his youthful dreams lost. A second figure of success is tortured by the fact that others refuse to believe in him. A third stands there, all he has yearned for safely clasped; but if one looks again, his dream too dissolves, although in comic innocence he clasps it still. There is yet another figure in the films of these years, superficially like none of these, superficially the very opposite of the Innocent, cast indeed as a villain, but again, if one looks, really the same figure—shown us in extremity.

In the films that feature him in this darker guise—for example, in *Dragonwyck, Undercurrent, The Strange Love of Martha Ivers* (each 1946)—it is ostensibly some other figure with whom we sympathize; but he remains the central figure of the piece. For in each film the story is of one who has fallen helplessly in love with him or with her. This villain has charms.

Dragonwyck and *Undercurrent* start out brightly. In each, a restless girl, still living at home, yearns to leave that home. The villain appears upon the scene and carries her off as if to the happiest of endings. In *Dragonwyck,* set in the past century, she is a girl on a small Connecticut Yankee farm, the villain a wealthy patroon, a distant cousin, who writes one day to engage her as a governess to his daughter. "Golly Moses!" she cries in ecstasy when her poppa allows her to go, and again when she sees her new home on the Hudson. (The patroon has never even counted his servants!) And when the grand visitors at his manor look down their noses at her, he, the patroon, takes her by the hand and waltzes with her at the ball before them all. "Golly Moses!" is all she can exclaim again. When his wife dies and he asks her hand in marriage, she is too breathless even to utter that exclamation. It is a dream come true for her.

In *Undercurrent,* she is a chemistry professor's daughter in a small college town, the villain a young millionaire captain of industry who visits the father to ask him for a new formula he has perfected and promptly returns to ask him for his daughter—because the meeting of these two has constituted a very special chemical event too, the father comments. "Judas!" this heroine exclaims when she sees *her* new home, Washington, spread out below their plane. "You've led me by the hand," she tells him, "into a strange and wonderful world"—she too breathing that it is "like a dream!"

Each of these heroines wakes from this dream—not merely to a sense of loss but to recognition that death lies all about her in the world into which she has been led. But she wakes slowly and incredulously.

In *The Strange Love of Martha Ivers,* the protagonist is not a wide-eyed young girl but a tough young man. As a kid he had hopped a circus train and run off from his home town (a terribly poor boy, he had had a rough time of it there). Now, passing through the town by chance, he discovers that his childhood sweetheart—who almost ran away *with* him that day—has become the reigning power there. The town has even been renamed for her. "Welcome to Iverstown," he reads on a sign, and "Maybe this time they mean it," he breathes. He is soon adding, "Yes, now I've got luck!" because Martha Ivers, though a married woman, is still in love with him, and if he wants to, it's clear, he can share that power with her. This hero too wakes to the fact that there is only death to be gained here, and pulls out—just in time. Each one of these protagonists is very nearly killed at the hands of the beloved.

In the first film I described in this chapter, the figure of success uttered vague cries about having perhaps injured other people. Here there is nothing vague about the fact that he has. Nor is his guilt ever wished away, as in the second group of films I described. And the estrangement that grows between him and his beloved as she learns of his guilt is never healed.

In *Dragonwyck,* the patroon (Vincent Price) is trying to keep his enormous land grant intact, but to do this he has to break the anti-rent movement spreading among his tenant farmers. In this fight he is gradually defined as altogether ruthless. He lacks an heir to whom he can leave Dragonwyck, and he is defined here even more clearly as a villain: we see him poison his first wife when she fails to bear him a son; we see him try to poison his second wife, the heroine. The captain of industry in *Undercurrent* (Robert Taylor) owes his fortune too to ruthlessness. It rests on a certain remarkable invention of "his" —which turns out not to be his at all but that of a little refugee

whom he has murdered for it. Taylor has also robbed his own brother
of his proper share in the business, rigging the books to make it appear that his brother was the crooked one. And this man too tries to
take the life of the heroine. In *The Strange Love of Martha Ivers* too,
the fortunes of Martha Ivers (Barbara Stanwyck) are founded on
murder. Martha, we learn, never ran off with the hero because in a
last-minute quarrel with her aunt she struck her and accidentally
killed her—the aunt toppling down a steep flight of stairs. Through
this accidental killing she came into her aunt's fortune. She secured
that fortune through a willful second killing. For she took her tutor's
advice and lied about her aunt's death—pretending to have seen a
stranger run off from the scene. And some years later she coolly "identified" as that stranger and sent to the chair an innocent man. Her
husband, the tutor's son, acted as prosecutor, and this gave him his
start on a political career. He is D.A. now; soon, it's predicted, he will
be governor—"whatever his wife wants him to be." We see Martha
try to take the life of this husband, when he stands in her way. And
we see her try to take the life of the hero.

This figure of success is carefully defined as a twisted character.
Vincent Price in *Dragonwyck* takes dope; Robert Taylor in *Undercurrent* beats his horse; Barbara Stanwyck—Martha Ivers—all but
beats her dipsomaniac husband. Each of them, we are told, is "sick."
Look closely, however, and the special case, here as always, becomes
the familiar case. Here is the same sick figure I have been sketching
all along—his sickness merely graver now. In this character, in fact,
the kinship of the two other figures I have been describing in this
chapter is confirmed, for their pitiful cries are interwoven here—the
cry of the first: "I am homeless!" and the cry of the other: "I am
doubted! Do not doubt me!" This latest figure adds the desperate cry:
"Believe in me or I will have to destroy you!"

As all is told, as usual, in terms of boy meets girl, look closely at
the gesture with which this villain approaches his victim. Here, for
example, is the scene in which Vincent Price proposes to Miranda in
Dragonwyck: Down the hallway his wife has just died—poisoned by
an exotic plant he has had placed in her room. Wasting no time, he
hurries to Miranda. He utters no villainish laughter, however, as he
approaches. Here is the familiar pathos. Face dark with suffering, he
comes to her—a suppliant. His line is dying out, his authority is no

longer believed in, Dragonwyck is threatened. Perhaps Miranda can give him a son. And she believes in him, believes in his dream. As Gershwin, toward the end, came to Julie, asking her to restore his lost life to him, the patroon comes to Miranda. Dressed in a dark robe, the crest of Dragonwyck embroidered over his heart, he approaches—and pours out to her all his anguish. "I wish I knew something I could say to help you," she tells him. "I want to so much!" "Do you, Miranda?" he cries. "You must have faith!" she tells him. And he? "As long as you are with me!" He knows, he says, that he has no right to speak at this time, but he cannot help himself. (Gershwin's desperate cry echoes here: "Hurry, darling, hurry!") When they are married soon after, "You will be with me wherever I am, always!" he cries. But Miranda in her turn fails to give him a son. And then as he begins to lose the fight against the anti-rent movement and as he grows more violent in his ways, she begins, too, to look upon him with a difference—to judge him. Frantic again—for "You shall not destroy Dragonwyck!" he has cried to them all—he feels driven to destroy Miranda too. She is rescued by a doctor, a leader in the anti-rent movement, who loves her. And the patroon commits suicide. The film keeps him a touching figure even at the end. As the shot rings out, as he gives one last look toward Miranda, who has been his hope and his loss, then slumps forward, all who stand there silently remove their hats.

In *Undercurrent* too, the villain approaches the heroine as a frantic suppliant, his appeal the same: he too wants her to restore to him a life that has somehow eluded him, a belief in himself that fails. Soon after their marriage, Robert Taylor pours out all *his* anguish to Katherine Hepburn. The story he tells is one of cruel injuries suffered at the hands of his brother, Robert Mitchum. Clinging to her like a child, he cries, "He can't hurt us if we hold on to each other! . . . We'll never let him come between us!" The heroine decides that she must learn more about this man who shadows her husband's life; and so his nature is gradually revealed to us. He turns out to be the very opposite of the person Taylor has pictured. Unlike Taylor, he has never had much money, "never cared about it"; but when Hepburn at last finds her way to his house, in contrast to the house to which Taylor has brought her (which is strangely "unused"—"a little grim, I'm afraid," Taylor has muttered), *Mitchum's* house is "like someone's home." (Taylor, in a jealous frenzy when he finds her in this place, starts throwing about the books, the records, the pipes, the various tokens of a life really lived.) And Taylor's sick hatred of his brother turns out to be more, too, than a matter of jealousy. His brother is the one who knows his guilt—who has guessed about the murder of the little refugee. Throughout most of the film, no one knows where Mitchum is. He has run away to avoid facing his brother with what he knows about him. He has joined the Army, hoping to be killed. But he comes out alive. And after he meets Hepburn (she doesn't recognize him—takes him to be the caretaker at the place), he goes at last to Taylor and confronts him; for she's "a fine woman," he tells Taylor, and mustn't be hurt. Taylor must tell her all the truth about himself.

"I can't give her up!" Taylor cries. "I'll give it all back—but not her!" "I can be all right!" he cries. "She loves me!" And as the brother still faces him, he promises that he will tell her the truth. But give him a little time—until he's sure of her. "To whom do you belong?" he has cried frantically to Hepburn. Then, as estrangement has grown between them, because of his weird behavior—his accusations that she falling in love with his brother whom she is not even aware of having met—"Please," he has begged her, "try a little old-fashioned trust, a little blind faith." And she has tried. But for Taylor too, as for the patroon, everything suddenly fails—here in a most ironical fashion. "Forgive me!" she cries to him one day. "I almost destroyed our happiness by doubting!" She confesses that someone had planted in her heart the suspicion that he had murdered his brother; but she has evidence now that he is very much alive. "I am deeply ashamed," she tells him. "I was going to go away and never see you again!" He asks her softly, "You couldn't have endured living with a murderer?" Unknowing, she has spoken fatal words. *"I'm going to see,"* he tells her, *"that you never have the chance to doubt me again."* So Taylor in his turn tries to destroy the woman who was once all his hope but has become instead a judgment upon him. This heroine escapes death even more narrowly than the heroine of *Dragonwyck*—escapes only because Taylor is trampled to death by his horse (the horse that was once his brother's and that he has tried in vain to master). And from the wheelchair in which she will have to stay for a while, the heroine comes at last to meet Robert Mitchum. Some day, we gather, when it becomes fitting to hold out his hands to her, he will lead her among humbler but happier ways.

Behind the figure of Martha Ivers there range themselves even more clearly in kinship those other lost figures I have sketched in this chapter—their gestures the same, here simply exaggerated, the malady turned acute. When Sam after the lapse of many years meets his childhood sweetheart again, now virtual sovereign of "America's fastest growing industrial city," he asks her, "Aren't you glad that you missed that circus train?" But staring at him she mumbles, "I don't know"—thrown quite off balance, her husband notes in amazement. He has never seen her lose her poise like that before. Martha drives Sam to the top of a high hill from which all her kingdom can be surveyed—Iverstown. (Martha's name had been Smith, but her proud aunt had insisted that she take *her* name, Ivers, if she wished to inherit her money; for her aunt had scorned Martha's father, who was a millhand.) Yes, her father had been a millhand here, Martha boasts to Sam, and now she owns the town. Now she employs thirty thousand workers at the mill, instead of the mere three thousand who had been employed in her father's day. "And I've done it all myself!" she boasts. Nor does she intend to have it taken from her. When Sam appears on the scene, she suspects at first that he has come to blackmail her—for she assumes that he was a witness long ago to the death of her aunt. Yet as she gazes down upon her conquest spread out before her, "It doesn't even look real," she breathes. "If anyone asked me, I would say that my name was still Martha Smith." Martha takes Sam to her house. And in this rich mansion that was once her aunt's and that she's had completely redecorated, one room remains untouched, "nothing changed since that night" when Martha almost ran off with Sam. "I come here often," she confesses (as Ronald Colman often fingered that little key dangling from his watch chain, while his spirit groped to remember the home he had lost). One thing that Martha craves from Sam is release from Walter—weakling, drunkard, "scared little boy," who is helplessly in love with her and whom she bullies as she likes, but who does "know her" and knows the history of her ascent to power. His inability to forget her guilt, which he shares, has *made* him a drunkard, and the daily spectacle of his distraction serves to keep her too from forgetting. Walter assures Martha that Sam too has come to remind her of that guilt—come with "blackmail in his eye." Actually, Sam had slipped away that evening just before everything happened, and never knew why Martha did not follow him. But now, his curiosity aroused by Martha's strange behavior (just as Hepburn's curiosity was aroused by Taylor's), he consults newspaper files, pieces together what he learns there with Martha's own remarks, and soon does know what happened and knows about the conviction, years later, of an innocent man. He faces Martha with his knowledge.

And now Martha must "be sure of him." The way in which she tries to win him is familiar, recalls Taylor's protestations as he paints himself the helpless victim of his brother, recalls too the protestations of the other heroes sketched in this chapter—the cruelly misunderstood heroes of all those Grade B musicals. She was helplessly swept along, Martha insists. Walter's father, her tutor, was the one responsible. Seeing the power he could gain for himself, he persuaded her not to confess; assumed the role of her mentor from then on; married her off to his son; arranged the trial of that innocent man; manipulated everything, right up to the day of his death—she quite helpless all this time and longing so for Sam to be there. And Sam lets himself succumb to this argument, as we have seen others succumb. The kingdom to be found in Martha's arms is a tempting one. On the hill above Iverstown, these two cling together in a frantic embrace. Sam has met a young girl in the town—a wanderer like himself, who has thought he might be moving on with her. She is now distraught.

Happily, Sam is not lost. He too wakes; is able at last to say, "You're sick, Martha," to tell her that he is leaving. When Walter speaks *his* mind about all those years and Martha then begs Sam to kill Walter ("You believe *me*, don't you?"), Sam suddenly hangs back. Martha bursts into further frantic self-justification. "I've put thousands to work!" she cries. Whole families, she cries, owe their livelihood to her. "Look what I've done!" (Her words match words spoken more casually by Ronald Colman in *Random Harvest*—explaining why he has stayed on in industry longer than he had intended to.) When she sees that Sam is no longer bound to her, "We can't let him go, can we?" Martha cries to Walter. And now she begs Walter to help her kill Sam. But Walter, so recently the proposed victim himself, hesitates, and Sam slips away.

If Sam has broken free of her, Walter is bound to Martha still. "You're insane," he too has told her—but has added, smiling, "and me too." He turns to her now: "Don't cry. He'll never tell." She tells him, "For the first time in my life I was afraid; I felt you were no longer standing by me!" He puts his arms around her and says, "It's not your fault." "It isn't, is it, Walter?" she begs. "It's not anyone's fault," he assures her. "It's just the way things are!" (the precise comfort, recall, offered by the musicals I described). "And you'll see," he continues, "things will be different now between you and me—just like nothing ever happened." "*You* believe me!" she cries. And Walter, who has always been rebuffed by her before, asks, "Will you kiss me?" And she kisses him; and in a kind of bliss the two commit suicide together. As she falls dying, Martha cries out, "Ivers Ivers Ivers!" but then, "No—Martha Smith!" And here too is an echo of *Random Harvest*. In that final embrace, too, things were to be as though nothing had ever happened. The same magic name, even, summoned bliss: "Smittie!"—two worlds here joined at last, and the amnesiac relieved of all his agony.

4. A shocking character—Verdoux

I have described a series of figures who are even monotonously similar. Whether the figure of success stands before us as hero, clown, or villain, it is a single likeness that confronts us: one who has not found himself but lost himself, one who has "arrived" only at distraction, a sick man. Let me stress again, however, that this likeness has been drawn unawares and that the general public never consciously recognizes this to be the portrait. The truth of this was obvious when one particular figure of success appeared upon our screens and was labeled at once a shocking and freakish character and denied a return appearance: Chaplin's Monsieur Verdoux (1947). Verdoux happens to be again the very figure I have sketched at chapter's length. But this time he is not painted for anyone's comfort. Here, for a change, is a work of art. The hero is summoned before us in sharpest outline, and Chaplin takes care to see that no one can mistake him for a man unlike the rest of us. Waiting, at the end of the film, to hear the death sentence imposed upon him, Verdoux turns to those who have watched the trial—turns too, in this gesture, to all of us sitting in the movie audience—and remarks, "I shall see you all very soon, very soon."

Verdoux is a devoted husband and father, and a successful blue-beard. Once he was a simple bank clerk; but losing this employment in the depression, and having a wife and little son to support, he has taken to marrying and then murdering for their money a series of other women. Many who saw the film complained that it was outrageous to make such a figure an object either of humor or of sympathy. This killer *is* made a terribly funny figure and he is also made sympathetic. Yet none of that blind sympathy is asked for Verdoux that was asked of us for the killer in *Dragonwyck* or *Undercurrent*; and in the end this comedy treats its central figure more solemnly than do any of those other films. Here is the real outrage. *Monsieur Verdoux* is a relentless study of a man's distraction, of the "half dream world" in which he moves—giving that world a long look from which we are not allowed to turn away.

He renders with a terribly funny accuracy the zest Verdoux shows for his work, the pride he takes in a task well done. He tells us everything in a gesture—as Verdoux, hand on hip, after the dispatch of some "job," picks up the telephone to call his broker, or sits at the piano to trill off an arpeggio, lips pursed in a self-satisfied smile; then returns home to his wife and son, the deed to their little house his at last—"*That* they'll never take away from us." More consummately still he shows the strain of the game. He gives us no shrill cries like the cries of those other lovelorn ones, but shows us this man's distraction in a thousand subtle ways. ("We were happy then," his wife recalls of the days when he was a bank clerk. "Aren't we now?" he asks. For it is only after his wife's death that he awakens to reckon, himself, the "numb confusion" of those later days.) The moment Chaplin shows us may be funny. Colliding with a dressmaker's dummy that belonged to a former victim, he mumbles, "I wonder where that ever came from." The moment may be more than funny—as Verdoux, pausing on the landing on his way upstairs to "liquidate" Lydia, gazes out at the moonstruck night and moans, "Endymion! . . . Our feet were soft in flowers . . ." Or one day, seated at a sidewalk café, he looks up with a pleased smile from reading about the success of a new poison he has tried—and finds himself face to face with the young girl he has spent a recent evening with, the two of them talking about the ideal they share in common, that has kept them at their labors; and he is unable to greet her. "You go on about your business," he cries; and to elude her, he scrambles onto the back of a passing bus—leaving her standing there, puzzled.

Verdoux had picked up this girl, meaning to test his poison on *her* (figuring that she was just a lonely tramp who would not be missed), but he had changed his mind—finding, in conversation with her, that she lived by the very religion he lived by. And this "religion," as they both name it—what is it? The girl's husband, now dead, had been a hopeless invalid; and it was for him that she had lived and worked. "I would have killed for him," she declares. Verdoux's wife, for whom *he* kills, is a cripple. Once again, the image the success boy holds in his heart of hearts turns out to be the very image of helplessness itself.

Monsieur Verdoux is not a work that is entirely controlled. The scenes of Verdoux at home are sentimental; Chaplin himself is held a bit rapt before the image of the cripple. And at the end of the film, after Verdoux's wife and child have died and he has "awakened" to the truth about himself and goes to meet his "destiny"—his trial and death sentence—this character seems suddenly just a little too all-wise. Chaplin succumbs to the temptation to step into the play himself. Verdoux at the end is actually no longer Verdoux but Chaplin, acting out—haughtily, prophetically—his own martyrdom at the hands of a public that does not know itself.

 5

"Don't you know me?!"
(some restless ones)

By its reception of *Monsieur Verdoux* the public showed that it prefers *not* to know too well the hero who engages its feelings in film after film. It wakes reluctantly to any daylight look at him and at that "half dream world" in which he moves — wakes as reluctantly as the bewitched heroines I have described. This is easier to understand if one studies in certain other films the drama of an imagined venturing forth from that world. At the end of *Dragonwyck, Undercurrent, The Strange Love of Martha Ivers,* one sees Miranda, Hepburn, Sam look eagerly toward a wider world that now lies before them. But here the final fade-out leaves one. "You are now leaving Iverstown," the road signs read in *Martha Ivers,* but one travels no further. In certain films, however, the story is entered at a later point, just as escape is planned.

In *The Chase* (1946), we meet the heroine, Lorna (Michele Morgan), already disenchanted, already aware that she has entered a world of death. Her marriage to the villain, Roman, a wealthy Florida racketeer, had meant her rise from rags to riches; but now if only he would let her leave, she implores him, she would happily leave as empty-handed as he found her. (This villain again, though painted a villain indeed—he keeps a great dog in his wine cellar, to tear his enemies to pieces for him—is painted a tragic, a suffering figure, like the villains of the last chapter, tormented by the fact that he no longer possesses this girl. We see him stretched out on his sofa, listening to moody symphonies, or racing his car through the night—a brooding fated creature, by no means placed outside the reach of our feelings.) The hero who wants to deliver Lorna from this man is Scotty (Robert Cummings), a war veteran who has wandered into the house to return a wallet he found on the street. Roman, amused by such honesty, has hired him as chauffeur. One of his duties consists of driving the distracted heroine around. And it is always to the same place that she asks him to take her: a lonely pier on the waterfront—where she stands and stares and stares across the waters. "What's out there?" she asks him; and he tells her, "Havana." And then one day she asks him to help her cross, and he agrees.

The tickets have been bought; the boat is to sail that night; the plans are set for escaping from the house; and Scotty lies down for a brief nap. He wakes—amnesiac. He cannot remember how he came there. He has a frantic feeling that there is something he has to do. He finds his eyes forever turning to the clock. But what the appointment is that he must keep he cannot recall. He hurries for advice to his former Navy psychiatrist. But the psychiatrist merely tells him to stop worrying: he obviously has an anxiety neurosis. He advises him to turn his clock to the wall and come and have a drink. The hands of the clock continue to circle; and at the bar where they go, Scotty finds his eyes still lifting to seek the hour; but no recollection comes. Only at the very last instant does Lorna's name, mentioned by someone in the room, recall him from this strange paralysis. He hurries to her and together they just barely do manage the escape.

What is the sleep from which he has risen, forgetful? Lying down to nap, he has dreamed a dream: He is on the ship with Lorna. They have made good their escape. Shyly, they declare their love for one another. They reach Havana. They are in a small café to which a guide has brought them. On the dance floor again they murmur their love. But suddenly she slumps within his arms and glides to the floor. He draws a knife from her side. And it is the knife he bought a few hours earlier at a pawnshop. But no—this is not his knife, he cries, but the mate to it, which he had also seen there! No one believes him.

He is charged with her murder. And when he leads his accusers to the pawnshop, to prove his innocence, the woman says that she has never even seen him before. He must manage an escape again and, wandering about this strange island, seek the evidence that will clear him. At last he tracks to his lair a certain agent of Roman's. He has known, of course, that Roman's hand has been in this. But as he is eavesdropping and the agent is giving the information that he needs, he makes some small noise. The man comes upstairs to look for him. The two scuffle together behind a dark hanging. One of them, then, drags forth the body of the other. The curtain parts and—it is *he*, the hero, who is dragged forth, dead!

Here he wakes (and here we wake, for the transition into this dream has been managed so smoothly that it is only now that we come to know it for a dream). Here he wakes into that dazed state that is broken only at the very end of the film. This has been the source of it: a vision of empty death across the waters has held him paralyzed on this shore.

Even the very end of the film fails quite to dispel the dream he has dreamed. The lovers make the boat. The villain, racing his car in pursuit, is destroyed in a crash. Their escape would seem to be complete. But in the final shot of the film the two sit murmuring their love—in front of that same cheap café it has been fatal for them to enter in his nightmare. And watching them from the driver's seat of their carriage—is the same little man who in that nightmare guided them there with malicious intent. The hero has been to Havana, we've been told, only once before in his life, years before, so that in a queer way this duplication of the very elements of his bad dream leaves us still entangled in that dream—intrudes a note, if not of death again, then at the very least of unreality.

In a whole series of films in which some hero tries to help a heroine to escape or tries himself to escape a condition of life in which they no longer believe, a similar vision of life across the waters shapes itself, a similar helplessness grips the protagonists. It is interesting especially to find this imagery in films in which the conscious eye of the film maker upon his material is, in each instance, a totally different one— to find it, for example, in Odets' *None But the Lonely Heart* and Capra's *It's a Wonderful Life*. Odets views the inability of his hero to escape from captivity very mournfully; Capra, rather like the doctor in *The Chase,* proclaims cheerfully that no captivity exists, no urgent appointment needs keeping. Yet at the heart of each film lies the same image—an image which neither Odets nor Capra quite intends to present.

In *None But The Lonely Heart* (1944), another heroine, Ada (June Duprez) longs to be delivered from her present mode of life. Again the man she has married is a racketeer (Mordoni). Ada has obtained a divorce from Mordoni, but she is not really free of him. She longs for a life somewhere out of his reach—"as small as this room" it could be. And when she meets the hero, Ernie (Cary Grant), she hopes he will carry her away to this life. And Ernie wants to. He too is "sick of this street" on which they live. "Let the wind come and blow it to pieces!" he declares; one who remains here has to be hare or hound, and he wants to be neither. His mother runs a little shop and she would like him to run it with her, but "squeezing pennies out of paupers" that is. It's something else he wants. In Ernie we meet again that restless hero sketched in the third chapter. ("Tramp of the universe, that's me," he says of himself.) But the more positive aspect of that hero, which was only hinted at there, is here presented to us plainly, for he is posed now in the same picture with that other, villainous figure, who sits in possession. He very clearly hesitates to settle down only because he quests "the free the beautiful the noble life." The boy with "perfect pitch" Odets names Ernie. There is in the film a girl, rival to Ada, whom one may match with the heroine of that third chapter, who wants to "plant trees in (the hero's) blood"; and here that heroine too shows a new face. "My house is yours whenever you want it," she says to him. "I'm here whenever you want me . . . I'd marry you quick"—a good nice girl, but playing in spite of herself the role of the siren (aptly enough, we see her always with a cello, usually plainting the tune which gives the film its title). She tries to detain the hero from that appointment he has with "the beautiful life," she tries to keep him here on this street. When Ernie at the very last does walk into her house, it means no happy ending but defeat. For though Ernie wants to leave with Ada, he never does. He returns to this girl next door; Ada returns to Mordoni. These two lovers, also, have glimpsed a frightening vision at the end of the road they have wanted to take.

Odets is very glib with verbalizations to explain this defeat. "You

Cary Grant and Jane Wyatt in *None but the Lonely Heart* (1944).

can't beat it, son; not in our day," Ernie's mama says to him. And what "it" is is named too, bluntly enough. "You can't beat me," Mordoni makes it clear, "I'm a machine." In literal story terms, Odets has Mordoni threaten Ernie with sudden violence if he should try to take Ada from him. But what is intriguing about this film is the discrepancy between what Odets thinks he is showing us—a hero unable to elude the too wary grip of the tyrannous Mordoni and that "machine" of which he is a living part—and what he really shows us, which is "the human spirit . . . on its knees" for quite another cause. It is not Mordoni who subdues Ernie; it is, just as with the hero of *The Chase*, his own too timorous imagination.

This hero moves about in no literal trance like Scotty in *The Chase*, and yet as dazed as Scotty. In terms of the story this film means to tell, the actions he takes are incomprehensible. It is only in terms of another, unwitting story that they become clear. Wanting at any cost to leave this street, wanting more and more to take Ada with him (every time he kisses her "it gets deeper"), Ernie takes a series of actions sure to bind him there. One of the very first things he does is go and hire himself out to Mordoni as a henchman—which soon involves standing by while old friends of the family are robbed and brutally beaten (Ernie is soon washing his hands a hundred times a day). Then he delivers himself up to Mordoni even more completely. The very first chance he gets, he blurts out to this man all his hopes for a future with Ada. Mordoni, naturally, responds to his confession with violent threats. Ernie could not have managed to make their escape more difficult. He has already had to put off their leaving because he has learned that his mother is dying of cancer, and he has to stay to try to make her last days a bit less grim. But his working for Mordoni hardly gives his mother ease; she dies a most unquiet death because of it. He has been told that she has only a few months to live. A few months' postponement of their escape would hardly seem to make the fatal actions that he takes necessary. It is nevertheless the scenes in which he learns that his mother is dying that do throw some light on his actions. It is from this point on that he moves as if spellbound into Mordoni's hands. His mother's old friend tells him of her condition and he walks out of this man's shop as if walking in his sleep. "A friend put something in my ear and I can't get it out! Buzz buzz buzz!" He wanders, in shock, all the day and all the night.

"Echo echo echo!" The next day he pretends to his mother that all is well—and then he reports to Mordoni for work. Some time later he returns from a violent day spent with Mordoni's boys to find that his mother has been sent to jail (desperate for money, she has begun to deal in stolen goods), and he hurries to the prison where she now lies close to death. She lies in the strange room, rain shadows making it still more strange to him, staring at him, in her shame, as if already gone from him. "Why are you here?" he cries wildly. "I'm the boy who needs you, loves you, wants you!" When he has to leave, he moves off again like one who is walking in his sleep. As if inevitably, after this, Ada fades from him for good, and he turns in at the little house where the cello raises its drowsy complaint. Not intentionally perhaps, yet clearly enough, Odets has sketched a hero struck helpless before the fact that he is to be left motherless; or call it, at that level of allegory Odets himself is always broadly hinting, a hero unable to make a new life for himself not, as the author thinks he shows, be- cause "no one can lick" the "machine" that's running things, but be- cause he himself quietly submits to that machine, struck helpless by the fear of parting with the familiar.

Superficially there is perhaps little likeness between the nightmare from which the hero of *The Chase* awakens paralyzed and this night- mare which unmans Ernie; yet actually—Ernie staring aghast at the once familiar figure of his mother, now made a stranger to him by approaching death; Scotty stumbling over a strange island, finding no one who will recognize him and clear him of the charge against him, staring at last aghast as his own corpse is dragged out, dead face up- turned—the shock involved for each of them may be reduced to the same shock.

If one looks at Capra's *It's a Wonderful Life* along with these two films, the likeness becomes more evident—ironically, since this film seeks no common ground with either; its moral (consistent with the enthusiastic title) is that the helplessness its hero thinks he suffers is really no such thing.

George Bailey (James Stewart) longs year after year to "shake the dust of this crumby little town and see the world." Every time he hears the whistle of a train, the motor of a plane, the sound of an anchor chain lifted, he stirs as restlessly as Scotty did in *The Chase*, watching the circling hands of the clock. There is an appointment he must keep! This town, he declares time and again, is no place for anyone "unless he is willing to crawl to Potter" (Lionel Barrymore), villain of this film, "richest meanest man in the county"—"a sick man," George's father explains it, who "hates anyone or anything he can't have." In *The Chase*, the villain has a peculiar pastime: he has rigged his car with special controls in the back seat, and when his chauffeur is driving him somewhere he loves suddenly to step up the speed to a hundred miles an hour, leaving only the steering of the car to the wild-eyed chauffeur. George feels, as it were, that anyone in this town clutches the wheel of such a car: sooner or later Potter, in the back seat, can be counted on to take over. And so he wants to leave. But year after year something prevents it. His father dies and he has to assume charge of the Building and Loans Company he has headed (and which has done so much for the poor of the town) or see it go out of business. His brother is going to take over for him, while he steps out, but his brother gets a wonderful chance somewhere else and again George stays. And then—there is Mary. The sequence in which George tries to resist proposing to Mary is intended by Capra as comedy, and he does make it comic, and yet—through the strain of trying to—he makes it more grim in its way than any similar sequence I have described so far in which hero resists heroine. The sequence builds to the moment in which George, who has been helplessly sniffing the fragrance of her hair, takes hold of her and begins to shake her frantically: "Now you listen to me! . . . I don't want to get married ever! What I want to do . . ."—close to tears—then suddenly in helpless further frenzy hugging her and kissing her. Cut to relatives throwing a storm of rice. And George "never does leave Bedford Falls." And at last, just as he has feared, the day arrives when Potter sits there in control. His Uncle Billy unwittingly sets down where Potter can snatch it up $8,000 of Building and Loans funds. Then he can't remember what he's done with the money. And without this sum, George's books won't balance; he is faced with the collapse of the business and a jail sentence. He has to crawl to Potter, begging for a loan. And Potter refuses it. At this point Capra forgets his comic touch, as George turns on his old uncle: "Silly stupid old fool! One of us is going to jail, and it's not going to be me!"—turns on his wife and children: "Happy family! . . . Why did we have to have all these kids?!" The only comedy here is that achieved when, at the bar to which he staggers, George mumbles out a prayer, is the next minute punched in the nose by a neighbor he has angered, and explodes, "That's what I get for praying!" George heads next for the river and is about to jump into its dark waters when Capra intervenes, introducing George's guardian angel and the happy thesis of the film.

With the appointment in heaven of this guardian angel (Henry Travers, who will "win his wings" if he can help George), the film has, in fact, started. George's life up to this moment has then been run through in flashback for the angel's benefit. He frustrates George's suicide by jumping into the water before him—George, without even thinking, leaping to his rescue. Then, "I'm your guardian angel," he declares. George, unconvinced, mutters, "This is the kind I would get." But the angel turns out to be brighter than he looks. "It would have been better if I'd never been born," George mutters on. "Wait, all right, you've got your wish!" the angel exclaims, seeing a way to show him (a way to show us) just how happily effective his life really has been. He leads him back into Bedford Falls—as it would have been if George had never lived. Now he makes point after point for George. This old druggist would never have been saved by George from sending the wrong pills that day: he is an old wreck of a jailbird. George's kid brother would never have been saved by George from drowning in the creek, would never himself have saved all those boys on the Navy transport years later. Building and Loans would have gone out of business and his old uncle would have gone to the insane asylum. His mother would have turned into a sour old boarding house keeper. Without him, in fact, the whole town would have fallen into despair and corruption—the people become real minions of Potter (Pottersville, the town has been renamed). Perhaps worst of all: his wife would have been a spinster, and a librarian, and worn glasses! "Please God, let me live again!" he cries. And *this* wish is granted him. "Yay!" he cries, running home as fast as he can. "You're now in Bedford Falls," the sign reads as he gallops past. "Yay!" he cries. "I don't care what happens to me!" And at home waits final proof of just how wonderful real life is: the neighbors have pitched in and contributed that $8,000 he needs. They surround him now, breaking into song: "Should auld acquaintance be forgot . . ."—and happily forgot is our earlier acquaintance with their evil-scowling faces, for these faces glow now with innate virtue. And the wee tinkling of a bell is heard: up in heaven, Henry Travers has received his wings.

Capra has labored a moral here that is the reverse of the moral labored in *None But the Lonely Heart*. But his moral fails, just as the moral of that film did, to contain the real substance of the drama. George, staring into the waters where he hopes to escape from what seems to him captivity, is shown by the angel a vision that is actually no different from the vision seen by Ernie, by Scotty. As George is led through the strange town which is and yet is not the town he knows, we are supposedly watching as the angel shows him what a difference his life has made to others. But actually we never do see George absorbing this argument; we never see him accept the basic premise upon which the argument rests: that this *is* simply a demonstration of what the town might have been. The real drama of this sequence is the drama of George's anguish as he tries to get one person after another to recognize him—an anguish very similar to Scotty's as he wandered through that other town, trying to make people admit that they had spoken with him that very morning. "Don't you know me?" George cries. "It's me!" "Mother!" he cries. "Help me!"—staring at her as Ernie stared at his mother when she lay dying ("I'm the boy who needs you, loves you, wants you!"). "Mary!" he cries, running after the poor spinster and seizing her in his arms—"I need you, Mary!" He staggers through the vacant house that was never his, he runs through the streets, wild-eyed, sobbing at last, "Please, God, let me live again!" Our relief, his relief, when that wish is then granted ("You know me!" he gasps to a friend) is much the same relief we feel in *The Chase* when the ringing of the phone dissolves the image of the hero's dead face and shapes before us the room in which he has been sleeping and now wakes. And when George, running home now past the window where Potter sits, shouts, "Merry Christmas, Mr. Potter!" his action matches the action of Ernie, returning finally to the girl next door, the action of Scotty when he turns the ticking clock face to the wall. Scotty, Ernie, George, each of these captive heroes, gazing, restless, into the waters, finds the face he sees there too unfamiliar, the new country before him too new, unreal, and he draws back, crying, Please, God, bind me securely here where I am.[1]

In certain other films, the hero does not draw back quite as promptly. We see him enter upon a new life, not in dream but in fact. And in these films the nightmare visions I have just described all come true.

In *Scarlet Street* (1946) and in *Nora Prentiss* (1947), two heroes actually cut themselves free from the old life. Edward G. Robinson in *Scarlet Street* is a cashier who has given twenty-five years of "faithful service." To the chant of "He's a jolly good fellow!" he has just been presented with a gold watch from the boss. Kent Smith (Trent) in *Nora Prentiss* is a doctor who has been practicing successfully for twenty years, has a nice house, a wife, two kids. Each of these "good fellows" is restive as the film opens; the place he has made for himself has suddenly come to seem meaningless. For each it is a fateful meeting with a young woman that has provoked in him the consciousness of something missed. Sitting talking with Joan Bennett —whom he has rescued on the street from a young man's assault— Robinson finds himself whistling back when a robin whistles. "I bet I haven't done that in forty years!" Trent finds himself just as strangely stirred, talking with Ann Sheridan (Nora Prentiss), who has knocked on his office door after a street accident. He finds himself suddenly laughing. "You should laugh more often," she tells him. For each of these men, face to face with this stranger, instincts long subdued, early dreams long dim, revive.

Robinson had once dreamed of becoming a great painter. He still does paint a bit at home on Sundays, but his shrewish wife mocks his efforts, threatens to give his work to the junk man. Now in the presence of this girl he feels inspired once again. Trent has dreamed less grandly, but once had built himself a cabin in the mountains. It sits there unused. He had played the piano once. The piano sits in the cabin, covered with dust. "How did you ever let it get that way?"

[1] In an article published in *Harper's* magazine in June 1948 ("Those Movies with a Message"), Siegfried Kracauer refers to a hero one may relate to the heroes of this chapter—the hero of certain "progressive" films such as *The Best Years of Our Lives, Crossfire*, etc., which, Kracauer comments, "upon closer inspection . . . reveal the profound weakness of the very cause for which they try to enlist sympathy." The hero, a "weary standard-bearer of progress," "seems . . . to be overwhelmed by a mood of resignation."

Nora asks him. Trent's wife is no shrew like Robinson's wife; she is a good woman. But like some of those other good girls I have described, she is his unwitting jailer. After his first meeting with Nora, Kent comes home to suggest that their lives have fallen into a rut. "It seems to me that we have a quite normal life," his wife replies. Nora—is a girl with dreams. Like Ada in *None but the Lonely Heart*, she may look a bit like a tramp but—she is "an amazing girl." She's just a night club singer, but when Trent sits at the piano and plays some Chopin, she knows right off which opus it is. Like Ada, she dreams of the better life.

These heroes too begin to dream. Robinson sets Joan up in a beautiful apartment, and there he goes to paint, free from his wife's baleful eye. One day a dealer sees his paintings and is impressed. Joan, to protect herself, pretends that they are hers, and so when they are given an exhibition it is her name that is soon circling the town. Robinson is happy enough about this. "It's just like we were married—only I take *your* name!" If only he could actually marry her! And then that chance too opens up for him. His wife's former husband, whom everybody had thought dead, turns up alive! This man is not eager to return to his wife, but Robinson tricks him into it, and he himself, with a little hop of joy, quits that home forever. Trent too, straining to escape his present state, but unable to bring himself to ask for a divorce, suddenly finds a way out. A cardiac patient staggers into his office and drops dead. With quickening breath, Trent notes that the dead man is his own height, weight, age. Changing clothes with the corpse, he places it in his automobile, sets the automobile afire, and pushes it over a cliff. Then he leaves town with Nora. With hop of joy, with quickening breath, each steps forth from captivity—into a state just as desperate.

Robinson bursts joyfully into Joan's apartment, to find her murmuring love to Johnny, the youth who was beating her up on the street the day he met her. For Joan all along has been helplessly in love with Johnny. It is upon his orders that she has been leading Robinson on, for what she can get out of him. Robinson, doggedly, returns after Johnny has left and proposes marriage to Joan. She greets his proposal with hysterical laughter. In sudden madness, he kills her. It is not he who hangs for the crime, but Johnny. Through a certain fluke, all the evidence points to him. But in the film's final

Edward G. Robinson in *Scarlet Street* (1946).

sequence, we see Robinson wandering the city's streets, a derelict. He has been fired from his job; for, to satisfy Joan's desires, he has been drawing funds that weren't his. He is known to the city cops as a nut, for he's always trying to give himself up as a murderer, and nobody believes his ravings. As the film ends, we see him shuffling down Fifty-seventh Street past the very gallery from which his portrait of Joan, "self-portrait," has just been sold for some fabulous sum. It is being removed at that moment from the window. As it is carried out, his hungering eyes follow ("It's me! It's me!"). Then the camera pulls up and off from the scene as he, a small ghostly figure, shuffles on down the street.

In *Nora Prentiss,* Trent, living in another city now, reads in his home-town paper about his own funeral, and is about to throw away his dark glasses when another article catches his eye: the D.A. suspects foul play and is ordering an investigation. Trent nervously goes into hiding again. But one evening—"I want to feel alive again!"—he does go out, and he is in an automobile accident. He wakes in a hospital to learn that plastic surgery must build him an entirely new face. "This is a godsend!" he cries. Now they really can begin a new life! But when at long last the bandages are removed and he walks over to the mirror—his face is a grotesque battered mask. "It's what I wanted, isn't it?" he cries. "No one can recognize me now!" The day holds more than this for him. A police officer walks into the room and declares him under arrest—for the murder of Dr. Trent! The D.A. back home, suspecting murder in the case, though never questioning the identity of the dead man, has followed the trail here. And Trent's fingerprints match the prints left at the scene of the crime. At the trial, his wife is among those to testify. Has she ever seen the defendant before, the court asks. She stares at him. "No," she declares, "never." And Trent does not speak out his true identity. Nor does he allow Nora to speak out for him. For it would only bring further distress upon his family; and, he declares, "I *am* a murderer, and I *have* murdered Dr. Trent."

Scotty, Ernie, George, Robinson, Dr. Trent—home for each one of these heroes means bondage, the death of the heart; and yet—"out there," across the waters, the new man he dreams of being stares back at each one of them with empty eyes.

"Where am I?"

In 1945, Walt Disney released a raucous and nerve-racking film called *The Three Caballeros*—a sort of comic-fantastic travelogue through Latin America, featuring Donald Duck as the eager traveler. "What hath Walt wrought?" one critic asked—as though Walt had conjured up a world of chaos all his own. But he had wrought what he had out of materials not at all private to him—simply with a gusto all his own. This film might be said to sum up in violent caricature the painful visions contained in numbers of other films.

In one grotesque sequence, Donald Duck is ardently pursuing various female faces and forms that materialize out of the sky above Mexico City. He hovers excitedly—"Oh boy!"—closes in for a kiss, diving at one pretty face after another. Each, as he closes in, fades suddenly, translated into a star or a guitar or a flower (his head goes through it as through a paper hoop, and he emerges wearing a clown's collar of petals); or the pretty face erupts into the two shrieking faces of his gay caballero comrades, Joe and Panchito. Poor Donald endures, himself, many strange and senseless translations, whirled at last into a striped Mexican pot, then back into his own self—standing now in an entirely new locality, among some obscene cacti. "Where am I?" he squawks.

In this piteous questing figure, the object of whose quest is always exploding in air, one can recognize every one of the figures I have described in former chapters, from the first two heroes, who don't want to be hurt again ("Leave him alone, Miss Ilse!" "Stop it, Helen, stop it, stop it!") to the heroes of the past two chapters, whom we see in the act of questing still: the success boy—who cries "Gotta make time!" but when he gets there, the cupboard is bare, the dreams of his youth vanished, "Part of me is lost!"—or the hero who tries to escape from the ruined street walked by the figure of "success," who seeks a new life, hurries to it, only to have this too turn to nothing in his arms, he too finding it difficult to recognize himself, squawking, "It's me! It's me!" The failure of the dream to bring the hero of the first chapter home, the frenzy with which the hero of the second chapter resists committing himself, the hapless clamoring of the heroes in all these films—"Who am I?" squawks Gregory Peck in *Spellbound;* "Where am I?" squawks Ray Milland in *Lost Weekend*—all becomes much clearer in the light of the frustrations endured by the heroes of the past two chapters. For between the one life no longer believed in and the other, unimaginable, where indeed does life wait for the heroes of these dramas? Who indeed are they? Every one of them inhabits a nightmare realm very much like that which Disney paints, where visions tantalize but deceive, what seems substantial may prove insubstantial, what promises life may bring death. Nothing is sure.

In film after film that I have named this nightmare realm takes shape, and also in many that I have not named—many, too, which fit no one of the general patterns I have noted. Here, for example, are five variants—in which the pattern is neither success story, exactly, nor the story of one who tries to break away from an established life. And the same image forms. In each, the hero seeks a life, seeks definition of himself, only to have belief in the life he grasps at suddenly shaken. The films, of course, feature love stories, and that image is to be discerned in these terms: within the hero's embrace, the beloved is suddenly translated, turns unknown.

The heroes of *I'll Be Seeing You* and *Enchanted Cottage* (1945) are both returned G.I.'s. The first (Joseph Cotten) is a victim of shock; the second (Robert Young) has been horribly disfigured. As

Ray Milland in *Lost Weekend* (1945).

Gregory Peck in *Spellbound* (1946).

we meet Joseph Cotten—Zachary—he has just been given an eight-day furlough from the hospital and has set out to try to prove that he can find a place for himself. ("You've got eight days to believe!" a voice sounds in his head.) He boards a train, uncertain where he'll go; for he's an orphan and has no home. And on the train he finds Ginger Rogers; they are seated next to each other and they get to talking shyly. She's getting off at Pinehill, she says, to spend Christmas with relatives. He decides to get off with her and pretends he has an appointment there himself. For this girl makes him "feel kinda good."

So he takes a room at the Y, and he calls on Ginger, and she begins to make him feel better and better. He tells her all the truth about himself. It's nothing to be ashamed of, she tells him. He knows, it isn't like having gone to prison or anything like that, but—"Can you make me believe in myself the way you believe in yourself?" he begs her. And the more time he spends with her, the more he does believe in himself. One night, back at the Y, one of his nervous attacks comes upon him; the room begins to waver, battle sounds fill the air, his face begins to twitch, a great pounding begins—his heart. But prayerfully he invokes her image; her voice seems to reach him through all that roar—"You must believe, you must believe!"—and the dissonance subsides, the room regains its shape. "I made it!" he cries. Now he is full of plans. And "You figure in all these plans," he tells Ginger.

But Ginger is full of apprehensions, and so are we. It is from Ginger that he has borrowed self-confidence. She herself seems to him so full of it—she "believes." "How do you know that it's not make-believe?" she has asked him; but she hasn't dared tell him that it is precisely that. "Dreams for the future are impossible," we have heard her moan to her aunt. For she is a jailbird, out on furlough herself, with two more years to serve. (An earlier dream has had this ending for her: A "party" to which her boss had invited her—ah, now she was on her way, she had thought—had turned out to be a "party" between just the two of them, and in the ensuing tussle he had plunged, by accident, out of a high window.) Ginger doesn't dare tell Zachary, for if the image of her that he clings to should be changed into the image of another wavering one—"I don't think he's strong enough to know," she cries. She has heard him speak those words: "I know, it's not as if I'd been in prison." And he has also said: "Without you, I'd be back where I started."

The very day he is leaving for the hospital, "sure of himself" and of her, Ginger's little niece lets the truth drop while Ginger is out of the room. We see his poor face crack. He rides to the station in a daze; and in a daze he climbs aboard his train, with hardly a word to Ginger. "Oh, I think I know!" she gasps as the train is pulling out, and runs beside it calling his name: "Zachary! Zachary!" But he just stares out the window.

In *Enchanted Cottage,* it is through Dorothy Maguire that the hero, Oliver, begins to believe once again. The disfigured G.I. has gone to a lonely cottage in the country to get away from everybody, and especially from his family. He has broken with his fiancée too. At the little cottage, Oliver is about to put an end to it all; he "can't face life like this, ugly and repulsive." But Dorothy, the housekeeper's helper, walks into his room and takes the gun from him. She has been in love with him ever since he paid a brief visit to the cottage before the war, and she senses what he is up to.

Dorothy herself, like Ginger, is the most uncertain of creatures. "There are some meant to be wanderers," she has mournfully agreed with the housekeeper. For she, like Ginger, has received a sentence: she is terribly terribly homely. But she is terribly terribly thoughtful and kind and understanding too; and when a letter arrives for Oliver one day announcing that his mother is coming to look after him— "There's no way to make them understand!" he cries—Oliver impulsively proposes to Dorothy. He is immediately ashamed, for it is not love that he offers the girl, it is just that he wants to put up "a last barrier" between him and the world he is "afraid to face." He begs her pardon. But she, caring as she does, accepts him. And then on their wedding night "something extraordinary" happens. Dorothy sits at the piano to play. She wants to try to make him understand through the music what he means to her. As she plays, she seems to see him standing there as she saw him on his first visit to the cottage —"Everything she had ever dreamed of." She breaks into tears and runs from the room. How could she ever be to him what he has been to her? Oliver follows her. He sees how cruelly he has hurt her. He will tell her that she is free. But when he draws near—she is beautiful! He takes her in his arms.

The two send for their neighbor, the blind man (Herbert Marshall), and they confide to him their extraordinary news. It must be this enchanted cottage, they tell him. (It is a cottage with a long history of happy honeymoons.) A miracle has occurred—"We are no longer as we were!" And the camera shows us the two of them—smiling, smooth of face, both just as pretty as Hollywood stars. They are terribly happy. We see Oliver in the morning bend over Dorothy as she lies in bed. "Shhh!" she tells him, "I'm dreaming," and she describes her dream. She is at a wedding and the groom is the most handsome man—"positively stunning!"—and the bride too is the envy of all the onlookers. Everybody is "so jealous." "That was no dream," they breathe.

But they are a little afraid, they tell the blind man. Their marriage did not begin as true marriages usually do. Maybe this cottage, "alive with memories," is taking revenge. Maybe this happiness is given to tantalize them and it will suddenly be taken away. "I couldn't stand being ugly again for Oliver!" she cries. Nor could *he* stand it, she fears. The blind man tells them not to be afraid; but he himself is full of apprehensions. When he learns that Oliver's mother is arriving for a visit, he manages to intercept her in the garden and to warn her. Pretend the change is as great as they think, he begs her. "Play a part with them!" He tells her a little legend about "a city in ruins" which those who live in it "see as a great and beautiful dwelling place" because they look upon it with "the sight of the heart." But the witless mother, well meaning but distracted, blunders in—as Ginger's little niece had. "If you're happy, that's all that matters!" she cries; and to the girl, "You've got so much to give—more than a pretty girl!" At her words Dorothy drops the fragile teacup that she is holding; it cracks into a hundred pieces on the floor. And her face and poor Oliver's face crack too. The camera shows them changed again into despairing ugliness.

There is another image from *The Three Caballeros* that can be said to sum up in caricature the substance of many of these films: A little bird is making a nest, carefully balancing twig upon twig—constructing a fragile structure that mounts in the air. Another little bird, the mischievous redheaded aracuan, places on top of it just one more twig, and the whole thing collapses as the aracuan laughs and laughs. In *I'll Be Seeing You,* in *Enchanted Cottage,* we watch, twig placed on twig, a precarious structure in the building—a new belief in life. And we wait in suspense to see the final twig placed that will collapse it all. Sympathetic ones stand loving watch. Don't tell him yet, Ginger's kind aunt counsels. "Play a part with them!" begs the kind blind man. But the mischief cannot be avoided. The frail venture fails.

But this is Hollywood. I have outlined only the plight that is presented and withheld the dream annulment of that plight. In *I'll Be Seeing You,* when Ginger returns to jail, Zachary is waiting for her at the entrance gate. The whistle of a train in the distance has just recalled her terrible parting from him when he steps out of a shadow there and embraces her. As soon as the train pulled out, he tells her, he understood why she had kept the truth from him. "I need you," he tells her, "and I want to feel that you need me!" When her term is over, he'll be waiting. And he'll be all cured by then, both of them ready for a new life. "Oh, Zachary, I love you so much!" she cries, and the music swells up—"I'll find you-oo-oo!" In *Enchanted Cottage,* after the mother leaves, the unhappy two run to the blind man: "Why didn't you tell us? You've known all along!" But "What is there really to be sad about?" the blind man asks, and he explains to them: A great change *did* come over them—they fell in love. "Love grants one a gift of sight that isn't granted to other people." And they must accept it. The spirits of those who lived in the cottage before them and scratched their linked initials on the windowpane have no wish to take vengeance upon them! They belong here! They must scratch their initials too. So Oliver and Dorothy turn again to gaze at one another, both again all Hollywood smooth, as an enchanted melody once more whispers through the enchanted rooms.

Studied at any remove, these final gestures seem precarious enough still: the two clutching each other at the gate of the jail, "There will be a new life waiting!"—the two in their faraway cottage scratching their initials, "They would want us to!"—frail figures clinging together in a void, insisting, "We belong somewhere!" We have seen belief fail before, the magic words "I love you!" prove insufficient. But Hollywood knows how to make us feel that in this final embrace at last the lovers *are* secure. It knows how to grant us "special sight," like that of which the blind man spoke, so that we can ignore the ruins that actually surround us. It draws us into the embrace with the lovers, into the magic circle. An enchanted music springs up to wrap us around; the edges of the screen blur; and the camera moves us hazily in. In this final close-up, the embrace is all-encompassing, a world unto itself; and with authority the magic letters form: FINIS. We are safe.

The comfort of this ending is not suddenly appended, of course. We have been led to anticipate just such a miracle. In *Enchanted Cottage,* the whole story is recounted in flashback by the blind man, who has announced it as the most enchanting chapter in the cottage's enchanting history. The film begins as he turns to us from the piano, where he has been fingering out some of that enchanted music. This music actually wraps us around from the start. And from the start we are drawn, time after time, into the lovers' own hallucinated circle. A moment such as that in which Dorothy dreams her pitiful dream about the envious wedding guests is presented in the same sort of blissful close-up. We never do measure the pity of it.

As the months go by, though, for these years, and film follows film,[1] this final relief must be waited for in more and more anguish. In a film like *Enchanted Cottage,* one never too seriously doubts how all will end. The title itself hints at eventual comfort. But just as in the film of "success" one can trace a certain darkening of the pattern, from the quiet sufferings Ronald Colman endures in *Random Harvest* (1942) to those very much more strident agonies of Robert Taylor in *Undercurrent* (1946), so here. The nightmare to be annulled sharpens. Titles like *Enchanted Cottage* and *I'll Be Seeing You* give place to titles like *Shock* or *Dark Mirror,* which give none of the same assurance. Belief fails more cruelly, fails often near the very start of the film. One wonders whether the magic can ever be woven.

Shock (1946) begins as the heroine arrives at a San Francisco hotel where she is to meet her G.I. husband, just back from overseas. For two years she has thought him dead—he had been officially reported killed. But suddenly she has heard from him. She hurries into the hotel and asks for the room she has reserved by wire—and they tell her that there must have been a slip-up: they never received her wire. "But it's the only place that we can find each other!" she cries. (Which isn't really very likely; but the film is straining here to create for us that image of living nowhere, of "a city in ruins," that lies at the heart of all these dreams.) A room is found for her at last. She is sitting up, waiting for her husband, clutching his photograph in her

[1] *The Clock* is another film that follows the pattern just given, *Spectre of the Rose* another.

hand, and she dozes off. The camera moves us slowly up on the photograph. And then—here could be a moment out of *The Three Caballeros*—suddenly it whirls dizzily into a spiral which, deepening, seems to suck us in. And in a dream now her husband calls to her from the other side of the door: "Let me in!" Calling his name in return, she rushes to the door. But the door retreats from her. "Don't go away!" she screams, but it retreats again. "I can't find you!" he calls. She gets to the door at last, but then she can't turn the knob. And on the other side of the door, her husband recedes down a long corridor. She wakes with a start, and struggling to free herself from this nightmare, she walks out onto the balcony of the room. But there the nightmare seems to continue before her eyes. Framed in a window across the way, Vincent Price is quarreling with his wife. "Whatever we had for each other is gone!" he is crying; he wants a divorce. But she is refusing. In a sudden rage, he raises a heavy candlestick and strikes her down. The heroine backs in horror from the balcony and sinks down upon her couch. In the brightening morning when her husband arrives, he hurries up to the room, knocks eagerly, and enters —and there she sits, staring in front of her blankly. He cannot rouse her. Face to face at last, they do not know each other.

In *The Three Caballeros*, poor Donald, seeing the bright image that he quests time after time turn to air as he approaches it, finds that he can no longer be sure of his own definition, finds himself sucked into one whirling gaudy vortex after another, pulled out of all shape. It is the same with the protagonists of all the films of this chapter—and most painfully in *Shock*.

There are no kindly helpers here—like Ginger's aunt or the blind man. The husband calls in the hotel doctor, who says that the girl is suffering from shock. And they are in luck, he says, because a famous nerve specialist is staying at the hotel. But when the specialist walks in—it is Vincent Price! When he notes the position of her window, he guesses at once that she has seen him kill his wife and he whisks her off to his sanatorium near by. His murdered wife has sup- posedly left on a vacation, and he has arranged everything to make her death look like an accident—whisked her corpse off too to an appropriate spot. He now sets about to try to drive the heroine insane, so that she can never bear witness against him. The hero alone could rescue her. But the hero hangs back—unsure of himself, unsure of his beloved. The doctor does not allow him to see much of her, and when he does he makes sure that she is under some drug. Once the hero gets in when the doctor doesn't intend him to, and the girl cries out what she has seen and why she is here. "Don't leave me; he'll kill me!" she begs. "Come back!" she implores him as the doctor enters to take him away. But he is unable simply to believe in her. The sight of her that morning in the hotel, just sitting there staring so strangely, has shaken him. "Janet the nervous and imaginative kind? Why no, sir! I grew up with her, in the same small town in Michigan. She was just a nice kid!" He doesn't know her any more. It is Vincent Price in whom he puts his trust—"You men know best." And Vincent Price is very persuasive, does *seem* most helpful. Janet has a persecution complex, he explains to him. It's the strain of the war, he explains. He takes him on a little tour, shows him a series of other patients—each of them convinced that the doctors want to murder them. The mind is a delicate and fragile thing, he tells him—almost as intangible as faith; and that is what he is going to need, faith. (Recall the soothing deceptive voice of Taylor in *Undercurrent*: "Try a little old-fashioned faith in me"; the soothing voice of the doctor in *Chase,* assuring Scotty that the appointment he feels he must remember is unreal.) The doctor walks with the husband in the garden back of the hospital. The birds twitter cheerfully, the sun shines down, the doctor is very calm, professional. And he gets permission from the husband to give Janet insulin injections—with which he plans eventually to kill her. In this queer world of bright deceptive voices, the lovers again seem doomed. The film now dwells interminably upon the doctor's dreadful interviews with Janet, she writhing and sweating under the insulin injections, he drilling at her: "Your head, your head! . . . Your mind is sick and it's getting worse!" (This film received a barrage of criticism, as one hardly designed to promote confidence in our mental hospitals.)

At the very end things take a turn. The D.A. who has been investigating the death of the doctor's wife mentions something in the hero's presence that suddenly fits in with all his wife has been trying to tell him. Belief in her returns to him, and together with the D.A. and another doctor he rushes to the hospital—just in time to prevent that final "accidental" overdose of insulin which was to finish her off. One might suppose her to be a little the worse for wear already, but "Don't worry, son," the other doctor comforts the hero, "she'll come out of it in a couple of hours." And sure enough,[2] Janet opens her eyes and gives her husband a smile. "Aw, Janet darling!" he cries. One in the audience recovers a little less abruptly—leaves the theater still in some shock.

The helplessness the protagonists suffer grows more pronounced from film to film. From film to film, the world that is painted is more and more treacherous, the face of things more and more impossible to read.

The Locket (1946) starts, in effect, from the bright center of the dream dreamed by the heroine of *Enchanted Cottage*. It is the wedding day of hero and heroine (of one of the heroes, for this film has a series of them); and the groom is positively stunning—blond Gene Raymond ("Nice!" exclaim the wedding guests); and everybody is so jealous of the bride, Nancy (Larraine Day). These two agree: they are "living in a dream world." And then, as in that earlier film, another character walks in and speaks the words that shatter that world. In walks a former husband (Brian Aherne). Had she ever told Gene she had been married before, he asks Nancy. She never had. "I hate to be the one to destroy your happiness," Brian tells Gene, but—you couldn't possibly build a life with this woman.

[2] Once the hero believes in her again, her recovery is virtually automatic in this dream. In a Hitchcock film called *Notorious* (1946), starring Ingrid Bergman and Cary Grant, another heroine suffers an almost fatal wasting when the hero is unable to believe in her. They are both FBI agents, operating in Latin America. She has been something of a tramp (shame about her father, who collaborated with the Nazis, had driven her to this), but now she loves the hero truly and wants to change, wants to marry him. But he can't believe it, even though he loves her too. So in despair she accepts the job of marrying a wealthy Nazi to try to extract secrets from him. Her husband discovers what she's up to and begins to poison her. Not until the very final scene does the hero come to her rescue. She is so sick by now that she can hardly sit up. But "Sit up," he tells her simply, "I'm getting you out of here! I love you!" "Oh, you love me?" she cries. "Why didn't you tell me before?" "I know," he cries, "I couldn't see straight or think straight. I was a fatheaded guy full of pain!" "Oh, you love me!" she reiterates—and on and on they whisper their love, though a servant has gone to summon the husband and his villainous friends, and it's a long long way from Ingrid's upstairs room to the front door. By any literal reckoning it is a very silly scene. In terms of the dream, however, it makes sense enough, for in terms of the dream her captivity and her dreadful wasting are simply the result of his failure to believe in her, and all that is indeed needed to revive her and to set her free in his declaration. Wrapped in that magic, the two easily descend the long staircase together and make the door.

"It's strange, but at the time I thought it was the luckiest accident that ever happened," he begins—and the film cuts in flashback to the time when *he* first met Nancy. At a vacation resort, his bicycle collides with hers. "From that moment, we were practically inseparable." And soon *Brian* is living in a dream world. Brian is a psychiatrist. "Despite my psychiatric training, I was unable to detect a flaw in her." If ever there was a perfect woman in the world, Nancy seemed that woman. They are married. And she decorates his apartment with such taste and ingenuity! Life seems complete. And then one day—in walks a man to speak the words that bring that world clattering down. Clyde, the portrait painter (Robert Mitchum again), walks into Brian's office. He too apologizes for the interruption, but, he says, a man's life is at stake. He is afraid he must tell Brian that Nancy is a murderess. Brian thinks that this young man is hysterical—another patient for him. Talk it out, he tells him. And within the one flashback, a second flashback unfolds.

"It's hard to remember not knowing Nancy," says Clyde. He saw her first when she visited one of his art classes, and "I must have looked funny staring at her." From that first moment he could not rest until he could paint her portrait, nor until he could have her love. He soon does complete a portrait of her, and instantly it wins him an important prize. And the evening of his triumph they go together to a little Italian restaurant he knows and there "You'd make somebody a wonderful wife," he tells her, and she has no objections. For him, too, life seems complete. But not for long. At the portrait's exhibition, a valuable bracelet had been stolen from one of the guests. Now he opens Nancy's pocketbook to get a few nickels for the jukebox— "Body and Soul" he wants to play—and there lies the bracelet! "Why did you do it? Why did you do it?" he asks her back at his studio. "I saw it lying there and just couldn't help myself," she tells him. "But make sense!" he cries. "Why why why? You must have thought of something!" And yes, at last, under his probing, she does remember. It was, of course, something in her childhood. And we are given a further flashback within this flashback within a flashback: the scene of a trauma she has suffered as a little girl. Some mean woman accuses her of stealing a locket she *hasn't* stolen—though she has yearned for it with all her heart. The next time she yearned for something, she must have felt subconsciously that she had nothing to lose by taking it because she would be punished anyway! "You poor kid!" cries Clyde, terribly terribly relieved. For this explains everything. And now, of course, she wouldn't ever do it again. And he'll send the bracelet back through the mails. The lovers kiss and once more "Life is complete." Until suddenly, months later, at a party they attend, another theft takes place and a murder (the murdered man has apparently surprised the thief) and—Nancy comes running to the hero from just that part of the house. She tells Clyde that, entering the hostess's room to powder her nose, she has found the corpse sprawled on a bed. But he mustn't testify that she has come from there. "Nasty stories" might result. He is worried that if they keep back their evidence the valet may be falsely accused; for he has been found leaning over the body *after* Nancy has come running from the room. But Nancy becomes so overwrought—he suspects her, she cries, doesn't he?—that finally—"I wanted to prove to her that I believed in her"—he testifies as she begs. The valet *is* convicted, however. When Clyde can't help feeling disturbed. Nancy again begins to insist that he suspects her. Crying, "Suspicious, neurotic!" she rages from his apartment and disappears out of his life. Now he does suspect her. And, he sums up, now that he has located her at last, he must save the valet's life.

The waverings of Brian begin; now we watch *his* piteous struggle to believe. He tries first to talk Clyde out of it. "You have a tendency to doubt people's motives. It indicates that you are unsure of yourself." Society, after all, has found the valet guilty. Can he prove him innocent? He gives him some pills to calm him. And, he asks, why doesn't he come up to the apartment later and talk this over with Nancy too? Back at the apartment, waiting for Nancy to appear, Brian paces about a little anxiously. But then she arrives and she admits at once that she knows Clyde, "Oh, very well." Is he still as sulky and does he still say that she ruined his life? She had loved that boy very much, until she learned how neurotic he was. When Clyde arrives, she is very gentle with him, though he rages on. "He is sicker than I thought" she murmurs to Brian. Finally Brian asks him please to leave. And he takes Nancy in his arms. "He should be helped," he muses, "but not by me, because we're in love with the same woman." The next day Clyde walks into Brian's office with his portrait of Nancy under his arm. It is Brian's now, he tells him. And he may be interested to know that the valet has just been executed. Turning, he leaps through one of the office windows to his own death. The portrait he has left for Brian is a strange picture: a bland face—with empty eye sockets. A terrible puzzle of a face.

Doubting has been a strain and the two leave together for a vacation in England. There the war catches them and both of them pitch in to help. Nancy drives an ambulance. They both work night and day. One weekend, they and some other war workers are invited to take a little time out for a visit to a rich country mansion. And just as they are leaving, Brian hears that the hostess is missing her necklace. The ride back to London is anguish for him. His eyes keep moving to her purse and he seeks one excuse after another to look into it, but she always casually prevents him. Then, back home, looking for her key, she dumps the entire contents of the purse onto a table—and no necklace is there. As he stands slack with relief, she reads his thoughts. "I'll say it for you. I'm no thief, darling." "I'm so ashamed!" he cries. And they embrace. "I love you so very much!" he cries.

That night he returns from an emergency call to find that bombs have leveled his house. Frantically searching among the ruins—he doesn't know where Nancy is—he stoops to something on the ground that glitters. It is the stolen necklace! And tangled with it are other jewels! Nancy comes hurrying; and as she draws near—the music begins to crash loud—he stares at her. Her face, lit by the dying fires here, is the very face of the portrait. The scene cuts to a room in a mental hospital; and the same wide eyes stare at Brian where he lies helpless in bed. Nancy has had him committed. She sits gently beside him with the doctor; and he is trying to tell the doctor the real truth, but the doctor is assuring Brian—as Brian had once assured Clyde: "*Look* at her! You are imagining things!" This final flashback unwinds. Brian, released at last, is pleading with Gene Raymond. Nancy enters and "Why, of course" she knows Brian, and she is so pleased that he's up and about again. Brian cries to Gene, "You're going to make the same mistakes I made, all over again!" and he leaves. "It's very depressing," Nancy murmurs. "He's not the only one who cracked up in London during those days." These two lovers embrace. It is time for the wedding ceremony to begin.

And then, unexpectedly, Nancy herself breaks down. Through a very strange coincidence, the groom's mother now approaches and gives Nancy a little present—and it is the very locket which, years before, she had yearned for so painfully. Nancy takes her place for the ceremony; she is walking down the aisle, and there stands Gene, blond and smiling, and she gives a scream and falls to the ground. The facts of her life have suddenly disclosed themselves to *her*. As the film ends, a doctor and nurse are—properly—in attendance upon this heroine. But they don't seem to despair of Nancy. "Can you go on loving her?" they ask Gene. He can. The suggestion is that in time, then, all can be well—for "it's love that she's needed all along." It's love that she lacked as a child, and jewels had come to symbolize love for her. But if he'll stand by . . . And so this film ends rather as *Enchanted Cottage* did: love again will build a world entirely new. But one can't help but be haunted just a little by the fact that in the old world two men lie dead because of Nancy, and the life of a third has been wrecked; can't help but remember just for a moment with a little shiver that face staring with empty eyes among the ruins as— flashback within flashback within flashback—one hapless lover after another drew near for a kiss.

In *Dark Mirror* too (1947), we enter a world that is dangerous for those who draw near the beloved—a world in which death can lurk even within the dreamed-of embrace itself. As the film opens, one victim sprawls dead in a plush New York apartment, a knife in his shoulder. The police get busy and all evidence points to a certain girl who was seen with him that evening and seen leaving his apartment shortly after the time of his death: Olivia de Havilland. "That's the girl all right!" a series of witnesses declare. When the police question the girl herself, however, she gives an alibi and the people she names positively remember seeing her where she says she's been. The bewildered cops turn up at her rooms to question her further—and are confronted by twins. This explains the confusion; but now neither twin will testify to which is which. And the law can't force them to incriminate each other. Obviously the innocent one believes her sister to be innocent too. The cops are stumped. And then the police lieutenant asks the hero, Lew Ayres, a psychiatrist, to determine by his own special means which must be the guilty twin. Ayres has his own reasons for accepting the job: he is close to being in love with one of them—if he only knew which one. The same terrible puzzle now

confronts this hero that confronted the relay of heroes in *The Locket,*
each of whom had to try to decide which of two possible women—one
a murderess, one near-perfect—the real Nancy was.

Ayres gets the two to submit to his tests by pretending that he
merely wants to add them to his "collection." Studying twins has
been his specialty. And he will pay them for their help. Hard up,
they agree. He puts them through an elaborate workout: Rorschach
test, association test, lie detector. (The film bases much of its appeal
upon the curiosity value here.) At first both twins are dressed identi-
cally, and one can't tell them apart at all. (They are, after all, both
Olivia de Havilland.) At a certain point they begin wearing little
name pins—"Terry" and "Ruth"—and they can at least be distinguished in this way. For a while the film does its best to be misleading
about which of the two is the girl to be loved, but at a certain point
Terry begins to be dressed in blacks and Ruth in whites, so now it's
easy—we think. Also, Ayres has begun to pay serious court to Ruth
and to squirm out of any dates with Terry, who is always pressing for
one. He goes to the lieutenant now and announces that he has
checked test against test and can be quite sure: Terry is insane and
she might well have committed a murder; Ruth would be incapable of
such a crime. Terry's trouble is paranoia, based on exaggerated jealousy of Ruth, for Ruth has always been the one people preferred.
This had been the murdered man's undoing, Ayres figures: he had
thought Terry and Ruth to be the same girl but had become troubled
about variations in her character and no doubt had just remarked to
Terry that she seemed strangely different that evening from the girl
he loved. No arrest can be made on the basis of Ayres' tests, but at
least everything seems to be clear and Ayres can approach the girl he
loves with his mind at ease.

He phones Ruth and asks her to meet him that evening but please
not to let Terry know. He plans to talk with her about her sister.
They arrange to meet at his apartment—about eleven, she suggests.
She puts down the receiver. The music begins to roar. And the camera moves up on the name pin on her blouse: it is Terry to whom he
has been talking. Just a moment later he realizes his mistake, because
Ruth drops in on him. Phoning the lieutenant from the restaurant
where he takes Ruth, he reports that he expects to play the role of

human booby trap before the evening is out. When he returns to Ruth, she says there is a question she would like to ask him: What is the cause of hallucinations? Could it be just nerves? No, he tells her gently; the cause is a sick mind. And may he explain something to her now? She would rather postpone it, she says; she is tired and would rather go home. "Of course, dear," he murmurs. What he does not know is that Ruth has been asking not about her sister but about herself. Terry has been working on her, trying to make her think that she is seeing things. There is an old wives' tale that one of a pair of twins is apt to be not quite right, and Terry has managed to worry her about this—by telling her each morning that she has heard her talking in her sleep; by using a concealed flashlight to wake her in the middle of the night with strange blinkings of light that she, Terry, pretends not to have seen herself. At the hero's words, Ruth is now close to distraction. But Ayres is blissfully unaware of this. He proceeds to his apartment to wait for Terry's visit, perfectly sure of himself.

As Terry leaves for the appointment, "Be careful, don't take too many sleeping pills," she slyly suggests to Ruth; then—first slipping something from a bureau drawer into her purse (as the music roars) —she sets out. The hero greets Terry as if he thinks she is Ruth. And he promptly announces that it's about Terry that he wants to speak. "You don't like her, do you?" she asks. "But I love you," he tells her. She replies that she is curious to know just what difference he can find between them. "For instance, kiss me," she proposes. He kisses her. And does he really think that he could tell that kiss from one of Terry's? "I think I'd know in my heart," he declares. And then he defines Terry's sickness for her; and he wants to persuade her to take her sister to a doctor. And if she refuses? "If *you* refuse, Terry," he suddenly levels, "I'm afraid I'll have to tell the police who killed" that man. He is still very sure of himself. But as she retreats to the couch and reaches in a lunge for her purse, the moment suddenly becomes nightmarish. The camera has eyed her purse steadily throughout the scene, and one expects her to pull a gun out of it. Instead, she pulls out a compact and begins nervously to powder her face. And stenciled on the compact is the name "Ruth." One knows, of course, that it *is* Terry who sits there. And yet—irrationally or not—one does not know it for sure. And in the next few moments her figure and the figure of her absent sister waver together in an entire not-quite-logical sequence of ways.

Putting away her compact, she looks up at him and asks, "Haven't you forgotten Ruth? She won't take this lightly." Ayres himself has warned the lieutenant that his job is a ticklish one, because twins are a strange phenomenon. He has cited an instance in which twin sisters, living miles apart, one of them serving a prison term, the other holding down a very respectable job, suffered identical toothaches in the same hour. Apparently the ties that bind twins are unpredictable and strange. Perhaps, one feels suddenly, perhaps in the last analysis twins *cannot* be entirely distinguished from each other. Perhaps these two sisters are so bound, one to the other, that Ayres cannot possibly attack Terry without evoking Ruth's bitter enmity. Perhaps this is Ruth herself speaking, one even feels, and Ayres has really misfigured. The next moment, the two figures waver together in still another way. In answer to some comment Ayres makes about Ruth, she replies lightly, "I doubt that anyone would take very seriously a girl who suffers from hallucinations." "What do you mean?" the hero cries, and for the first time he realizes that Ruth had been asking about herself earlier that evening. As he grabs at the girl, "Look closely," she challenges. "Are you so sure you know whom you have kissed? Look closely!" And even if both Ayres and an audience know well enough that this is Terry, if they stop to think, her words have their effect. Because it is Ruth whom Ayres has pretended to kiss; and the image of this girl he loves has suddenly become confused for him.

And now his beloved recedes from him more cruelly still. The phone shrills. At the other end is the lieutenant. He has decided to call on Ruth, to check that *she* was all right, and he has found her dead from an overdose of sleeping pills. As Ayres stands there at the phone, speechless, his death seems near too. Terry's eyes steal to the sharp scissors lying on a table top. One can see the film ending, aria da capo, with this overeager man, in his turn, sprawled dead on the carpet.

But this film too manages a happy ending. The scissors are simply forgotten. Ayres turns to Terry with the news and the two leave quickly for the twins' apartment. There Terry goes into a cunning act: swearing that the dead girl, "poor darling," is Terry, she "makes a clean breast of it," names her the murderess, and turning Ayres' words against him she defines her sister's "sickness" in just the terms he has recently used. Then the lieutenant opens a door and in steps the real Ruth, who is not dead after all. The lieutenant has been playing a brilliant hunch. Terry, at the sight of her, goes quite out of her head, and gnashing her teeth, picks up a heavy object to hurl. Once again we expect to see the hero lose his beloved—and happiness so very near! But the missile falls wide of its mark. Terry is led off. And as the curtain falls, Ruth and Ayres are smiling at each other across the teacups. "How does it happen that you are so much more beautiful than your sister?" he is asking her brightly.

But above the music that swirls softly around these lovers, a question still lightly echoes: *"Are you so sure you know whom you have kissed?"*

"I'm still alive!" (tough boy)

There is one hero, featured in many films of these years, who is set down in a world more frankly nightmare than any I have yet reported —a world bristling with dangers, where *no* voice is to be trusted and the seductive treacherous female truly reigns, death lurks most surely in the center of the embrace. This hero is the familiar "tough boy" hero of thrillers derived from the novels of Dashiell Hammett, Raymond Chandler, and their like. He is usually a "private eye," hired to perform some apparently routine job, to locate missing person or missing heirloom, but involved before the tale is out in matters more unusual. Murder enters the picture, of course. And invariably as murder there enters some deadly-fascinating lady. But this hero is not the hapless hero of the past chapter. Here too (as in *The Locket* and *Dark Mirror*) there occurs the moment when the lady stands before him, suddenly, as his enemy. She has seemed all innocence, wide-eyed and sweet, and suddenly there she stands behind the pointed gun, or there she stands above the gleaming loot or in the enemy's midst, one of them. For the hero of the past chapter this moment was a fatal one. The poor lover, finding his beloved so utterly changed, endures a fatal change himself and topples to destruction—or so very nearly so that his survival seems a miracle. Because he has been taken by surprise. Everything has seemed so sure. But *this* hero comes armed for just such surprises. "Hello, angel," this hero drawls. "I thought I'd find you here." As standard as the scene in those other films in which the hero gapes in surprise (as stunned as Donald Duck, mouth wide) is the scene in which—even before she has made her move—this hero addresses her: "Sorry, it won't work"; "You've put on a good act, but it won't work"; "Don't try to be cute. I know you, babe." Her wild reproofs echo from film to film: "You don't trust women one bit, do you?" "You don't trust anybody but yourself!" His reply always matches that of the hero of *Calcutta*, who quotes for the lady an old Gurkha saying, "Man who trust woman walk on duckweed over pond." The lady in *Calcutta* chides the hero for not being more like his friend—to whom she was engaged until someone murdered him. He has nothing in common with that boy, she reproves him; he is cold, unfeeling, sadistic, suspicious . . . *"And I am still alive,"* he closes the list.

He *is* different. She is right. He is one who survives, who boasts of this. The minor characters in these films are familar enough. Each hurries to his destruction. Like Clyde in *The Locket,* who "has to have" Nancy, each one "has to have" something and scrambles after it in a fever. It is a woman, or it is power and wealth, or the two quests are interwoven. In *Murder, My Sweet,* there is the deadly Velma and some priceless jade; in *The Glass Key,* Janet Henry ("I want Janet Henry more than anything in life!") and high political stakes; in *The Maltese Falcon,* Bridgid—"Oh, she's sweet!"—and the jewel-encrusted falcon ("It took seventeen years to locate . . . I wanted it . . . I got it . . . Now I haven't got it . . . but I'm going to get it!"). They scramble in frantic relays, gripped by their sharp hungers ("My love for you is incurable"). And as always, what they seek eludes them as they draw near. Velma, Janet, Bridgid—"Every guy's seen you somewhere," as the hero says to the girl in *The Blue Dahlia.* "The trick is to find you." In *The Maltese Falcon,* they think they have their hands on the jeweled bird. Trembling, they unroll the wadding in which it is wrapped. With quick knife they scrape at the protective coating of enamel—then scrape at it, scrape at it, faster and faster, the music getting wild; and then begin to scream at each other and to sob: "It's phony! It's lead!" And the real bird? "Its fate remains a mystery to this day." But the hero—he watches them, eyes flicking; he stands outside the feverish circle, quietly watching. "Why so frantic, little man?" he drawls. And, deadpan, he moves among the corpses that soon strew this cruel landscape. Because he can boast that *he* is still alive, the frantic motions of the other characters can be shown more starkly now than in former films. Stark too are those scenes in which these frantic motions come to their dead-end. Certain still-lifes now are an invariable: the corpse fallen in some tiny room, where an electric signboard from across the street blinks coldly upon it, or the single bulb above swings over it a dreary light and shade; or fallen in some luxurious apartment, splayed out like a design among the overturned furniture, not "hurt much, just snapped," like the buttonhole flower dropped near it; or a tumbled figure on the sidewalk, where curious passers-by gather. The camera lingers, surveying the scene with a pitiless eye. For *he* is intact. This hero is the knowing one. As the others hurry toward death, "You've got brains—yes you have," he drawls, a smile just baring his teeth.

And yet—the picture I have just given is misleading; for one can wonder at moments just how many brains this hero has, himself. This question is often put to him, in fact. The young girl in *Murder, My Sweet* exclaims, "I think you're nuts—barging about without any clear idea of what you're doing!" "You are as dumb as they come," the hero of *Ride the Pink Horse* is told. Here is no unruffled Sherlock Holmes. If he is "still alive" at the end of a film, he endures before the film is out many a senseless beating. The scene in which he stands there, smiling, and drawls, "I know—" is standard in these films; but standard too is the scene in which he walks right into one of those traps he knows so well about. If one sets film next to film, if one sets, even, incident next to incident in any one film in this series, the roughings-up, the workings over this hero endures assume very nearly comic proportions. Again and again the scene recurs in which, blackjacked, doped, punched in the kidneys, kicked in the temples, he blacks out; and again and again he drags himself to his feet, studies his battered self in the mirror, and then, face set, returns for more. "Sock-me-again Bowman" the hero of *The Glass Key* is tagged. "Bouncing ball . . . Little rubber ball is back!" Nor does the necessity for this bouncing back always seem obvious. And as invariably as he walks into the enemy lair—into blackjacks, into rabbit punches—

he walks into the deadly embrace of the "babe" he knows so well. The necessity of this seems often as questionable. When he finds her at last in the enemy's midst and drawls, "Hello, angel, I thought I'd find you here," the remark might be said to cut two ways. This hero seems "too smart for his own good."

The hero himself, questioned as to why he does "take" what he does, is apt to reply that he is paid for it, "Just a small businessman in a messy business"—"I have to eat." Others sometimes make the same point: "He's not a detective, he's a slot machine." One might ask whether he couldn't transact business in a somewhat less risky manner. Does he always have to go where he goes alone, for example? But the explanation leaves more unanswered than this. If the hero were really moved by money, it would occur to him—in film after film— that he finally could make more money by retiring from the case than by sticking with it. For there are always people who would gladly "sugar him off" the case. In many of these films a moment arrives when the person who has hired him decides to discharge him, so no money is coming in at all. In each of these cases he refuses to retire: "There's no law that says you can't work a case without a client."

The very look of the office space this hero occupies belies any claim that money explains him. As one of his clients, in *The Big Sleep,* remarks disdainfully, there's "not much front" to it. It is always the barest of possible rooms, in the cheapest section of town. Bare walls, uncarpeted floor, a desk, a couple of chairs, a phone; wash basin in the corner—in which to bathe bruised temples, swelling eye; mirror above—in which to squint at the damage; that is about all. Nor does the room where he sleeps at night—when he does sleep—boast further graces. Bed, chair, bed table, ash tray, phone, alarm clock. If this hero is out for the money he can make, then he *doesn't* have a very clear idea of what he is doing.

There is another answer this hero is apt to give those who ask why he keeps "poking his nose into trouble," "asking" for a rough time. "I like it that way," he says. Here again one can mention facts that seem to contradict his statement. For this hero steps into danger with no jaunty smile upon his lips. He moves in, his face taut, the sweat starting upon his brow; looks down and sees that his hand is trembling, peers into a mirror and sees that his mouth is twitching. As he bends to embrace the treacherous lady of these films, his face darkens as though he were approaching death. As he walks down the corridor toward the room where the enemy waits, he moves each limb as though it were painful to do so. He wears, in fact, the look of the wandering hero of the third chapter—the look of one very much afraid of being hurt. This hero *is* different from the other heroes I have described; but the difference is not casual.

Here are the films themselves, however. Here is the hero in motion —a knowing one ("I'm still alive") and a fool ("dumb as they come"), who "likes it that way" and yet draws near with a look of pain. In motion, these scrambled elements unscramble and his true nature can be deciphered.

The Maltese Falcon (1941) is the original of the series and the most lively. The hero is Humphrey Bogart—Sam Spade. The film opens on the bare office Sam shares with a partner. "Yes, sweetheart?" he asks Effie, their secretary. She has a visitor to announce—Miss Wunderlich (Mary Astor). She enters, dressed in demure black. And she needs someone to trail a certain Mr. Thursby for her. She has a sad little story to tell, about a sister in trouble. Spade listens, his teeth showing in a smile that might just possibly be a sneer. "Uhuh," he grunts. Then in blunders his partner, Archer. And "grinning from ear to ear," Archer takes the bait and claims the job for himself. After she leaves, gazing at the money she has left, Archer gloats, "There's more where that came from!" and "Oh, she's sweet! . . . I spoke first!" Spade looks on quietly. "You've got brains," he drawls. The camera lowers to the shadowed reflection on the floor of their two names in lettering. "Yes you have," he drawls. And the next clipped shots show us feet approaching through the dusk, a gun pointed, in close, and Archer rolling down a long dusty incline at the edge of town. Then the curious are gathering, flashlight cameras coldly exploding. Spade is there too, quietly looking down upon the scene. "Have the Spade and Archer taken off the door and Samuel Spade put on," he instructs Effie.

But now? Off goes Spade himself, looking for trouble. Face twitching queerly, he telephones Miss Wunderlich at her hotel. She has checked out. The next day's papers announce the death of Mr. Thursby too. Back at the office, Spade silently waits for a call. It comes. Can he hurry right over? The name to ask for will be Miss Leblanc. Effie's face is puckered in distress, but off he goes.

She has a "terrible terrible confession" to make, Mary Astor begins. "That story I told you . . ." He didn't exactly believe her story, he cuts her short—"Miss . . . ?" "Bridgid O'Shaunessy" is her real name, she tells him. And poor Mr. Archer, she laments—only yesterday so alive. He cuts her short again: there's little time for nonsense, because "out there" are a flock of D.A.'s with their noses to the ground. She asks, Do they know about her, do they have to? "Will you shield me?" she cries. He tells her, "I've got to know what it's all about." She cries, "You've got to trust me! I'm so alone and afraid—with nobody to help me if you won't!" He tells her, "You won't need much of anybody's help—you're good." She deserves that, she replies, suddenly meek; but the lie was in the *way* she said it. Yes, it's her own fault if he can't believe her now. "Now you *are* dangerous," says Spade. But if she wants his help, she must give him a "line" on Thursby. She tells him that she met Thursby in the Orient, and the two of them had just lately returned from there together. Then he had taken advantage of her dependence upon him to betray her. How betray her, he asks. But she shakes her head. It was Thursby who murdered Archer, of course, she tells him. And who killed Thursby, he asks. She doesn't know at all. "This is hopeless," says Spade, coldly scanning her. But—he'll take what extra money she has about her, and he'll be back.

The police meanwhile are knocking at Spade's door. But they get nothing from him. Spade has checked with his lawyer, who's told him that yes, he can hide behind the right of a client to anonymity. Back at the office, Effie announces another visitor. The calling card she hands him smells of gardenia. "Quick, darling, in with him!" cries Spade. And enter Joel Cairo (Peter Lorre), fidgeting gloves and cane. Mr. Cairo wants to offer condolences upon the death of Archer. And could there be any relationship between that death and the death of a certain Thursby? His curiosity is not idle. He is trying to recover "a certain ornament that has been mislaid"—a black figure of a bird. He is prepared to pay five thousand dollars for it, no questions asked. Spade tells Effie that she can leave for the night, and she has hardly gone when "You will clasp your hands together, please, behind your head," lisps Mr. Cairo, leveling a gun. Spade with deft motion disarms him, knocks him unconscious, and searches him. When the little man opens his eyes again, Spade explains, "Imagine my embarrassment at finding that your offer was hooey." But the offer is genuine, Cairo insists; he has merely tried to spare the owner some expense. Here is one hundred dollars as proof of his sincerity. Say two hundred, says Spade. Then he has the bird? When Spade says no, Cairo opens his eyes wide: why, then, did he just risk serious injury? "I should sit around and let people stick me up," says Spade. "Please, my gun now," says Cairo. Then he is once more lisping, face furiously grimacing, "You will clasp your hands together, please, behind your head"; and this time Spade, laughing, tells him to go ahead and search the place.

"You aren't exactly the sort of person you pretend to be, are you?" says Spade to Bridgid, back at her rooms. This schoolgirl manner . . . "By the way," he says, "I saw Joel Cairo." Her face changes and she starts moving around the room, straightening things, poking at the fire. Then—"What did he say about me?" she asks. His bluff has worked. "Nothing," Spade tells her. "He offered me five thousand dollars for a black bird." Ah, she cries, that is more than she could ever offer, if she must bid for his loyalty. Loyalty is a wonderful word from her, says Spade. What has she ever tried to buy him with but money? Should she offer herself, she suggests. Smiling, he walks up to her, his fingers dent her cheeks, and he gives her a contemptuous kiss, then draws back. "I don't care about your little secrets," he tells her, "but I can't go ahead without a bit more confidence in you." She wants to speak with Joel Cairo, then, she says. But not here! He mustn't know her address! So Spade arranges a meeting for the three of them at his own apartment.

Cairo, upon arrival, nervously informs Spade that there is a boy down on the street, watching his window. Spade has noticed it himself. The kid has been shadowing him. He assures Bridgid, when *she* gets excited, that he has shaken him each time before visiting her rooms. "I am delighted to see you again, madame," says Cairo. And "I was sure you would be," says Bridgid. And Spade watches the two of them spar. She has been told of his handsome offer, she says. How soon can he have the five thousand in cash? The money is ready, says Cairo. No, not in his pocket. And the bird? No, she doesn't have the bird at the moment, but in another week . . . For she knows where Thursby hid it. And why a week? And why is she willing to sell? Because she's afraid—after what happened to Thursby. Spade's eyes flick. And what exactly did, asks Cairo. "The fat man," she murmurs. At which Cairo leaps to his feet; and his eyes move to the window. "You might be able to get round the boy the way you did that one in Istanbul," says Bridgid. "You mean the one that you couldn't get to?" Suddenly the two are slapping at each other nastily, and Spade has to break it up. Then they are at each other again, scratching and kicking. The cops walk in on this; they have returned to question Spade further. Spade has to do some fancy talking to get rid of them again. One of the cops doesn't care for the way he talks and takes a cuff at him. Spade, shaking, yells at the other one to get him out of there fast. He does.

Cairo takes a hurried leave too, and Spade and Bridgid are left alone. And now she can do a little talking, Spade announces. She must be going, she says. He asks her: How about the boy outside? She sits again—"You are a most insistent person . . . You are the wildest, most unpredictable person." What makes this black bird so important, Spade asks her. She's never been told, she says. Cairo and Thursby had offered her money over in Istanbul if she would help them to get it. Then Thursby and she had found out that Cairo meant to run out on them with it, so they had run out on him instead. But then she had found out that Thursby didn't intend to give her anything, and so she had come to Spade for help. "You *are* a liar," Spade tells her. And "Yes, I am," she abruptly confesses. Well, says Spade, coffee will be ready soon; they have all night. At that, she stretches out on the shabby couch and "I'm so tired," she sighs—"of lying and thinking up lies." Spade gazes down at her darkly. Then— his look is a strange one, a savage and suffering mask is drawn upon his face—he bends over her in an embrace. Beyond them, past the thinly blowing curtains, down there in the street, the camera shows us the boy still at his watch.

The next day Spade brings Bridgid in to Effie and asks could she put her up for a little while, for safety's sake. Then he seeks out the little gunman, who isn't hard to find, carefully insults him ("I won't forget you," says the kid) and tells him to take word to his boss that he, Spade, plans to have a talk with him. Back at the office, he waits for the fat man's call. It comes promptly. So off goes Spade now to meet this one. Gutman, the fat man (Sidney Greenstreet), looks Spade up and down haughtily as he mixes drinks for the two of them,

and he asks: Whom is he representing—Cairo or Miss O'Shaunessy?
It must be one or the other, he persists, as Spade is noncommittal.
"There's *me*," drawls Spade. The fat man chuckles. But, he guesses,
Spade doesn't know what the bird is, does he? And if *they* don't
know—this he guesses too—"I'm the only one in the whole world
who does!" "Tell me, and there'll be two of us," Spade suggests. "You
know what it is, I know where it is." And then suddenly he gets to his
feet; he knocks something off the table with a vicious blow; he sends a
glass crashing to the floor—the fat man just sits there—and he had
better do any talking he wants to do that day, Spade yells, or he's
through! He'll give him until five o'clock to be in or out for keeps!
And he rages out of the apartment. In the lobby he slows down, grinning, and looks down at his hands. They are trembling briskly.

The fat man does send his gun boy, Wilmer, to bring Spade back.
On the way, Spade "rides" the boy some more, removes his guns from
him—"This will put you in solid with the boss." He hands them to
the fat man at the door—"A crippled newsie took them away from
him, but I made him give them back." "An amazing character,"
laughs the fat man a bit wryly. And now, he tells Spade, he's going to
hear a most astonishing story. He pours two drinks again. The Maltese falcon, it seems, was sent as a gift to Charles of Spain from the
crusaders to whom he gave the island of Malta—a golden bird en-
crusted from head to foot with precious jewels. But on the way to
Spain it was waylaid by buccaneers. In 1840 it turned up in Paris,
overlaid with a coat of enamel, and in that disguise it kicked around
from dealer to dealer until a certain very great dealer, in an obscure
shop, recognized it for what it was. Then he, the fat man, got wind
of it. That was seventeen years ago. Just as he was on his way to see it,
the dealer was murdered, the bird stolen. The fat man spent seventeen years tracing the bird again. And he had it—but he hasn't got it
now. His agents, it seems, had their own ideas. "But I'm going to get
it," he says. "And now, sir"—he will give Spade an immediate twenty-
five thousand dollars for it, or if he cares to wait and take half of what
can be realized on it, this might well amount to a quarter of a million.
But as the fat man talks on, dangling before him this fabulous prize,
Spade begins to blink, the face before him begins to blur, the bulking
body to loom hazy and mountainous. Spade, hand to his head, staggers to his feet. The liquor has been doctored. Wilmer steps from the

next room cheerfully, trips him, and as he lies there dazed, gives him a vicious kick in the face. Cairo joins them from the bedroom, stepping gingerly over the body. The fat man casually finds his hat and the three take their leave.

When Spade comes to and hunches himself to his feet, he gets Effie on the phone. Effie has news: Bridgid has never turned up at her place for safekeeping. Spade, grimacing and shaking, ransacks the fat man's quarters and finds a news clipping about the docking of the "Paloma" that afternoon. He gets there fast. But the ship, when he gets there, is empty and in flames—the firemen are still doing their best. Maybe the damn bird doesn't exist at all, he suggests to Effie, back at the office, as she bathes that bruised eye for him. But just then a final visitor arrives and stands wavering in the doorway: the dazed figure of the ship's captain, Jacobi, a package, swaddled in newspaper, hugged in his arms. He thrusts the bundle at Spade and falls dead. Spade, teeth bared, grips Effie so hard that she cries out. He yells at her, "We've got it, angel!"

The phone shrills and Effie answers it. She tells Spade: it was Bridgid and her voice sounded awful. "You've got to help her!" She gives him the address Bridgid had screamed out and Spade taxis out there. (But first he thinks to check the bundle at the bus terminal and to mail the check to himself, care of general delivery.) The address, at the end of town, is false. There's only an empty lot there. Spade returns to his own room. At that address, Bridgid is waiting for him, however—cowering in the doorway. He helps her upstairs. Upstairs, the others are waiting too—"Well, sir, we're all here": the fat man and Wilmer and Cairo. Bridgid gives a little scream. Spade eyes her with a smile. And he asks the fat man: is he ready to make a first payment? The fat man takes out ten thousand dollars. They had been talking about a lot more—"but there are a lot more of us to be taken care of now." And maybe Spade does have the falcon, but they certainly have him. There's something else to be discussed, though, Spade suggests. Three murders have been committed, and "a fall guy" will have to be chosen from among them. He would suggest Wilmer—who actually did commit two of the murders, didn't he? He is perfectly willing to discuss either of the others, of course, Spade drawls, his arm around Bridgid ("Feeling any better, precious?")—if the fat man thinks that a persuasive story can be concocted. The fat man reluctantly surrenders Wilmer; and Spade, as a practical measure, knocks Wilmer cold. But before he sends for the bird, he'd like some details, he says; for if the story for the cops doesn't hang together, he's likely to take the rap himself. The fat man obliges: Thursby and Bridgid had been allies. He, the fat man, had tried to make a deal with Thursby, but Thursby had been "determinedly loyal" to Bridgid. (Spade smiles at her.) So Wilmer had dealt with him. Cairo had then recognized the advantage of getting in touch with the fat man. And it had been Cairo who had thought of the "Paloma," for he had heard that Jacobi and Bridgid had been seen together. They had walked in on the two of them down at the dock and had persuaded them, so they thought, to come to terms (and Wilmer had accidentally set things on fire), but on the way back to the hotel the two had slipped through their fingers. By the end of the afternoon, they had found them again, and Wilmer had managed to get a shot in at Jacobi, but Jacobi had gotten away, and with the falcon. They had captured Bridgid, though, and persuaded her to tell them where Jacobi had headed and then to phone Spade, in an attempt to draw him away. But it had taken too long to persuade her. And the fat man has a bit of advice for Spade. If he doesn't give Bridgid as much of that ten thousand dollars as she thinks she should have—be careful. And now they would like the falcon.

So Spade calls Effie and tells her how to get the bundle, once it is daylight. And they all sit down to wait. But when Effie arrives and they surround it and with trembling hands unroll the black bird from its wrapping and scrape at the enamel—they scrape and scrape, wilder and wilder, and then begin to sob like children, for the bird is fake, it is lead. The man whom they had duped to get it originally seems to have duped them instead. "Well, sir," says the fat man, first to pull himself together—he's off to Istanbul again, to find the *real* falcon. Suddenly they discover that Wilmer has slipped away. The fat man and Cairo hurry off after him. But first the fat man, pistol leveled, asks Spade to return that ten thousand—"Your hard luck, sir." Spade tells him that he is keeping one thousand, for time and expenses. Spade and Bridgid are left alone again.

Spade steps to the phone and calls the cops. He suggests that they pick up Wilmer for the murders of Thursby and Jacobi. And Wilmer has been working for Gutman and Cairo, he tells them—who will be trying to "blow" town. With a drawn look he turns to Bridgid now, and she had better give him "all and fast," for "we're sitting on dynamite," he tells her. The cops will soon be here too. What about Archer? She had hired Archer, she cries, to trail Thursby—yes, hoping to frighten him off, so she wouldn't have to share with him. But she had warned Archer that the man was dangerous! Spade corrects her. Archer wasn't dumb enough to be spotted by the man he was trailing. She had killed Archer herself, hadn't she—hoping to have Thursby sent up for it? "You know I didn't!" she cries. But he interrupts her. She hadn't known the fat man was in town, or she wouldn't have wanted to be rid of her gunman; but when Thursby was killed, she had known it must be he, and she had needed another protector, and so she had had to come back to him, to Spade. Well, if they hang her, he tells her, he'll always remember her. "Don't say that, even in fun!" she cries. "You say such wild and unpredictable things!" He knows very well, she cries, that it was love that brought her back to him. From the very moment they met they had known that they were meant for each other. Spade doesn't deny it. "Maybe you love me, maybe I love you," he tells her. And the sweat is standing on his forehead. But "I don't care who loves you . . . I won't play the sap for you . . . I'm not Thursby, I'm not Jacobi. I won't walk in their footsteps . . . I won't," he tells her—and the smile on his face is a grimace—"because all of me wants to, regardless of the consequences, and you can count on that." She flings her arms around him and presses her mouth to his mouth. When the buzzer rings and the cops walk in, she is still in his arms. But—"Here's another for you," Spade says. "She killed Archer." He hands over the thousand dollars, too. "I was supposed to be bribed with this." One of the cops picks up the black bird and asks, "What is this?" "The stuff that dreams are made of," says Spade through his teeth. And he walks to the elevator with them. As the cage groaningly descends, her face, through the grillwork, upturned to his, vanishing reproachfully, he turns and—the music is groaning too, but triumphant—he walks away.

What, then, *has* this "wild and unpredictable" character been after? Bridgid, in that final scene, raises the question shrilly. Would he be doing this to her if the falcon were real and he had been paid? He tells her, "Don't be too sure that I'm as crooked as I'm supposed to

be." Is it revenge that moves him, then? Did Archer mean that much
to him, she cries. He was a son of a bitch, says Spade, and she didn't
do him, Spade, a damned bit of harm by killing him. Then why is he
doing this to her, she asks—"Why, *why?*" In my synopsis I omitted
one thread of this story: Spade has been playing around with
Archer's wife, and this is why the cops treat him as a suspect. Has he
been moved, then, to clear himself of a possible murder charge? But if
he had told the cops at once what he knew of Archer's errand, he
could easily have diverted suspicion from himself. Instead, he did
everything to antagonize them. "I won't play the sap for you," Spade
explains to Bridgid. He doesn't just mean that he's not going to go to
prison in her place. He means that he intends to remain a free agent.
If one names *this* the compulsion that moves him, one confronts
again, of course, that original riddle I noted: Why does he entangle
himself with this woman to begin with? The moment they meet, he
knows her for what she is; he doesn't exactly believe her story. "This
is hopeless," he says—then takes the case. "Loyalty is a good word
from you!" he mocks—and then walks into her embrace. This is the
sequence of things. And then finally, "I won't play the sap for you,"
he says, "because all of me wants to," and he painfully disentangles
himself from her arms. A curious sequence.

And yet there is a logic to be traced in it. It is the logic of the
endurance test. This hero takes the hopeless case, enters the deadly
embrace, to prove to himself that he can emerge intact. All about him
he watches others rushing to destruction. He is determined not to
follow in their steps. He sees the eager and the timid alike lost to
themselves, because nothing remains in which they can believe. This
hero has trimmed belief to belief in his own definition, in his own
powers to endure. "There's *me*," Spade says to the fat man. His
words may be read beyond their context there. Here is a creed. This
creed demands precisely the rigors of the tale I have just recounted.
For until that self is tried, this hero too is no one, is nowhere. It is
appropriate that he is shown always at the film's start sitting in that
stark room, waiting. "In with him!" he cries when the client is announced. His trial is about to begin. From here on he asks for it, he
walks into trouble nonstop; he provokes every assault upon his integrity possible. It is not shrewd of Spade to provoke the police, to provoke the trigger-happy Wilmer. He is under compulsion to do so, for

only in this way can he define himself. The trial that this hero endures is very real. In film after film he is shown staring into the mirror at a battered countenance. He is always on the verge of breaking. A face rigidly controlled, but a telltale twitch in his cheek marks him. And when Spade, cuffed by the cop, yells, "Get him out of here!" or, the falcon suddenly in his hands, yells, "We've got it!" for a moment even that control is gone. This hero is to be understood as one who could easily enough, if he should relax in discipline, join the ranks of all those other frantic ones.

The assaults that he endures, and that he provokes, are various. On one level is sheer physical battering. The test is to get up onto his feet again after *anything*, shake himself, and go on his way. The test at another level is to avoid ever acting as another's tool. Even when it would not particularly hurt to, he must never let himself be turned simply to the client's purposes. He "should sit around and let" Cairo search him!—even when he knows Cairo would find nothing. If Cairo offers him a hundred dollars down, he takes two hundred; he takes a thousand from the fat man for "expenses," even though he will then hand the money over to the cops. Clients never tell him all they know, and here too lies a test. He must untangle the truth, must piece together the real story. But most rigorous of all the trials through which he puts himself is that of retaining his self-possession in the face of the various lures that are dangled before him—the lure, here, of the fabulous Maltese falcon; and the lure of Bridgid. He must be able to do without, to have the falcon in his hands, to have Bridgid—and to disdain to need them, sufficient to himself.

Bridgid in *The Maltese Falcon* and her counterpart in other films may be said to contain in her person all these trials in one. When the hero takes her on, he takes it all on. When Spade accepts Bridgid's case, he asks as it were in that very gesture for Cairo to walk in on him, for Wilmer to pick up his trail, for the entire arduous history that follows. (The camera is sometimes eloquent here: when, with a dark look, Spade enters Bridgid's arms, the camera, recall, over his shoulder, picks out the tiny figure of Wilmer waiting in the street below. Perilous encounters that will certainly follow are contained here within the very motion in which he bends down to her.) When at the last he withdraws from her embrace, to let her be taken away, everything is said. Here is *the* crucial motion, *the* trying moment. He can extricate himself from anything now, put anything from him, and there will still be *he*.

Film after film since *The Maltese Falcon* has put its hero through these same fires. But films featuring this hero tend to plots so very tangled that I shall detail only one more at full length. Though the plot of *The Maltese Falcon* is not a simple one, even as I have condensed it here, it is far simpler than most. It is possible to walk out of the theater after seeing a film in this genre and to find that one is incapable of recounting which character has been involved with which other character for what reason, and just how the frantic activities of each have crossed and crisscrossed. The hero alone, it often seems, is capable of holding in his mind's eye that entire complexity. The films are less marred by such confusion than might be expected, precisely because the trial through which the hero must pass is in part this very trial—of finding his way through a landscape in which the truth never does lie composed for one to see. These are among the most vivid of the films of the forties, make up probably *the* most lively genre, just because even in their grotesqueries they grope boldly for that image of disorder which most films struggle to gloss over as quickly as they can.

Here is a simplified version of *Murder, My Sweet* (1945), based on a Raymond Chandler novel, the hero this time a private dick named Marlowe—played by Dick Powell. Here is a typical intricacy:

The story is told in flashback as Marlowe, questioned by the cops about certain murders (the film opens to the hot glare of lights turned in his eyes as they put their questions), tells them of the job he has just been on. The job was to try to find somebody for someone; but he has found out only how big a city it was, he begins. The camera moves now past a bewilderment of neon signs, in through an upper window of a shabby building, to the offices where Marlowe, the night in question, sits looking out at the street. The lights from the street blink onto the window glass the image of a visitor. (It has begun.) The visitor is a giant by the name of Moose, just out of jail after an eight-year stretch, and he wants Marlowe to help him find Velma, who used to be his girl—"cute as lace pants" she was. So Marlowe sets off through the city. He visits the cheap café where she once worked, but the café has changed hands. He locates the widow of the man who formerly ran the place, and this "charming lady with a face like a bucket of mud" remembers Velma all right, but Velma is dead, she tells him. She doesn't remember any Moose, she insists—with too great emphasis? He takes a photograph away from her that she has tried to hide, or pretended to try to hide (it is signed "Velma"), and he leaves. The woman all this while has appeared to be drunk, but listening outside her place now he hears her at the telephone and she doesn't sound drunk any more but wide awake—and like somebody busily making funeral arrangements.

He returns to his office and finds another client waiting. This one smells real nice, says the elevator boy. Mr. Lindsay Marriott has no more seeming relation to Moose and his Velma than Cairo had to Bridgid. He has to meet some men that evening at a certain lonely spot and give them some money, and he'd like company. He asks Marlowe not to carry a gun, though; and he can't go into what it's all about. Why should he risk his neck without knowing what for or what the risk is, Marlowe asks. Marriott, reluctantly, adds a few details. A jade necklace has been stolen from a friend of his, a lady, and the thieves are offering to return it for a given ransom. He's offering Marlowe a hundred dollars just to ride along. Marlowe says that he, not Marriott, will drive the car; and he wonders, he adds, why he has waited until the last moment to call on him, and also where he got his name—but he will take that hundred. At the rendezvous, Marlowe steps out to reconnoiter. A sudden apparition confronts him as he plays his flash; but it is only a deer. He returns to the car and gets a blackjack behind the ear. The screen blurs. The blur clears and a girl's voice asks, "What happened?" But voice and girl vanish before he has been able to get a look at her. In the car, Marriott is doubled up, very dead.

The cops have some questions to ask Marlowe (all this is still unfolding within the supposed telling of his story later to the same cops). They learn very little from him, but he picks up a clue from them. They let something drop about a Mr. Amthor, a "psychiatric quack" who had had some connection with the dead man.

Marlowe returns to his office and finds still another visitor waiting. ("Business is getting prettier," says the elevator boy.) She is a newspaperwoman, she tells him, and she has come to get some details about the Marriott case. "Do you do your own typing?" Marlowe asks, watching her hands. Then he dumps her handbag onto the desk and

finds in it her real name: Anne Grayle. She isn't a newspaperwoman
at all. And now he does the questioning. The jade, it seems, belongs
to her millionaire father, or rather to his wife, her stepmother—of
whom she doesn't seem to be very fond. Marlowe flashes the photograph of Velma, but she doesn't recognize the face. He suggests a
little visit to the Grayle mansion.

As the elderly Mr. Grayle talks to Marlowe about jade, which is his
hobby, and about the necklace in question, an irreplaceable one, Mrs.
Grayle, much younger than her husband, eyes Marlowe, and Marlowe eyes Mrs. Grayle—who is dressed to permit it. "Do you think
you can do anything for us?" she asks. When father and daughter
take their leave, "You'd better sit over here beside me," she tells him.
Marlowe does so without coaxing and puts some questions to her
about "poor Lin" Marriott. And how many others Marriotts are there,
he ventures. He asks about Mr. Amthor too. She tells him that she
had gone to Amthor for help with her "centers of speech," and so had
Marriott, because he'd had some trouble getting started, some fear of
failure. "I wonder if Amthor would take my case," says Marlowe; and
when Anne peeks in, the two are locked in a fierce embrace.

That evening Mrs. Grayle takes Marlowe to a night club. They
have hardly arrived when she leaves him, to powder her nose, and
never reappears. But Marlowe finds himself confronted by the daughter. She will offer him double whatever Mrs. Grayle is paying him if
he will stay away from them. He declines. At which point—these
various figures appear and disappear as apparition-like as that deer in
the night—Moose stands there, beckoning to him, and he wants him
to "ditch the babe" and come with him. He wants him to meet a
guy.

The "guy"—whose swank apartment they approach by a back elevator run by an armed henchman—turns out to be Amthor. The
threads of the story begin to interweave now—to our confusion.
Moose asks Amthor to ask Marlowe to tell him where Velma is. He
seems to think that Marlowe knows, and Amthor seems to be encour-
aging him. Marlowe takes the occasion to tell Amthor that he can
guess the racket Amthor is in, a dirty blackmail game, Marriott once a
collaborator. When Amthor calls him a stupid little man, he hits
Amthor in the face—and is treated to the trouble he has looked for.
Again everything goes black, the screen blurs. And this time the blur

clears only after a crazy nightmare in which someone pursues him with a hypodermic needle and then he has to break through a gray web woven by a thousand spiders. He wakes, weak and dizzy, on a cot in a bare little room. He walks and walks that room, to clear his head. And the cot looks much too inviting; it is only through the greatest effort of will that he keeps from crawling back into it. "And now let's see you do something really tough," he tells himself, "like putting your pants on." This labor accomplished, he manages to rip a bed-spring from the cot, yells, and when the roughneck set to guard him comes running in, floors him with his improvised weapon and makes his escape. Or rather, he disdains escape. Though his head still spins, though he can hardly stand, though every moment is still a battle against losing consciousness, instead of simply getting out of that place, he walks in on Amthor's assistant, a Dr. Sonderberg, and con-fronts *him* with a few impertinent questions. Dr. Sonderberg is al-most his match: in persuasive psychiatric tones he assures Marlowe that he is just about to pass out—and Marlowe nearly succumbs to the suggestion. But he just manages not to, somehow has his say and takes his leave.

Out on the street, Moose materializes once again. "I'd like you to keep looking for Velma!" But some remark Marlowe drops about Amthor sends him hurrying off again. And Marlowe heads for Anne's apartment near by. He would like a little black coffee. And he would like a little talk with her. As she is reluctantly playing hostess, sud-denly it occurs to him that he has heard her voice before: this is the voice that spoke out in the night, then vanished, leaving him alone with a corpse. What was she doing there, he demands. "I didn't kill him!" she cries. Had she been following her father? "You must be-lieve my father!" she cries. He thinks he will have another talk with Mr. Grayle.

He finds the old man in a desperate state. Mrs. Grayle is missing. The police have been there, questioning. And this whole thing has gone too far! He blabbers on about the happiness he once thought he possessed—having such a beautiful wife, and his jade. And now this irony: because of his jade, he is losing his wife. He doesn't under-stand any of it, but he will pay Marlowe well to see that the whole matter is closed. Anne too begs Marlowe to stop right there. But Mar-lowe refuses. They have talked about a beach house on the Grayle estate. He demands a key from Anne. And at the beach house, as he has guessed, he finds Mrs. Grayle.

That was a pleasant little blind date she fixed for him with Amthor, Marlowe challenges the lady. She is sorry, she says—but she had thought he might have the jade. "Was it bad?" she asks. "He almost made me mad," drawls Marlowe. And how about explaining a few things now? She will tell him everything. Amthor is blackmailing her—his game as a psychiatrist is to uncover a good basis for this. And she wouldn't want to hurt her husband that badly. Amthor had asked for the jade. But before she could get it to him, it was stolen. Quietly turning off the lights, she moves to Marlowe, and please, she tells him, she wants him to help her kill Amthor. "I haven't been good," she cries, "but"—he must help her to find peace; "I need you so!" Face darkening, Marlowe, like Spade, moves into the embrace. "All right," he tells her, withdrawing from her arms—he'll look up Amthor in the morning. "How would you like not having to earn a living?" she whispers as he takes his leave.

But the next morning when Marlowe walks into Amthor's apartment again, he finds Amthor crumpled among the overturned furniture—not hurt much, just snapped. Moose has been there. He has guessed that Amthor has been playing with him. Marlowe finds Moose back at the office. "I gotta find her now; I gotta go away," Moose tells him. Marlowe shows him the photo he took from the old lady, and this is Velma, isn't it? But the photo is a phony—as he has come to suppose. Now he does know where Velma is, he tells Moose, if he would like to come with him.

Back at the beach house, he makes Moose wait outside for a signal. ("Like lighting dynamite and telling it not to go off.") And he enters, himself. Mrs. Grayle moves to him through the dark with glittering arms outstretched, but quietly extricating himself, he confronts her with his version of events: The jade has never been missing at all. She had not wanted to whet Amthor's appetite. And it was not Amthor who killed Marriott, as she has implied; she killed him. "You can't mean that!" she cries. She killed him, he continues, because he agreed to help her commit a murder but then turned scared. He agreed to help her kill a certain nosy private detective whom she didn't want finding her for a guy named Moose. "Oh, it's all true," she moans, "but I was trapped! Now I'm so close to peace!" "Sorry, it won't work," he tells her. It worked once, eight years ago, on a guy named Moose. What had she taken Moose into—was that murder too? It's not just men she fears her husband might find out about. Suddenly, as might have been predicted, she stands there behind a pointed gun. "It's too bad it had to be like this! I could like you a lot!" But then as suddenly Mr. Grayle and Anne appear in the doorway. And "It's gone too far, and I'm so tired!" the old man cries—and he shoots her. Now Moose breaks in. "You've got a refund coming," Marlowe breathes. Moose gazes at his Velma—"She's hardly changed! Only more fancy!"—then swings on the old man: "You shouldn't have killed her!" And though Marlowe tries to get in the way, and does manage to stop one bullet (everything goes black for the third time), the two poor lovesick ones ("I loved her too much!" the old man sobs) kill each other. Back at the police station, the flash-back at last unwound, "That's all," Marlowe sums up—which, one could say, has been quite enough.

Emerging from this intricacy—barely emerging (he sits there heav-ily bandaged, telling his story)—this hero, like the hero of *The Mal-tese Falcon,* has little that is tangible to show for his labors. He is just barely not in trouble with the cops. He is nearly broke. From Moose, from Marriott, from Velma he has had some cash down, but he has refused every offer of real money along the way (and toward the end has loaned money to Moose). But—he has what he has labored for: his own integrity, that sense of himself as all-surviving, intact at the end of no matter how many blackouts, able to struggle free from whatever web is set to entangle him. He has refused to let weariness, blows, drugs stop him. He has found his way through a bewildering maze of lies. Above all, he has gazed upon Velma, has entered those glittering arms and disentangled himself again—Velma, for whom Moose, for whom Pop, for whom Marriott, and even Amthor lost themselves. Nothing—not even Amthor, though Amthor did almost make him angry, not even Velma with all her charm and all her wealth—has been able, quite, to make Marlowe forget himself.

But I have omitted the very end of this film. At the very end it departs from the example of *The Maltese Falcon* and holds out a special prize to its hero. Marlowe says that he can't believe the cops are taking his word for how things happened. His hunch is right. It turns out that Anne has backed him up in his story. He muses aloud about Anne: a nice girl; too bad he had to kick her around. "And she probably thought I liked that blonde." All the while, who should be sitting there in the police station, hearing every word he says, but Anne herself? And as the film ends, these two are riding off together in a taxi, twined in each other's arms. Here is a rather less stark triumph than poor Spade's. And here suddenly, if one wants to take it, is a more obvious explanation than the one I offered above of why Marlowe has submitted to the rigors he has. I have omitted also a little passage between the two in which Anne for the second time begs Marlowe to quit. "You take some horrible satisfaction in seeing people torn apart, don't you?" she challenges. But he replies, "If you stick with a thing, Anne, it smacks you sooner and cleaner." One might say that he has refused to drop this case, and taken what he has, for Anne's sake, to cut her clear of the tangle—a prince eager to rescue Sleeping Beauty from the confusion caused by a wicked stepmother.

This conclusion is inserted in a number of films of this genre. In some, in fact, the girl for whom we are to suppose he has stuck it out is not the stepdaughter of the temptress but that central figure herself, the counterpart of Bridgid and of Velma. She turns out to be really just the victim of a spell, who has been waiting for the hero's kiss to wake. In *The Brasher Doubloon* (1947), in *The Big Sleep* (1946), in *The Lady in the Lake* (1947), the final embrace hints just such magic. *The Brasher Doubloon* ends as the hero picks up the telephone, about to accept another assignment, and this lady reminds him: her own case has not yet been solved. The telephone is returned to its hook and "It will be," he assures her, taking her in his arms. In *The Big Sleep,* the hero puts down the telephone after obliging the cops with the resolution of the case and the lady says, "You've forgotten one thing—me." "What's wrong with you?" he asks, pulling her toward him. "Nothing you can't fix," she assures him. *The Lady in the Lake* ends as the two start off for New York together. And the tickets are one-way, she informs him. "Scared?" one of them asks. "Sure, but it's a wonderful feeling," the other replies—for the spell in which she is caught is no longer a dark spell.

A certain doubt as to just how "one-way" a trip this hero could very well be taking intrudes itself if one stops to recall that the hero of all three films, though he's played each time by a different actor (George

Montgomery, Humphrey Bogart, Robert Montgomery, respectively),
is supposedly the one quite singular person: Philip Marlowe (who
was also the hero of *Murder, My Sweet*); whereas the ladies are
several. But there is more to belie the credibility of the ending than
this. It reverses everything that has set the drama in motion; it denies
the essential nature of the attraction this hero feels toward the lady
the moment he meets her and throughout the course of the film. In
Murder, My Sweet, Marlowe's relationship with Anne is actually
very similar to his relationship with Velma. At their first meeting, he
unmasks her roughly; at their third, he unmasks her again. A little
later (in a scene I skipped over), he kisses her, then draws back to
inquire, "Did you decide to be nice when you couldn't buy me off?" "I
think I'm wrong," he does add, and in each of these films remarks are
inserted that give some warning of the ending to be; but these remarks do little to disturb the real pulse of the film. What draws this
hero toward the girl is always precisely that she is, and he knows it,
deadly, a trick, a test—impossible to possess and death to those who,
once in her arms, forget it.

In the opening scene of *The Brasher Doubloon,* the basis of the
relationship between these two is clearly stated. A telephone call takes
the hero out one night to cover a new case. It is a nasty night and the
hero curses himself for going, but "I knew it was the voice of the girl
on the phone that got me," he tells us, narrating the story for us.
When he gets to the address he has been given, it is not that girl but
her employer who wants to talk with him—an unpleasant old woman
who wants him to recover a rare gold coin that has been stolen. She
will give him no pertinent information, however, and the hero is on
the point of refusing the case when an encounter with the girl decides
him to stick with it. The girl seems overeager to have him take the
case. Why, he begins to probe. What is the coin to her? And what is
the old woman to her—why does she jump so at her voice? Did she,
Merle, take the coin herself? "I don't know," Merle mumbles. "You
just don't remember!" he taunts her. Suddenly he spots a gun lying in
an open desk drawer. "Thinking of shooting someone?" he asks. He
starts to put a hand on her and she recoils as from a snake. "I just
don't like the touch of men," she explains—adding, however, "That
doesn't mean I wouldn't like to get over it." "We'll take it very slowly,
then," he tells her. And she can tell the old lady that he'll take the

case after all. As he leaves the house, "There was a bad taste in my mouth all the way back to the office," he says. "I couldn't figure the switches she pulled."

It is "the switches" she pulls, it is a bad taste in his mouth, which always "gets" this hero. This is very much so again in *Lady in the Lake*. In this film, Marlowe has submitted a story to a magazine chain and has had a letter from them asking him to come in. The letter is signed: A. Fromsett. The hero narrates the film this time with a difference: the camera gives us the action as if we were seeing it through his eyes—his own face appearing only occasionally in mirrors. "Maybe you'll get the answers to things quickly," he teases us first. "Do you think you will? You've got to watch them all the time." And he repeats in ominous tones the name: A. Fromsett. So we walk down the corridor into the offices of "True Horror," "Monster Stories," etc. and confront A. Fromsett—who turns out to be a lady (Audrey Totter). Miss Fromsett first pretends to Marlowe that she doesn't know where she's put his story. "It's underneath that magazine there," he informs her. She quickly begins to chatter about it then: Are there really detectives like the one he writes about, and is it possibly autobiographical? Quit being cute, he stops her. It's a private operator she's looking for today, isn't it, not a story. He's right, she confesses. She wants someone to locate her boss's wife, without his knowing. The wife is a terrible woman who has run off somewhere and must be found, because her boss wants a divorce. Marlowe stops her again. A tricky female, isn't she? Wants to knock off the wife so she can marry the boss herself—isn't that it? "You don't really need any help there, darling, not you," he tells her—and he'll take the case. He soon confides in us, "What I liked least about it was A. Fromsett." What he likes least about it and what has therefore involved him irresistibly.

In *The Big Sleep*, the lady's millionaire father hires Marlowe. He hires him to get rid of a blackmailer, but it becomes clear to the hero very soon that what he and a lot of other people really want is to learn the whereabouts of a certain Shawn Reagan, who had been the father's bodyguard. Marlowe soon finds the blackmailer—murdered—and soon after that the father sends word that he considers the case closed; but as Marlowe remarks to a friend, there's no law against working a case without a client. The millionaire has two daughters, "one wonderful, one not so wonderful," and Marlowe hints to his friend that it's for "Wonderful" that he is sticking with it. Here are the general outlines of his association with this wonderful girl: Her own father has described Vivien as "spoiled and ruthless." Her not-so-wonderful sister is not only spoiled and ruthless but a dope addict and a nymphomaniac, and Marlowe has quite a time with her too. In fact, the number of women whose lures he must survive in this film reaches comic proportions. But it is Vivien with whom he is chiefly matched. At their first meeting she tells him that he is a "mess," and she doesn't like his manners; he replies that he doesn't care for hers, either. She tries to pump him about what he's up to and he manages instead to extract certain information from her. In their next interview he manages to bluff her into telling him even more, and he has to hold onto her wrists hard to avoid getting slapped. Lightning and thunder outside the window accompany this duel between them. She pays him the next visit, to ask for his help in a certain matter. He challenges her story and soon proves it to be an elaborate lie. She tries to "sugar him off" the case then, and he responds with some merciless cross-questioning. "Wonderful," meanwhile, has been turning on her charms. What does he do when he's not working? Could it be stretched to include her? Marlowe stretches it, enters the lady's arms. "I liked that; I'd like some more," she suggests. But Marlowe ends a kiss with another sharp question, which catches her off guard. She very soon tries to trick him off the case with a report that Reagan has been found in Mexico. But Marlowe spots this as a lie too. And one evening, barely on his feet after a very thorough slugging received from the henchman of a certain gambler he's been keeping an eye on, he walks in on the gambler's hideaway, gets hit behind the ear with a fist full of ballbearings, and when he comes to finds "Wonderful" there in the enemy's midst, smiling. "Hello, angel," he says, smiling back. "I thought I'd find you here." It is from this point on that the film makes its turnabout: Marlowe, tied up, and left with "Wonderful" to guard him, tells her to come close, kisses her—as the music gets magic—and she gets a knife and cuts his bonds. When he has his final gun encounter with the gambler, she is there by his side; and when the truth is out we learn that she has been his adversary unwillingly, has been an innocent victim all along—victim of her not-so-wonderful sister. It is her sister who has caused Reagan to disappear—

she's shot him with her little gun. "Wonderful" had felt that she must share her sister's guilt. Marlowe magically releases her from this obsession.

In *The Brasher Doubloon,* Marlowe's adventure with Merle reduces itself to the same pattern: the "bad taste" in his mouth lasts through most the film. The second corpse he stumbles upon is crumpled over the gun which shot it, and this gun looks very much like the gun he had seen in Merle's desk. When he pays her a visit to confront her, she tells him her employer has just wired him that the case is closed—the brasher doubloon has been recovered. Marlowe is not interested in the wire, he lets her know. It lies, anyway: he has the coin himself, at this point. Merle soon returns his visit. Would he like her to tell him why she's come? "Yeah, then I can concentrate on the real reason." She wants the coin, she tells him. If he likes her, he'll help her. She likes *him* very very much. What about her little phobia, he asks. It responds very nicely to treatment, she tells him. And so he enters *this* lady's arms. But again he ends a kiss with a sharp question that takes her by surprise. He leaves the room to bring her a drink, and when he returns, there she stands pointing a gun at him—she wants that coin. He reminds her that she has told him she is fond of him. "That wouldn't stop me from shooting you," she tells him. He has to take the gun from her. The next corpse he finds has scratches up and down its arms that could only have been made by a woman's nails. And Merle is standing right there beside it. Then in the end it turns out not to have been Merle who killed any of these people. She too has been a helpless victim in the whole affair—victim, here, of the old woman, her employer, who has nearly succeeded in driving her insane, in making her believe that she *has* been a murderess. Again the hero has released her from delusion, and again it seems magic indeed.

The Lady in the Lake too proceeds from thrill to thrill, and one can call each new thrill essentially that of surprising the lady a further time at her tricks. Again he takes her in the lie, again he comes upon a scene of death and finds her insignia (here an initialed handkerchief). Each time, he lets her know that he knows: "You're just a nice clean campfire girl, aren't you? I know you!" At the end of this film, the turnabout effected is a supposed total reformation of the lady. She *had* been a tricky one, it is acknowledged, out to marry her wealthy boss by whatever means necessary. But "Everything is different now!" From now on she just wants to take care of him. "This is what the world is really like, isn't it?"

In each of these films, here is the essential dramatic progression: He perceives the deadliness of the lady at once and, to prove himself, takes her on. They contend with each other and, for all her wiles, he is able to resist her. One gesture sums it all up: the gesture in which he enters her embrace but then disengages himself and—not unmanned as others have been whom we have seen, but still himself— proceeds to disarm *her*. (This gesture in *The Lady in the Lake* is given a novel twist: "What would happen if I kissed you?" Marlowe asks Miss Fromsett—*we* ask her—and "Why don't you try and see?" she replies. So we step into the embrace: her eyes shut and her face swims toward us amorously. Then suddenly we back off, and her eyes snap open as we mock, "Do you always close your eyes for a kiss?"— and cut in quickly with a whole bombardment of questions we want her to answer.) Though each of the last three films manages to avoid the stark ending of *The Maltese Falcon*, in which Spade, disengaging himself from Bridgid's arms, turns in that motion to put her altogether from him—by delivering her up to the police; though the gesture of renunciation is cut short in these films, it remains essentially that same gesture.

Certain other films of this genre appear to offer us another explanation of why the hero "sticks it out": he has to revenge someone near or dear to him. This is so in *Calcutta* (1947), *Ride the Pink Horse* (1947), *The Blue Dahlia* (1946), *Cornered* (1946), and *The Glass Key* (1942). In the first two films his best friend has been murdered; in the next two, his wife; in the last, his boss has been framed for a murder. In each case the hero has decided to do his own investigating. For he is not invariably a private detective; he may simply adopt the role for a time. In *Calcutta*, he is a commercial pilot; in *Ride the Pink Horse*, *The Blue Dahlia*, and *Cornered*, he is a returned G.I.; in *The Glass Key*, he is a political henchman. One could say of him in any of these five films that he is just out to "square things" and that one doesn't have to suppose any more complicated motivation than that. But this explanation too proves at second glance inadequate.

In *The Maltese Falcon*, when Bridgid asked Spade, "Did Archer mean that much to you?" Spade told her, "You didn't do me a damn

Dick Powell in *Cornered* (1946).

bit of harm by killing him." He did add that a man wasn't supposed to sit around and let his partner be murdered. Avenging Archer constitutes one part of the challenge to his person that Spade feels bound to take up; but it can hardly be said to exhaust that challenge. The same is true for the heroes of these other films.

This is clear enough in each instance if one looks twice at the hero's relationship to the person to be avenged. In *The Blue Dahlia*, he feels no more love for his wife than Spade felt for Archer. Everything between them has "blown up in his face," and he has just walked out on her. In *The Glass Key*, everything has just blown up between the hero and his boss. In *Cornered*, he has no quarrel with his wife, but he has known her so briefly that he can't quite remember what she looked like. In *Calcutta*, there has been only a slight rift between the hero and his murdered pal—because of the latter's engagement—but the scenes about their friendship lack any spark at all and the film only comes to life when he meets the murdered man's fiancée—and faces the challenge of managing to survive the lady's charms himself. In *Ride the Pink Horse* too, the hero is supposed to have been fond of the friend, Shorty, who has been murdered. But it is clearly not this affection that really moves him now. Spade has mocked Archer, "You've got brains—yes you have." And the hero of this film is always making the point about Shorty that he had "no brains." He is clearly concerned above all to prove that *he does* have them. This is the heart of the relationship of each of these heroes to the person who has been destroyed. He sees in the other's destruction a doom that could threaten him as well, and he means to prove himself indestructible. In *The Glass Key*, when the hero walks out on his boss, he cries, "I'm tired of everybody outsmarting you!" His boss, who's a politician, is infatuated with the rich daughter of a reform candidate for some high post. To win her, he has decided to throw over all his former allies and back her father. He boasts that he practically has a key to the house now. "Yeah, a glass key," the hero mocks him. "Be careful it doesn't break off in your hand"—which of course it does. Soon after he's become engaged to the girl, he finds that he's been framed for the murder of her brother—and the person who has accused him turns out to be his beloved herself. The hero too is soon involved with this girl; in fact, he soon "has it bad" himself. But as he says to her when she asks him whether he doesn't want her, "It wouldn't make any difference if I did want you." [1] *He* is *smart.* And he survives.

There are certain late films in this genre, I should note, in which the survival of this hero is much more tenuous than in any of the films I have described so far. These films slightly alter the character of the hero. His chief task is to clear his name, for he is suspected of murder. Spade in *The Maltese Falcon,* recall, was under some suspicion of having killed Archer. In certain films—*Dark Corner* (1947) and *Dark Passage* (1947) are two examples—this suspicion is *the* crucial trial the hero must endure. And it is one he very barely does emerge from intact. The heroes of these films seem always on the verge of wavering into the lost-to-themselves characters of other chapters.

This hero is "framed" in deadly effective fashion—"easier than Whistler's mother"—and he cannot understand how. "I'm backed up in a corner and I don't know what's hitting me. Something's closing in on me, but I don't know what it is." He blacks out; he comes to, and a weapon is in his hands and a corpse is sprawled there by his side; and how it has all happened he doesn't know. He is not too sure of his ability to "keep his head up" and to find his way out of the dark. "Look at me," he mocks himself as his shaking hand lets a glass drop. "I'm a tower of strength! With nerves of steel!" In both *Dark Corner* and *Dark Passage,* though a temptress is included in the cast, the hero never becomes particularly entangled with her. There is no need for it. He is sufficiently "involved" already. The central female role here is that of a girl who stands by him through his ordeal. Hers is a role not unlike that of the heroine of the third chapter. Here too the hero tells her that she had better "do herself a favor" and "clear

---

[1] Here is another film that at the very end arranges a happy turnabout. It builds to the familiar gesture: the hero disengages himself from the girl's arms and soon afterward turns up at her house with a warrant for her arrest—for the murder she has been trying to pin on his friend. But suddenly her father confesses: *he* has done the killing, though accidentally. The hero has guessed it all along and accused the girl in order to "make the old man crack." He can now take the girl back into his arms again. *Calcutta,* for a change, allows the gesture of renunciation its follow-through. The lady in this film too has "really got under (the hero's) skin," but withdrawing from her embrace, he delivers her a swift relay of slaps that sit her down hard in a chair, and then turns her over to the cops on a murder charge—and doesn't take it back. And in *Ride the Pink Horse,* the hero puts the lady from him once and for all.

out." "If you're sharp, you'll get out now, fast," the hero of *Dark Corner* tells her. When she asks him what a certain person has "got" on him, "Nothing, and nobody has," he tells her, "and nobody's going to—you either . . . I'm as clean as a peeled egg," he boasts. And "now get out of here," he tells her again. But she won't. "I want to help you," she tells him. And as the curtain falls, "He hasn't asked me yet," she is telling a friend, "but I've told him. I'm bagging him for keeps." He'll hold his head up by himself, this hero has boasted; but by the end of the film the heroine has persuaded him—as that other heroine persuaded the sufferers of Chapter 3—that his pride, his wanting to play it "tough and lonely," is weakness. "You're sick," a girl cast in a minor role in *Cornered* tells that hero. "You're hurt so deeply that you don't trust anyone but yourself." The heroine of *Dark Corner* tells the hero, "I've cracked you wide open." She has indeed, for to trust no one but himself has been this hero's credo.

The alteration of this hero is effected, really, all too easily. He may be the most positive of all the figures I have described so far (and as such, by the way, the most lively of all these roles for an actor to play); but he remains an ambiguous character. All the questions asked him by other characters—who want to know which side he is on, what he is really up to—these questions are relevant, after all. Stare at this hero at the moment in which he is most himself, making the gesture of renunciation that most clearly defines him. Even this gesture is always a little ambiguous.

It is revealing to set up in perspective, behind this hero, not only the unhappy hero of Chapter 3 but the heroes of other chapters. It is appropriate, for example, to recall Sam, hero of *The Strange Love of Martha Ivers*. Sam withdraws himself from Martha's arms and from all the wealth that could have been his, in a gesture indistinguishable from the gesture I have just been tracing.[2] Sam's gesture is in one sense clear enough. It is clear that he is turning away from a corrupt offer. One can ask, however: does he turn away because he has

[2] Sam could very well be named the very "tough boy" with whom this chapter has been concerned. The film puts him through the familiar endurance test. I did not sketch his ordeal in full detail in Chapter 4. It includes the usual terrible physical battering: Martha's husband, afraid that Sam is out for blackmail, has his men pummel him black and blue and dump him twenty-five miles outside Iverstown; and Sam picks himself up and walks right back into town, asking for more trouble.

weighed the good and evil involved, or is he merely concerned to save his skin—seeing how risky it is to play with Martha? This hero is tough enough to resist the temptation of all those luxuries that Martha offers; it is easy enough to name him tough enough too to do without the luxury of believing in right and wrong.

There is another figure it is revealing to set by the side of this hero: Rick of *Casablanca*. These two heroes are very closely matched. The credo Rick announces corresponds exactly to Spade's credo, "There's me"—"I'm not fighting for anything any more, except myself." Rick is presented to us in cynical guise and the film proceeds then to reinterpret him for us more happily. One of the films I mentioned in this chapter, *Ride the Pink Horse,* labors for much the same kind of final rereading. Its hero, Gagin, blurs altogether with Rick. Here is the very same disillusioned warrior—or rather, here again is a man we judge from his talk to be that. Gagin declares that the war has been fought for the profiteers. One of them, a certain Hugo, has murdered his pal, and Gagin has come to Mexico to confront this man. He has a canceled check that is proof of Hugo's crooked dealings. He tells Hugo that he'll let him have the check for thirty G's. On the scene is a government agent who wants to bring Hugo to trial, and he needs that check as evidence; but Gagin responds to his appeals much as Rick responded to Lazslo in *Casablanca:* "I've seen enough of flags. Tell Uncle Sam to go take a walk for himself." In the end, in spite of all his bitter words, he hands over the check to the agent—forfeiting all the thousands he might have pocketed. But the gesture, again, remains ambiguous. Did he really have any choice, once the government man knew all about him? Gagin even jokes about this, himself: "A fat chance I had to collect, with you around," he tells the agent, as the two of them leave town together.

Questions hovered, of course, even over the final moment of *Casablanca*. Rick puts from him in a strong gesture not merely gold but Ingrid Bergman—sets her on a plane for America, where he can never follow. There is here something of the moment in which the hero of *The Big Sleep* and the hero of *The Brasher Doubloon* frees the heroine from a cruel enchantment, wakens her with a kiss to the sense of right and wrong which she has helplessly forgotten. Rick too puts "everything in order" here, and then he steps off into the night. A decisive moment. And yet—one can ask: where exactly is he stepping? Many of his doubles in other war films find it a relief in the end to annihilate themselves in battle. Even though the drama has been composed specifically around the task of answering the riddle of "what Rick will do and why," the question hovers still. The ending of *The Strange Love of Martha Ivers* is similar. Sam is headed West now, he's said. When the homeless girl he has befriended asks him what the West is like, he tells her, "Big." Big too is the choice that is open to us of what to name the life ahead of him, and what to name the spirit in which he sets forth. Rick, Sam, Spade—each of these figures wavers before our eyes, from light to dark, from positive to negative, from bold face to face of one who's "broken up inside." That decisive gesture of disengagement is a gesture, after all, strangely indistinct.

In studying that gesture, and in studying that final moment—as Rick stands watching Ilse's plane turn to a speck, as Sam turns away from Iverstown ("Don't look back!"), as Spade stands watching the descending elevator carry Bridgid out of sight—it is important to look at still another figure, in many ways a figure kin to these, and in whose gesture there is decidedly less ambiguity.

 8

"Maybe I know a way to get clear of the mess!" (the nihilists)

It was always "a bad taste in his mouth" that excited the hero of the past chapter to take on a lady, take on a job. The same may be said of the heroes of *Double Indemnity* (1944) and *The Postman Always Rings Twice* (1946). These heroes too go asking for trouble.

Walter Neff (Fred MacMurray), in the first of these films, is an insurance salesman. On his rounds one day he stops in at a big house covered with honeysuckle vines—"Murder sometimes smells like honeysuckle" he tells us, narrating the story. There he comes face to face—or person to person—with Phyllis Dietrichson (Barbara Stanwyck), a blonde for this picture, and a hot blonde. Neff eyes her hard, and she eyes him. He is there to check on her husband's insurance; but her husband is away, so he gives her his sales talk instead. Between bantering remarks, she lets drop a funny question or two about accident insurance, and she tells him to come back the next day when her husband will be there. And will she be there too? "Same perfume, same anklet?" he asks. "I wonder if I know what you mean," she says, and he, "I wonder if you wonder." When he comes back, her husband isn't there, of course, and it's also the maid's day off. She serves him iced tea, very ladylike. And she brings up that accident insurance again. She worries a lot about her husband, she says; and the trouble is he'd be hard to persuade to take out a policy for himself. Couldn't she perhaps take it out for him, without his knowing? And without the insurance company's knowing that he doesn't know, she means, doesn't she? And "You want to knock him off, don't you, baby?" he asks. She tells him to get out—"I think you're rotten!" He does— "You bet, baby!" "She didn't fool me for a minute," he tells us. ("I know you, babe.") "I stopped off at a drive-in for a bottle of beer . . . to get rid of the sour taste of her iced tea . . . I knew I had hold of a red hot poker," he tells us, "and the time to drop it was before it burned my hand off." But back in his room, the taste of her tea is still with him and "I was holding onto that red hot poker," he tells us. And he knows: "This wasn't the end between her and me. It was only the beginning."

When the bell rings, he knows who it is, and it is Phyllis all right. "You must never think anything like that about me, Walter!" And— his face a grimace—he walks into her arms. Over a bottle of bourbon, she tells him now how mean her husband is, and how he won't give her a divorce, and how sometimes, yes, she does wish he were dead, but Walter mustn't think that she would ever "do it." "Not if there's an insurance company in the picture, baby," he lets her know; for an insurance company always finds out. There's a guy up there at his office—a guy named Keyes. In three minutes he'd know it wasn't an accident. She begins to weep. "Just stop thinking about it," he tells her, and he takes her in his arms again. But "Maybe she had stopped thinking about it, but I hadn't," Neff tells us. For "It all tied up with something I had been thinking about for years . . . In this business . . . you're like the guy behind the roulette wheel, watching the customers to make sure they don't crook the house. And then one night you get to thinking how you could crook the house yourself and do it smart." ("There's me.") "And suddenly the doorbell rings and the whole setup is right there in the room with you . . ." And as she rises at last to go, "You're not going to hang, baby," he tells her, "because you're going to do it the smart way. Because I'm going to help you."

So this hero asks for it too; he too walks into the lady's arms, asking in that motion for all the rigors that follow. "That was it . . . The machinery had started to move," he says, "and nothing could stop it."

Frank (John Garfield) in *The Postman Always Rings Twice* is a guy whose "feet keep itching to go places"—until, hitchhiking along the California coast one day, he stops at a little hamburger joint and gas station and there comes face to face, person to person, with Cora (Lana Turner). Nick, the middle-aged Greek who runs the place, has left Frank to watch a hamburger on the grill while he's gone outside to give another customer gas—and Cora steps in, in a white playsuit, and gives Frank "that look." Frank forgets to watch. The hamburger burns itself black. He suddenly smells smoke. Nick has a "Man Wanted" sign out, and Frank goes out to him now to tell him that he'll take the job. "I'll tell my wife," says Nick, tossing the sign onto the incinerator—at which Frank starts to pluck the sign back out of the fire. But then he lets it drop again, stands there and lets it burn. This hero too knows well enough what he is "holding on to." His eye on Cora now is taunting. And she high-hats him in return, for any number of days. But the day comes when they move helplessly into each other's arms. Frank suggests that they run off together. But Cora wants to make something of herself; she won't be a tramp. "Aren't we ambitious!" says Frank. And again he knows: "Right then I should've walked out of that place." ("This is hopeless!") But he doesn't. One night he is lying in his little room and the door opens and it is Cora. "Do you love me?" she asks. "There's one thing we could do that would fix everything." "Like pray that something would happen to Nick?" he asks. "Something like that" she says. "I'm not what you think I am!" she wonderfully adds. "But I want to be something. I can't do it without love." This is it too. The machinery starts to move.

These heroes suffer now as long an endurance test as the heroes of the past chapter. From here on each successive moment inflicts its shock, and not to "go soft inside" is sweating labor. The two in *Double Indemnity* decide that the death shall be made to look like a fall from a moving train; for a double indemnity clause covers such an "accident"—they could collect twice the sum. The plan is for Neff to kill the husband in the car one night as Phyllis drives him to the station, then to board the train in his place and jump off the observation platform at a spot where Phyllis waits with the body, which they will leave on the tracks. First, of course, they have to trick the husband into signing the policy they want without reading it, and this isn't easy. But they accomplish it; everything is set—and then the husband breaks his leg and is not going to take the trip. There is the danger that he will find out about the policy he has "signed." Phyllis calls Neff at the office for advice and he has to give it to her in veiled casual words, with Keyes standing right there in the same room. Her husband is persuaded to take the trip anyway. The murder goes as planned, and Neff, on the murdered man's crutches, boards the train and hobbles back to the observation platform—to find a stranger sitting there, who will not leave. He has to think of a way to send him off. These crises, too many to detail, are nonstop. And the hardest thing for Neff to cope with is Keyes up there in the office; is talking over the case with him now and not showing anything; is facing Phyllis in his presence when she's called in for questioning. Meanwhile, Keyes begins to figure that something is wrong somewhere, and Neff and Phyllis dare not see each other much. And as it begins to look as if there's no chance of collecting, Phyllis grows nasty. Neff suggests that they had better "pull out" altogether, but "nobody's pulling out," says Phyllis. Now he begins to find out certain things about Phyllis's past and to guess that murder is an old game with her. The threat from this lady herself begins to grow—in familiar fashion. And through it all, Neff must try to "hold (himself) together."

In *The Postman Always Rings Twice*, the hero has to go through the nerve-racking act of murder twice, for the first attempt miscarries. Here he is actually brought to trial and barely escapes conviction. In place of the figure of Keyes looms the figure of the local D.A., suspicious of him early in the game and always trying to catch him off guard. And meanwhile the feeling that he cannot trust Cora grows, and for this hero too that is what makes it hardest for him to keep hold of himself. One day Cora declares in a jealous rage that she wants to see him in the death house and is going to give the D.A. the facts about him. "Take it easy; you're going to need *all* your strength now," she taunts him.

And each of these heroes begins to dream of a way out, "a way to get clear of the whole mess." These films too feature the gesture of disengagement, the gesture through which the hero stands at last clear of it all, "clean as a peeled egg."

The hero of *Double Indemnity* calls up the lady and makes an appointment to see her late at night, alone, at her place. And "I guess I don't have to tell you what I was going to do," he tells us. A guy named Zachette has been dropping in to see her a lot lately. Neff reckons now that her plan has always been to brush him off as soon as she had her hands on the money; and no doubt she's counted on Zachette to "take care of" him. "Then somebody else would have come along to take care of Zachette." But Neff has his own plans. Keyes has begun to suspect Zachette. Later this very evening, Zachette is headed for the house to see Phyllis, and the cops will be behind him. Which all fits nicely. Neff has a gun in his pocket and he's "getting off the trolley car right at this corner"; he's "got another guy to finish (his) ride for" him. He walks in and "Hello, baby," he says. He tells her what he's been thinking about her—"That's the way you operate, isn't it, baby?" And he tells her his plan ("I won't play the sap for you"). "This is goodbye," he tells her, and "it's you that's going, baby." When she begins to protest, he cuts in with "That's cute. Say it again." The window is open and music from a radio down the street drifts in. "I don't like this music any more," he tells her. "Do you mind if I shut this window?" And he crosses and shuts the window and draws the curtains and turns.

And now the film manages an ending that one could call the reverse of any of the endings in the past chapter. As he turns, there stands Phyllis with a gun in *her* hand. And she quietly shoots him. And then he shoots her, dead; and not quite dead himself yet, drags himself off to the office, where he gasps his story into the dictaphone, for Keyes' ears, before collapsing. (It is to Keyes, not to us, strictly speaking, that this tale is told.) And one could say that he has failed to get "clear of the mess"—could say that frustration takes the place here of the triumph the hero of the past chapter managed to wrest. But a less superficial reading of the scene than the one I have just given diminishes the difference and reveals this ending too as triumphant—the music here, too, behind the scenes, exultant if groaning.

As he stands there at the window, Phyllis calls to him in a strange low voice. And he turns. And there she stands with a gun in her hand. And she fires. He stops, motionless, gazing at her, and then begins to move toward her slowly. "Why don't you shoot me again?" he asks her. "Maybe if I came a little closer. How's that?" But she just stands there, and he takes the gun out of her hand—she is meek now, staring at him strangely. "Don't tell me . . . you've been in love with me all this time," he says. And "No, I never loved you, Walter," she tells him, "not you or anybody else . . . I used you, just as you said. That's all you ever meant to me—until a minute ago. I didn't think anything like that could ever happen to me." And "I'm sorry, baby, I'm not buying," he says. But "I'm not asking you to buy; just hold me close," she says. And he does. He takes her in his arms and she presses her lips against his in a sort of bliss. And *he* stares at *her* now strangely, stares at her in a new way. And "Goodbye, baby," he breathes—very gently now—and the gun explodes again. She swoons in his arms, dying. Tenderly he gathers her up and puts her down upon the sofa, gazing down at her.

And something has "happened" here to these two—something new. Love has been born in that dark room. The encounters between these two have always been harrowing encounters, each rending the other. But here at last, when they have succeeded in rending from each other life itself, here at last their long mutual ordeal is rewarded, they earn Bliss, they earn Peace.

Peace is tasted twice in this film, in fact; this final Grace is redoubled. Neff, putting his hand inside his coat now, and feeling the blood there beginning to spread, hurries from the house and down to his office, for a last interview with the other person who has been his intimate and his adversary throughout the film: Keyes. Here, actually, the film has opened—as his car rockets up to the curb and he, teeth clenched, sweating profusely, makes his way to the dictaphone at his desk, there to begin his story: "Dear Keyes . . ." Now he sits there, limp from the exertion of telling it, and the bloodstain on his jacket spread wide—and Keyes enters. The janitor, sensing something wrong, has sent for him, and he has been standing outside the door for several minutes—"long enough," he tells Neff. "You're all washed up, Walter," he breathes with a sort of passionate sadness. Neff declares that he's going to make a try for the border, and he, Keyes, will give him a few hours' leeway, won't he? But "You'll never make the border," Keyes tells him. "Watch me," says Neff and starts for the elevator, but his knees buckle, he sags to the floor. Keyes comes and kneels beside him. "How you doing, Walter?" And, smiling, Neff looks up at him. "You know why you didn't figure this one, Keyes?

Let me tell you," he says. "The guy you were looking for was too close. He was right across the desk from you." "Closer than that, Walter," says Keyes—as the eyes of the two meet. "I love you too," says Walter. He fumbles for a last cigarette, cannot get a match lit, and Keyes gently performs this office for him as the scene fades out. A second time, Love has descended, like Grace, joining *these* two in a tender exalted moment.

The film closes to a thrill of music. For the fact that he *is* all washed up, that he stands clear of life itself now—and the ambitions and desires that afflict one in life—is this hero's relief.

The note that closes *The Postman Always Rings Twice* is the same. These two lovers too arrange a rendezvous together. And maybe they can be happy again, *"maybe I know a way,"* one of them breathes. He takes her down to the beach where they used to swim together in the early days of their passion for each other. And let's swim way out, way way out so that we can barely get back, one says. So they swim out beyond the surf, out toward the horizon, until finally, treading water there under the blank of the sky, "This is far enough," one says. And all hate and all vengefulness has left them. She tells him that if he doesn't trust her, he can swim back to shore without her now, for she's tired and couldn't make it back by herself. But he gathers her in his arms and swims back with her. "Are you sure now?" "I'm sure." They roar along the shore road together in his car. When they get home, there will be kisses "that are from life, not death," he says. "I've been waiting a long time for that kiss." And all of a sudden—he is looking at her, not at the road—he runs the car into a fence. And Cora is dead. And Frank will soon follow her, for the D.A. has been waiting for something like this. The jury is out only five minutes. Frank is condemned to the chair.

If one wanted to be literal, one could call their final destruction accidental, call the automobile crash an ironic wrecking of the happiness they have just found out there beyond the surf. But for anyone watching this film who is caught up in the drama, the two events together compose one image—the meeting of hearts at last out there where the shore has been left behind, and the meeting of hearts in death, one meeting. There will be kisses now "that are from life, not death," says Frank; but even before we see the fence rushing toward us, his words sound in our ears with the ring of paradox: life, we have sensed, can only be found when it has been left behind—there is true happiness for us only when we have passed beyond *that* surf.

There is even a little scene in this film comparable to the scene between Keyes and Neff. Frank has been talking with a priest, because he is distressed at the thought that he is to die for killing *her*. But the D.A. enters and tells him: he's not going to the chair for killing Cora but for killing Nick. An undelivered letter has been found, a letter Cora had written to him just before their reconciliation, saying that she was going to run off somewhere forever. And "it was a very beautiful letter, Frank," the D.A. tells him—written by a girl who loved a man very much. But it contained just enough of a confession to convict him of Nick's death. So it's not for killing *her!* cries Frank. And "No, laddie," the D.A. tells him—a gentleness about him that is new. And Frank asks the priest—asks all of us now—to send up a prayer for him and Cora. "Make it that we're together, wherever it is." The note is again one of Grace earned, all that long torment they have asked for at last rewarded, quietus given, Love descending to transfigure the scene. Murder has become an irrelevance. For it is precisely out of the ruins of all that is earthly that Peace is seen to be born.

If one turns back to the beginnings of these two films, one can see that just this final victory is tasted in advance by the hero. This is the promise contained, for Neff, in the "sour taste" of Phyllis's tea, for Frank in the taste of smoke as Cora stands before him—the whole story a story of the quest for this promise, a breathless intent walk into this vivifying death.

The victory wrested by this hero and the victory wrested by the hero of the past chapter are, literally speaking, far from the same— the one fulfilled in death, the other boasting that he is still alive—and yet the two are very close. Look again at Spade at the end of *The Maltese Falcon*, as he puts from him not life itself but, of what is earthly, everything for which he feels desire, everything that "all of" him wants—it is a death of sorts. One cannot quite ascribe to him that pure nihilist delight one can ascribe to Neff, to Frank—a delight that negates this life and its values altogether. And yet this shadow certainly touches him. In weighing what he is, it is necessary to know this other figure.

The shadow of this other figure falls too across all those other heroes whom I have described. Again and again one can discern in them this death-seeking gesture. It is easy to discern, of course, in the war hero. The obvious burden of the dream which features him is to annul the gesture.[1] This is clearly, too, the labor the heroine of Chapter 3 performs. Many films can be said to invite us to thrill to the possibility that the gesture may attain its end. In a film like *Love Letters*, when Singleton begins to pry into the past, or *Spellbound*, when Ingrid makes the hero ski with her down the slope where Edwardes died—we are told that the heroine is seeking a new chance in life for them both, and supposedly we are hoping against hope for this, but the thrill the moment actually holds for us is the thrill of the possibility that they may both be destroyed. In most such instances, this thrill is unacknowledged and it is cut short before its proper climax; the alternate satisfaction of the more orthodox happy ending is substituted at the last. Therefore, films like *Double Indemnity* and *Postman*, that allow the theme its natural culmination, light up these other films for us.

Even in *Double Indemnity* and *Postman*, of course, much is veiled. One could give a literal synopsis of *Postman* and call the death of the two lovers an accident. One could make the same sort of synopsis of *Double Indemnity* and deny that Neff *meant* to walk to his death that night when he walked into Phyllis's darkened house. We who are in the audience see her slip a gun under her pillow before he enters but—to be literal—he does not.[2] And when Neff leaves that house, an episode is inserted that I have omitted: He meets Zachette on his way to visit Phyllis and carefully sends him away, so that the police *won't* find him there. He hands him a nickel and sends him off to phone Phyllis's stepdaughter Lola. "She loves you," he informs him. It is this very nice girl whom Zachette really loves, but Phyllis has managed to estrange them. One can take it that Neff then goes off to make his confession so that Zachette will be cleared and the two lovers can be happy—take it that we are witnessing the triumph of Neff's better nature. And yet one is not really moved to take it that

[1] Or to rename it an act of heroism.
[2] However, identifying with the hero as we tend to (for he is narrating the story), we tend also to transfer to him our own breathless anticipation of her using it. And as narrator, of course, he does know well enough what he is walking into. From the very start of this film we move with the hero toward a known fatality.

way. If in these films too, as in so many others, certain gestures are blurred, at least they are allowed to complete themselves, and the pattern comes clear enough.

The characters in *Double Indemnity* and *Postman* should also be set next to the heroes and heroines of the chapter dealing with stories of success. Cora in *Postman* wants "to *be* something"; in *Double Indemnity* they're going to "do it smart." One could classify the stories of these two films in a sense as stories of success that manage in a special, a perverse way to quiet the final dolorous cries I recorded throughout Chapter 4. Actually the characters in some of the success stories in that chapter manage to win a strange peace not too dissimilar to the one I have been describing here. Think of Martha and Walter in *The Strange Love of Martha Ivers*. When all their earthly hopes were stripped from them, an ecstatic tranquil love suddenly blossomed between *those* two—perhaps that strange love to which the title refers. When I described *Rhapsody in Blue, Incendiary Blonde,* and *Humoresque,* all of which have unhappy endings, I did not specify in what sense the dream granted an audience relief; but it is again in just this peculiar sense. *Rhapsody in Blue* ends with an outdoor memorial concert for Gershwin. Julie is in the audience, and as the music mounts, her face begins to register bliss. The camera begins to climb, off off into the air; and now that the earth has been left far below, we somehow feel, the souls of Gershwin and Julie can at last meet. One feels (if one lets oneself be carried away) much the same assurance in *Incendiary Blonde* when Tex marches off down the long blank hospital corridor toward her death. And *Humoresque* grants such feelings full scope. The night of John Garfield's big concert, Joan Crawford phones him from their beach house. "It's so quiet here . . . There's a smudge of smoke almost at the horizon . . . I wish I were on board that boat," she cries, "so far out that we couldn't see anything but sky and water, nothing more . . ." "I love you!" she cries, and when they have hung up and the strains of his concert begin to swell over the radio (*Tristan* it is, conveniently), she runs down to the beach—the music, of course, still reaching us—and into the waves. A huge wave curls right over our heads, thrillingly. Just before the concert she has visited Garfield's mother, who has ordered her not to marry him. The mother hasn't gone to Joan, Joan has gone asking for this. She has stared into the mother's dark forbidding eyes

Joan Crawford and John Garfield in *Humoresque* (1947).

with much the same eagerness with which she stares into the dark waves before she enters them—the mother, one could say, like Keyes for Neff, like the D.A. for Frank, a convenient obstacle, convenient Doom, against which to break her life.

The peculiar satisfaction offered by such endings[3] can be summed up, perhaps, in the image on which a third film opens, worth describing here: *Duel in the Sun* (1946). Like other films of its kind, this film grants us a preview of the fatality toward which we then breathlessly move. The camera poises above a desert landscape, slowly descends. "Deep among the lonely sun-baked hills" of Texas, far from any human dwelling, a voice informs us, at the site of a great weather-beaten stone known as Squaw's Head Rock—"time cannot change its impassive face"—two wild young lovers held a final fatal rendezvous. The two were never to be seen again. There, we gather, they destroyed each other. But, we are told—and the voice of the narrator takes on a hushed tone—out of the desolate crags, at that very spot where their lives were spilled, a wild blossom has sprung, a flower known nowhere else. The camera reverently approaches the little blossom, before cutting us back to the beginnings of the story. This is precisely the perverse promise each of the films in this chapter holds forth: out of the dissolution of lives, of living hopes, there blossoms something wondrous and rare.

Duel in the Sun offers us this rare satisfaction with more gusto than any of those other films I described. Its heroine seeks it out more hungrily than any of those other heroes and heroines. Pearl Chavez (Jennifer Jones) is a half-breed girl, the daughter of Herbert Marshall and a no-good Creole woman who is the poor man's undoing: she provokes him into murdering her and he is hanged. "One thing at least is certain: this life flies." But before he is led away, "Listen to me, darling," he says to Pearl; she must go to live with his cousin, Laura Belle McAnles, a great lady (whom he had *wanted* to marry), and Laura Belle will make a lady of her too. "Promise . . ." So Pearl goes to live on the McAnles ranch. Laura Belle has two sons: Jesse (Joseph Cotten), a fine and honorable youth, and Lewt (Gregory

---

[3] *Humoresque* does not quite end on this note, I should add. It strikes another, alternate note. Garfield himself, at the last, emerges from a very similar mood to declare that he intends to carry on, to keep working. This alternate note is sounded too, of course, in *Martha Ivers,* as Sam and his girl turn their faces away from Iverstown.

Peck), another no-good. Jesse would like to help Pearl to be like Laura Belle. Lewt is not interested in the project. One can tell what Lewt is from the first look he gives her—sitting on his big horse and grinning down at her. And her first night there he walks into her room and takes a kiss. The camera features the advance across the room of his slim legs, spurs jingling—that jingling exaggerated for us into an interminable sound: Here is Doom. "I hate you," she yells, of course, and pulls out a handful of his hair, and spits after him as he leaves. But the next morning when he dares her to ride his horse bareback, she quickly enough accepts the dare. He gives the animal a great slap and off it bolts and soon has bucked her to the ground; and Lewt is standing over her—spurs jingling—as she writhes there in pain. "Maybe him and me ain't your style," he suggests. But "Let me ride him more!" she asks right off. When he suggests a milder animal, "I like this one," she says. It is clear enough what he likes. (In *Humoresque,* soon after the two lovers meet, they go out horseback riding and that heroine too is thrown and when the hero runs to her writhes up out of this hurt into their first embrace.) The image of a hurt suffered is not irrelevant. The passion contracted here is a wound received, fatal and precious—precious because fatal. The slow death now ensues, the sweet rending, long drawn out.

The film soon features a violent scene of rape, with an electric storm for accompaniment (and of course the intolerable jingling of Lewt's spurs). And now there is double rending for the heroine. Jesse walks in on them. And now Jesse would never marry Pearl. He is leaving the ranch (because he has quarreled with his father) and "I might as well say it," he reveals to her, "I loved you . . . Somehow you touched me . . . I was going to come back for you some day." "Oh, I never knew! . . . You'll forget, won't you?" she begs. But "No, I don't think I'll forget," he says. Married to Jesse, she could have become a lady like Laura Belle! "Trash trash trash trash!" she sobs.

Now she asks Lewt to marry her. But "No woman is going to tie onto me," he tells her, "least of all a little half-breed like you." So to show him, she becomes engaged to Sam Pearce. But "She's got another man's brand on her," Lewt lets Sam know—and shoots him dead. Lewt must leave too now; he is an outlaw. But by night he drops in on Pearl whenever he feels like it. "I'm going to kill you,

Lewt McAnles," she tells him. But he just walks up to her, spurs jingling, and takes the pistol out of her hand. She asks him again to marry her, or at least to let her go away with him. He knocks her to the floor for that. When she hangs onto his boots, dragging across the floor after him, he kicks her off, leaving her bruised and bawling.

And now Laura Belle dies; and the chances of any sort of life for Pearl seem for a while to die with her. But there must be more to rend from the girl than this; the sweet torment of this story must be protracted further. So Jesse turns up again, with a wonderful offer. He is married by now to a lovely girl named Helen. "And I told Helen long ago that I wanted to get you out of here," he says. "She's a lady, ain't she?" Pearl asks. "Like you're going to be," he tells her. She's going to come and live with them and learn to embroider, to waltz, to make small talk. Or does she love Lewt? "I hate him!" she cries. So Jesse takes Pearl away. But of course Lewt hears about it. He sends his messenger to Jesse. Let him come out and meet him in the street. Jesse walks out, unarmed, to meet his brother, and Lewt shoots him down. Jesse doesn't die. "And you *will* come to live with us, won't you?" his wife asks Pearl. But then Lewt sends his messenger to Pearl. He'll get Jesse the next time, he says. Now he's going to hightail it for a while and if she wants to kiss him goodbye, let her meet him at Squaw's Head Rock.

The time has come for the final interview between these two. Pearl travels on horse now for two days, under the terrible glare of the desert sun. Hairy lizards creep across her path, bleached bones strew the way. She travels far far out into this desert land, until she reaches that nowhere on which the film opened—nothing there but sky and sand and the great impassive face of Squaw's Head Rock. ("So far out that we couldn't see anything but sky and water"—way way out, beyond the surf, so far that we can barely get back.) There she fires two shots into the air, and Lewt springs up on a rocky hillside, facing her. She takes aim and fires at him. And yelling curses, from cover now, the two begin to exchange shots, under the fiery sun. This final scene is protracted as in none of those other films—and in technicolor: blood, when it spurts at last, is lurid red for us. She doubles up first, clutching herself, and spilling blood on the sandy ground. But she creeps on forward, fires again; and up on his rock *he* staggers—"You got me that time." "You're lying like you always do," she yells. But

"There's no use lying . . . I can't shoot no more, honey, honest," he calls to her. "I'm through!" And "Ain't you coming up?" he calls. She drops her gun and, gasping, starts to climb the cliff to where he lies. For now at last it has happened to *these* two. Never has the word "love" been spoken between them—only the word "hate," endlessly; but now as their blood begins to spill from them, as life is left behind, now "I love you, I love you!" they call to each other. She clambers up the sandy cliff. The sand is loose and she slides back, again and again, and feverishly must reclimb. (We *wait* for that sweet quietus in this film.) But at last, inchingly, she reaches the top and drags herself across to him, and at last their blood-red mouths, in technicolor, meet; and as they swoon away, the camera lifts up, off off into the air, the earth left far below, this life at last thrillingly exploded.

9

"You can't kill me—this is the end of the picture" (some comic heroes)

The sweet release of seeing everything go to pieces is granted in certain other films too—but granted in terms rather different from those described in the past chapter. The Grace that descends to mark the hero's final moments is not invariably Love. Here, for example, is *The Treasure of the Sierra Madre* (1948):

Three tramps set out to look for gold in the hills of Mexico. One of them, Walter Huston, is an old man who's been "scrambling over mountains" looking for gold before; and he has found it in his time. He predicts at the start how this will all end. Why is he dressed in these rags? "That's gold." He's seen what it does to men. But will he go with them to look for it again? "Of course I'll go." The story takes just the course he has persuaded us—if not his companions—to anticipate. The three set forth "a noble brotherhood," but out in the hills this brotherhood dissolves. They strike their gold; the pile, as the two have dreamed, grows bigger and bigger and they start home—"Goodbye, mountain! Thanks!" But before they find home again, one of them (Tim Holt) has been shot and left for dead by one of the others, who walks off with the treasure; that other (Humphrey Bogart) has been murdered by bandits; and the gold has been thrown out by the bandits—mistaken for sand: when Huston and Holt (who's not quite dead, after all) reach the old ruins where the bandits spilled it from its little sacks, it is a faint glint blowing in the air. The two stand for a moment staring at the blown litter of sacks, staring at the ground and into the wind—and then Huston begins to laugh. He sits and leans his back against a bit of broken wall and laughs and laughs and laughs. "It's gone back to where we found it! . . . A great joke that's been played on us!" Roaring still, his laughter an echoing explosion among the ruins, "It's worth ten months of suffering and trouble, this joke is!" he cries. Again, at the other side of frustration, a rare gift is granted. But this time the miraculous flower is not love but laughter.

The joke here may well be called a very special one. And yet here is, in essence, the joke at the heart of all the comedies of this period. In all of them, laughter comes as everything that has been given is taken away again. The laugh always comes among ruins.

As in the past chapter, one's pleasure is in seeing that which is frantically sought, and sometimes almost grasped, elude the seeker. The subject of an animated cartoon short, for example, is usually the pursuit of one hectic small animal by another—cat after mouse or bird, dog after cat, spider after fly, wolf after sheep, ad infinitum. Over and over the pursuer catches up with his intended meal. He has him sitting on his plate, garnished and seasoned to taste. As he bites down, the expected mouthful escapes him. Closing his mouth on emptiness, the poor beast frequently knocks his teeth together so hard that they spill out (*Flirty Birdy,* 1948, *Uninvited Pests,* 1947). Or the quest is for a kiss. The laugh comes as, for example (in *Flirty Birdy*), the little bird, hopelessly enamored of a cat in bird disguise, swoops at it, and when it ducks, kisses away all the bricks of the chimney behind it. (Recall the passage from Disney's *The Three Caballeros* in which Donald Duck attempts to close in on one elusive female vision after another.) Or the film may show a dog trying to quiet a faucet's dripping, so that he can get some sleep (*Malice in Slumberland,* 1942). He ends by tampering so violently with the plumbing that the whole house is lifted into the air on a geyser.

In slapstick shorts which feature live comedians—the Three Stooges, Edgar Kennedy, Andy Clyde, El Brendel, and others—frustrations like this are duplicated. In *His Wedding Scare* (1943), El Brendel, who is on his honeymoon, tries in vain to get to kiss his wife. At the reception, too many admirers crowd around her to claim kisses for themselves. "Susie! Susie!" he calls, but he can never reach her. On the train for Niagara Falls, thinking himself alone with her at last, he lunges forward with puckered lips—but lands the kiss on the porter, who happens to be passing through. And when the conductor arrives, he turns out to be a former husband: Susie falls into his arms with joy, to reminisce. At the hotel, another former husband material- izes. In desperation, Brendel sets out with Susie for a little island in the middle of the sea. Again he puckers his lips for that kiss—when a submarine surfaces and "Yoohoo, Susie!" cries a man from the deck. Brendel holds his nose and jumps into the sea. Or three actors are desperate to find a job (the Three Stooges in *Rhythm and Weep,* 1946). They have just been thrown out of their twenty-sixth theater. They climb up to a roof top to end it all—having relieved some of their feelings first by assaulting each other—when they hear music and see an old man seated up there at a piano. He introduces himself as an unhappy millionaire who has to sneak up here to play because his family won't let him play at home. And he's just composed a musical, but he can't find the right actors for it. The Three Stooges of course offer themselves. But he can pay them only a thousand a week, he deplores. They accept his terms. And they run through a rehearsal of the show for him. The little old man is wild with delight. He's going to double their salaries. They, in turn, are wild with de- light—utter the beastly squeals in which these three comedians spe- cialize. "The way I'm throwing my money around, I bet you think I'm crazy!" says the little old man—and explodes in maniac laughter as an attendant hurries up to take him back to Dr. Dippy's Retreat. The three knock their heads against the walls, hit themselves on the heads with sandbags, shaken with the same horrid laughter them- selves.

In full-length comedies it is the same. In any of the pictures featur- ing Bob Hope and Bing Crosby—*Road to Morocco* (1942), *Road to Utopia* (1946), *Road to Rio* (1947)—Hope and Crosby, in lively competition (these two count fingers after shaking hands with each other), seek riches, and also the favors of a lady who is always Dorothy Lamour. The laugh comes as the riches and Lamour prove unattainable. Or perhaps one of them wins both riches and the lady, but once he has them no longer wants them. In *Road to Morocco*, Lamour is a princess. The one who marries her will share her kingdom. Hope wins her hand—and then discovers that she has only said yes because the court astrologer has seen in the stars that the first man she marries will die violently within a week. So he offers his place to Crosby.

We laugh, however, not simply at the individual venture which comes to nothing. We laugh as a total world explodes before our eyes. At the end of *Road to Morocco*, Hope and Crosby are on board a freighter headed back to New York with Lamour. Their rivalry has revived when it has turned out that the astrologer saw not the conjunction of stars he thought but a couple of flies stuck in his telescope. But before either could marry her, an amorous sheik ran off with her into the desert. They have recovered her and are headed back home— when Hope lights a cigarette in the powder room (misunderstanding the sign on the door) and the whole ship goes up. In the last shot of the film, as they sit somewhere in tatters, "You ruined the only good scene in the movie," Bing rebukes Bob. With that remark, the very framework of the reality we have supposedly been witnessing is exploded: nothing at *all* remains. An ending like this is frequent in cartoons. In *The Three Caballeros*, a little gaucho narrates the story of the race he won with a winged donkey. At the very last, as he is reaching for the bag of gold that is the prize, he is suddenly dragged off into the air by the donkey. And "Neither he nor I was ever heard of again," he informs us. In *No Mutton fer Nuttin'* (1944), a wolf has finally captured the sheep who has been eluding him; he ropes him to the platter and is about to take the knife to him when the sheep comments, "You can't kill me. You ain't got time. This is the end of the picture."

This delirious bursting of the bounds of the world we have been assuming is not reserved for the end in these comedies. The film may open with some little creature crying, "Do all spook pictures have to begin this way? Oh no no no!" (*The Fly in the Ointment*, 1943). In the course of a film a character may address the camera, "You might as well move on; I don't move from here all through da pitcha" (*The Shooting of Dan McGoo*, 1946), or he may threaten the audience with a gun because, presumably, someone won't sit down and keeps bobbing a shadow upon the screen (*Daffy Duck and Egghead,* 1946). "Lay you six to one that we meet Dorothy Lamour," Bing sings at the start of *Road to Morocco,* and references of this sort punctuate those *Road* pictures. In *Road to Rio,* Lamour plays the part of a certain Lucia. Questioned about Lucia's ability to sing, Bean Belly (Crosby) remarks, "If she looks like Lamour, she can sing like Lamour, can't she?" And casual allusions are often made to her role in the earlier film which brought her fame: *Jungle Princess* (1936). A huge jungle cat crouches by her throne in *Road to Morocco;* in *Road to Utopia,* one of the men gazes at her against a background of snow and murmurs, "She doesn't seem to belong"—and suddenly the familiar tropical background fades in: Lamour stands there again in her sarong.

But these comedies find a hundred varied ways, often doubled one upon another, to demolish before our eyes—in the name of laughter —all that has stood there the moment before. The demolition may be as literal as the explosion of the ship in *Road to Morocco.* It may be a matter of suddenly reversing some dramatic statement the film has just made. "Come with us to beautiful old Switzerland, land of peace and quiet," simpers the narrator in *Dear Old Switzerland* (1945)— and a great racket of yodeling interrupts him. Or the very laws of the physical universe are shattered. In *The Screwy Truant* (1944), a truant officer pup, to be inconspicuous, crosses a bit of lawn one piece of body at a time: leg, arm, nose . . . The truant he seeks, screwy Squirrel, to thwart the pup, pulls a pool of water from under him as though it were a rug. At the end of a Three Stooges film, *Idle Roomers* (1944), the three, trying to elude a wolfman loosed in their hotel, shut themselves by mistake into the same elevator with him. He takes over the controls, and in the final shot the squealing four of them are shooting skyward in the elevator cage, gravity left behind. In any Three Stooges film, the laws of nature are violated again and again. A foot is twisted around and around, then spins back as though it were only a mechanical thing. A man barks like a dog. A baby belches like a man. A whole series of shorts called *Speaking of Animals* specializes in animal shots with lip movements dubbed in, the animals made to talk—and say ridiculous things. Or perhaps it is a former cultural era that is demolished. *Flicker Flashbacks* specialize in ridiculing our early movies. Or a cartoon may turn the world of some familiar fable topsy-turvy (*Red Hot Riding Hood*, 1943, and *Nursery Crimes*, 1943).

The subtitle which Chaplin appended to *Monsieur Verdoux* could be applied to all these comedies: it is A Comedy of Murders.

The accusation was leveled against *Monsieur Verdoux* that murder is not funny. Many of these films that call themselves comedies are very barely so. The line between the laughter they evoke and an outcry of pain or hysteria is a thin one. It is a very thin line, for example, as we watch one of the Three Stoogers have his foot twisted around and around, or watch another one of them receive an electric shock and drop to the ground in a spasm, his companions trying to relieve him by sticking screwdrivers and electric bulbs in his ears. Or as we watch Edgar Kennedy in *Rough on Rents* (1942) ask some tenants to end a wild party, and then see them tear most of the clothes off him and stampede out, trampling him underfoot. The laughter wrung from one who sits watching such humor tends to be all too akin to the blubbering into which Edgar Kennedy dissolves or the squawl of maniac laughter which shakes the Three Stooges: the laughter of one who at last gladly surrenders his senses, quite literally just lets himself go. This is the laughter of Donald Duck in *Clown of the Jungle* (1947). He has been trying to photograph jungle birds and—"Oh boy!"—he has sighted many lovely shots, but each time the mischievous aracuan bird has thwarted him—upset his tripod or jigged in front of his subject or entangled Donald in lengths of celluloid. Donald erupts finally into helpless squawks, blubbering his lips with his finger, running distracted in his tormentor's wake. The familiar foundering squawks of Donald Duck might, in fact, be said to epitomize the laughter of which I speak. It should be noted that these squawks of his have altered over the years. In an early Disney like *Mickey's Band Concert* (1935), Donald was a figure who could survive any cataclysm, unmuffled and only a little ruffled. His squawks in those days proclaimed that ability. Today they seem to say simply: I give it all up!

If this is the laughter that sounds most often through these comedies, it is not the only laughter, however. If the most frequent image in these comedies is that of the hapless victim of a world that falls asunder, another character does make an appearance. Donald Duck epitomizes the one character; the little redheaded aracuan bird featured in various films with him epitomizes the other. And insofar as we laugh with *this* character, our laughter is of a different sort; for his relation to the same world is a special one.

This little bird has already been introduced briefly. He was Donald's tormentor in *Clown of the Jungle.* He appeared in *The Three Caballeros*—in which he placed that final one-too-many twig that collapsed the nest of another little bird. But my description of him so far has been slighting. Here is our first sight of him in *Clown of the Jungle.* The film is mimicking a travelogue and a narrator with honeyed voice has already introduced us to various rare birds. He tells us "a treat awaits us behind every twig and vine," and the panning camera suddenly frames the aracuan: an ugly little bird with a spray of red hair in disorder and dressed in an abbreviated nightshirt out of which skinny arms and legs protrude. He is stretched out languorously upon a branch, one leg crossed upon the other, one arm behind his head, dandling a yoyo. And here is our first sight of him in *The Three Caballeros:* Donald is watching still another film about rare birds. A scissortail bird has just snipped off another bird's pompadour; Donald's shadow, bobbing on the screen, has startled a third bird; then two toucans with clumsy beaks have had trouble kissing each other and one has tumbled off the branch into a pool. "What's that?" Donald suddenly cries from the audience—and around and around the poor toucan who flounders in the water we see the little aracuan circling, with a casual backstroke. His lack of concern is sublime. With a similar hauteur, soon after, he places that final twig on the nest of the little "craftsman" bird and watches it fall into bits.

At the very end of *The Three Caballeros,* Donald Duck collides with a toy Mexican bull and the scene explodes into fireworks. Donald is seen mounting with these fireworks and clinging to them in the air, until he is flopped at last, disheveled, into a serape that his comrades hold out—and the fireworks inscribe "El Fin," the End. Here is exactly Donald's position: as everything goes to pieces, there he is, caught helpless at the center of the explosion. The position of the aracuan is the reverse of this. The aracuan lounges at ease, clear of the trouble, superbly intact. In *Clown of the Jungle,* Donald tries to get rid of this infuriating fellow once and for all; he sets up a machine gun and aims it straight at him and fires a prolonged burst, then

Donald Duck in *Clown of the Jungle* (1947).

Charlie Chaplin in *Monsieur Verdoux* (1947).

Bugs Bunny.

Walter Huston in *The Treasure of the Sierra Madre* (1948).

Bing Crosby and the Andrews Sisters in *Road to Rio* (1947).

stares: the landscape lies in ruins, but the aracuan, smiling, untouched, reclines in a little beach chair sipping a cool drink through a
straw. There is a sequence in *The Three Caballeros* in which the
aracuan erupts into the scene, snatches a cigar from a parrot and runs
off with it—ostensibly right into nowhere: he seems to run right off
the very film that we are viewing (a bit of sound track is indicated to
one side, then sheer blackness). This image sums him up. The aracuan is simply not a native of the world before us, as others are, or
subject to the rigors of this world. In *Clown of the Jungle*, the moment after we have sighted him stretched out upon the branch, he
rises and runs about the tree, his head popping into sight from every
impossible angle—from the right of us, then instantly from the left,
from below us, then upside down, from above—uttering all the while
a little song: "Allapoppapoppapoppapoppapoppapoppapop!" "You'll
find him most everywhere," the narrator comments in *The Three Caballeros*. And this ability to turn up where he wants, to run quite wild,
is his essence. He can go anywhere. He paints a little open door on
rock and runs through; Donald, giving chase, runs hard against it.
The aracuan disbelieves in the laws of this world. He inhabits some
magical remove. And so all the commotions which surround him are
simply intriguing displays for him; the havoc sketches itself in air as,
in the films of the past chapter, those final landscapes sketched themselves far off below us, peaceful to behold.

The aracuan is not unique. There are others who assume his stance
—though often they maintain it imperfectly. The majority of those
little cartoon characters who are the torment of other little characters
attain this special perspective at least for moments. What else is it
when the little sheep in *No Mutton fer Nuttin'* cries, *"You can't kill
me . . . This is the end of the picture"*? Some of these creatures
maintain more consistently than others a likeness to the aracuan. This
is true of Bugs Bunny, Little Lulu, and Heckle and Jeckle (two
crows). Casual saboteurs, they look on unperturbed as the world goes
up in smoke all around them. The two skinny crows yawn luxuri-
antly; Bugs Bunny chews at his inevitable carrot; Little Lulu licks at
her inevitable lollipop. Nothing can spoil their appetites or their ease.
One can, in fact, trace the same bodily posture of ease in each of these
characters as in the aracuan: the lolling disdainful posture already
sketched—arms behind the head, one leg crossed upon the other.

The role is rarer in films featuring live actors, but it is to be found there. It was precisely the role of Walter Huston in *The Treasure of the Sierra Madre*. He even looks rather like the little aracuan bird. And this skinny old man with a shock of hair in disorder seems to his companions to be invulnerable, seems able to disdain the laws of nature. The two younger men have wondered before starting whether he will be able to keep up with them. But as the three of them strike into the wilds, we see the two younger ones laboring along, tongues out; and always above them on the slope, goat-nimble and perky, the old man—"Look at him climb!" At the end of each day the two young ones drop by the fire, too dead to stir, while the old man squats, lively and talkative, gobbling down beans—"Hey you fellows, how about some beans? Want some beans? Rough country tomorrow! Better have some beans!"—then lolls at ease, squeaking a tune upon his harmonica. "We ought to give up," the two groan one day and just drop where they are; at which the old man executes a saucy jig, squealing with laughter—"My, my, what great prospectors!" He could be that little bird incarnate here. Bogart, in dumb rage, nearly kills him with a stone—until Huston tells his news ("You're so dumb, you're so dumb!"): the two have given up at the very spot where there is gold to be found. All the while the old man watches them with knowing mischievous eyes. He knows what is to happen; he knows what always *does* happen. The events of the film unfold for him a spectacle so familiar that it is as though he himself were not even involved. The two young ones grow edgy, then—one of them—murderous; the whole venture blows to the wind. He just leans at his ease against that bit of broken wall and laughs and laughs and laughs—to see it all "go back to where it came from."

Bing Crosby is another who achieves this luxurious long-distance eye on events. "Do you want to be the best man?" Hope asks him in *Road to Rio* when Hope is expecting to win Lamour. "I always was," Bing retorts serenely. Best man he is: he moves through the *Road* pictures with a wonderful ease, the air of one impossible to destroy or disconcert. And the secret of his ease is again a cool heretical eye on events—as of one who assumes that he is not really a member of this world and so can watch it fall asunder with perfect calm. There is a sequence in *Clown of the Jungle* in which four tiny hummingbirds, "little songsters," huddle in the air and, a sunflower for a mike, "blend" for us "unforgettable harmonies." Donald sets up his camera to capture this sight—"Oh boy!"—but the aracuan erupts before them, all arms and legs, to execute a wild Russian dance—"hike!"— and destroy his picture. There is a sequence in *Road to Rio* in which the Andrews Sisters, in a song and dance number, blend for us *their* unforgettable harmonies and Bing dances along beside them. Just very lightly, with none of the violence of that bird, but his gestures very delicately mocking theirs, Bing destroys *that* picture, works a wonderful havoc. Many a tedious passage in these films is enlivened in these terms. Eyes lazily wide, his look works constant sabotage. This look is all-encompassing, does not omit Miss Lamour, the film in which he finds himself, Paramount Pictures, the movie audience. He even smiles away his own image. He is cast as one who has only to stroll beneath a lady's balcony in his immaculate attire (he bears little physical resemblance to that aracuan bird), has only to open his mouth and croon a little song, and the lady melts. But even as he softly warbles some irresistible lay, Bing smiles the whole act away. In *Road to Rio,* at the end of one song and dance he executes, he murmurs lightly as the audience applauds, "Thank you, you fools, you." His is the smile of the magician, dealing in illusions. Recall for a moment the comic hero of earlier days, the Innocent played by Keaton, a certain power of belief sweeping that hero to triumph, marshaling a chaotic world to his will. This later hero triumphs, "best man," through the power of disbelief, through a refusal to count himself as subject to that chaos at all. He can step out of it at will.

Here is of course a precarious perspective. Those who attempt it tread on air. Even Bing does not sustain that magic ease without a break. Bugs Bunny, Little Lulu, Heckle and Jeckel—each of them can appear to us at moments quite as destructible as others. The aracuan bird himself seems at times a bit too frenetic about his mischievous work to be termed quite disinterested. At the end of *Clown of the Jungle,* Donald Duck, victim of the sassy little bird, erupts into a crazy helpless imitation of the aracuan's song, and surrendering even his own natural motions to mimicry of the motions of his tormentor, runs crazily about our field of vision, a demented duplicate of the aracuan. At the end of another cartoon, *Daffy Duck and Egghead,* an unhappy hunter, forever eluded by sassy Daffy Duck, suddenly gyrates off across the waters and vanishes at the horizon, in the likeness of Daffy. This conceit, in which the two opposed figures are abruptly elided, is not inept. For the aracuan may well enough read in that other unhappy figure his own essential likeness.

Chaplin's *Monsieur Verdoux* dramatizes just this equation. Verdoux is knowingly defined as at one and the same time both figures, one stance relaxed all too easily into the other. For long sequences he is wonderfully that saucy and invulnerable little bird—as he pursues Mme Gronet nimbly about the bedroom, tumbles backward out the window but scrambles the next moment back in; or as he lunges amorously toward her corner of the sofa, teacup in hand, and miscomputing the distance, lands on the floor but arises without having spilled a drop of tea. The aracuan and his like have a way of turning up here, there, on the map, according to their whim, in a swift relay of disguises. Verdoux outdoes them all. And as he stands regarding a prospective victim, his is a detachment that is unmatched. But I have described in an earlier chapter certain moments in which this ease drops from him. And it fails him almost consistently with loud unwieldy Mme Bonnare (wide-mouthed Martha Raye). Here is a woman whose behavior he cannot predict as he can that of other women, and in her presence the face he shows us is again and again that of acute malaise—acute as that of any distracted creature in an animated cartoon. The subtlety of the film is here—in Chaplin's eye on the infirmity of this posture.

(In the last sequence of the film, his vision of this weakens. After the trial and conviction of Verdoux by a hypocritical public, when Chaplin in effect steps into the play himself—impelled to exhibit his disdain for that public—one could call the posture that *he* now assumes the very same posture. One can even note here the aracuan's bodily pose, as Chaplin lies stretched out languorously on the jail cot, one knee up, arms behind his head.)

This stance is a precarious one and negative. In this it recalls the stance of the hero of Chapter 7, the Tough Boy, whose boast was also "You can't kill me." Of all the heroes this book has arrayed, these two heroes alone manage in a broken world to hold themselves intact, if precariously. Of all those others, here are the conquering heroes. One might add to their ranks the "conquering hero" whom Sturges presents—the stammering Innocent. His victory was shown of course to be an empty one. Yet so, one could say, is the victory of these other

two heroes. Their victory consists in an act of disengagement from
this world. Where then do they themselves stand? What affirmation
can one credit to them?

Certain of the films that featured the Tough Boy attempted to
strike a more positive note, as I have recorded—to show the hero in
the role of a healer, a Prince who awakens captive ladies with his kiss
and leads them forth to a new life. This note, however, always rings a
little thin. *The Treasure of the Sierra Madre* attempts to show its
comic hero playing a rather similar role. This mischievous old man too
is presented to us as a Life-giver. In the last half of the film some
Mexicans come to his camp for help. A young boy has been found
half drowned, and no one in his village has been able to bring him
back to consciousness. Huston goes off with these people, and the film
shows him patiently working over the boy—who finally opens his
eyes and sits up, as the grateful villagers remove their hats to Huston.
(Later they invite him to settle with them.) And the note is struck
another time. Up in the hills the three encounter a fourth gold-
seeker, who demands the right to dig there with them. They agree to
kill this stranger—though Huston demurs; but bandits kill him first.
On the corpse they find a letter from his wife, begging him to return
home—for, she writes, they have already found "life's real treasure."
Holt is touched and declares that he will send the woman a portion of
his gold; Huston agrees to do the same. Then the gold is scattered to
the wind. But at the very end of the film Huston remembers
the widow. Holt has just said that he has no idea where to head next,
and Huston suggests that he could bring the woman news of her
husband's death. The hint is that he will find a new life in the process. The widow lives on a fruit farm and we have heard Holt murmur
that life on a fruit farm is his idea of happiness. So again—as Huston
sends this younger man forth from the ruins, forth from the false
dream which he has laughed away for him—we are invited to see him
as one who helps others to life. But these moments are strangely labored. That first great explosion of laughter rings true—as Huston
throws back his head and laughs and laughs and Holt stands gaping
at him, mouth open, dumbfounded. Here the film might very effec-
tively have closed. Instead, the younger man joins in the laughter; the
two sit rocking side by side; and then the younger, rising, supposedly
reborn, sets forth to find a new life for himself. And the drama falters.

 10

"This is hopeless!"

This book ends darkly. The figures I have presented seem together to form a hopeless circle. The hero who sees nothing to fight for; the hero who despairs of making a life for himself; the hero who achieves success but finds it empty; and the malcontent who breaks with the old life, only to find himself nowhere—each mourns a vision of happiness that eludes him ("How long was it we had?"). Two figures, one grim, one comic, boast survival of a sort among the general ruins, but this survival is a precarious victory. It is worth recalling the warning with which I began this book. Our films, I wrote, grant us a vision of the Hell in which we are bound, but cannot grant us a vision of our better hopes. The figures cast upon this country's movie screens may indeed falter in any gesture of promise. This does not mean that certain bolder motions are undreamed of in these times. Fortunately, there are dreams that are dreamed outside the confines of our movie houses.

In Dante's *Inferno,* when Dante, guided by Virgil, reaches the very depth of that region, they begin to climb down Satan's body and out of Hell. Dante describes how at a certain moment Virgil laboriously turns the two of them around, so that their heads are where their feet had been, and for a while Dante climbs on in anguish, because it seems to him that he is now climbing back into Hell. But they emerge into the open air, and he sees the feet of Satan sticking out of the ground: they have arrived at a new region, where perspectives are reversed. In Hell, the figure of Satan towered; here it is turned upside down. Within Hell, that world seemed intact, the darkness complete. But "here it is morning, when it is evening there." And in this morning light, new figures make themselves known.

Index

This book was set on the linotype in Fairfield.
The display face is Spartan Light.
It was set, printed and bound by H. Wolff, New York.
Designed by Jacqueline Schuman.